SHIELDING ASPEN

Delta Team Two, Book 3

SUSAN STOKER

CHAPTER ONE

Brain sat back in his chair in the bar and watched as Aspen Mesmer completely charmed his friends. He hadn't wanted to come out tonight. He'd wanted to wallow in self-pity about his lack of a love life. Thank God he'd dragged himself to the bar at the last minute.

If he hadn't, he would've missed meeting Aspen. And what a first meeting it was.

After walking into the bar, one second he'd been looking around for the guys, and the next, a woman was walking straight toward him with a nervous yet determined look on her face. He had time to appreciate the fact that she was almost as tall as he was—about five-nine or so—and probably around his same age as well. She wore a pair of black jeans that clung to her body in intriguing ways, Converse sneakers, and a T-shirt that said, "Will give medical advice for tacos."

Brain was shocked when she walked right into his personal space and put her arms around his shoulders.

1

"I'll give you twenty bucks if you kiss me right now like you mean it."

Her voice was husky, and Brain could swear he heard desperation. He didn't have time to say he'd happily kiss her, but not for money, when she put her hand on the back of his head and moved in.

At first their kiss had been awkward, merely a mashing together of their lips. But then Brain wrapped an arm around the woman's waist and took a step forward, bending her backward. She gasped in surprise and switched her hold from around his neck to latch onto his biceps.

Brain took advantage of her mouth opening, changed the angle of their lips just slightly and kissed her as he hadn't kissed a woman in a very long time. Long, slow, and deep. The little moans she made weren't helping him stop anytime soon either. He could tell she was muscular and strong, but at the moment, tilted backward, she was completely helpless in his arms. And he liked it a hell of a lot.

"All you had to do was tell me you'd moved on, Aspen," an irritated voice said from behind her.

The woman licked her lips and sighed in frustration. Brain saw her mouth "sorry" to him before she cleared the emotion from her face and turned to confront the man behind her. She wrapped an arm around Brain's waist, and he had no problem tugging her against his side.

"I did tell you, Derek. I told you a month ago when I broke up with you. I told you at least three times over texts. And I told you again tonight when you showed up here, begging me to get back together. I've moved on. It's time you do the same."

The man looked to be in his mid-thirties, and the pout on his face definitely wasn't doing him any favors. But it was the glimmer of pure, unadulterated anger in his eyes that made Brain nervous.

"When did you meet him? I mean, you're training with the Rangers every day."

"We've known each other a while," Aspen lied.

Knowing things could get awkward very quickly, Brain held out his hand toward the other man. "Name's Kane Temple. But people call me Brain."

Derek looked in disgust at the hand Brain was holding out to him then frowned at Aspen. "Brain? Seriously?"

She merely shrugged.

"Fine. I hope you aren't going to come crawling back to me when he breaks your heart," Derek bit out.

"I won't," Aspen told him perkily.

"I think it's time you run along," Brain told the other man, annoyed he wasn't taking the hint.

When Derek opened his mouth to say something he'd probably regret, Brain was done. He wrapped an arm around Aspen's shoulders and tugged her closer. "Come on, baby, I see my friends. I'm sure they've saved us some seats." Then he walked away from the heartbroken—and pissed—man and steered Aspen toward his teammates.

"Thank you so much, and I'm so sorry for involving you in that," she said. "But he wouldn't leave me alone and the only thing I could think to do was give him concrete evidence that I'd moved on." She started to reach for the small purse strung across her body.

"If you even try to pay me for that kiss, I'm gonna be pissed," Brain told her.

She froze and looked at him with wide eyes.

"How about we start over?" Brain asked. He took a step back and held out his hand. "I'm Brain."

"Aspen Mesmer," she said, grasping his hand with her own.

Brain shook it, then brought it up to his lips and kissed the back.

"You really don't have to hang out with me, I'm sure he's gone," Aspen said.

"Don't be scared of me," Brain ordered, not liking the nervous look in her eyes.

Her shoulders straightened and she stood taller. "I'm not scared of you."

Brain had liked that answer.

He hadn't expected to walk into the bar and have a beautiful woman beg him to kiss her. Even if it was only to get an ex-boyfriend off her back, it wasn't a hardship. The woman was lovely.

Aspen had light brown shoulder-length hair and chocolate-brown eyes. She wasn't wearing much makeup, maybe some lip gloss and something on her eyes. Brain wasn't an expert in women's cosmetics, but he knew he didn't like it when it looked like a chick's face was caked in the stuff. Since they were similar heights, he loved that he could look her in the eyes, and he even liked the slight wrinkles at their edges, letting him know she probably smiled and laughed a lot.

Overall, Aspen looked like the girl next door...which Brain loved.

He'd brought her over to his friends not only for show, in case her ex hadn't actually left the bar and instead was watching her, but also because he was genuinely interested in getting to know the intriguing woman. She'd been bold and confident, but also nervous and wary when she'd approached him. The contradiction was captivating. She'd gotten his attention for sure.

"So you're a combat medic?" Trigger asked Aspen. He had his arm around Gillian and, for the first time in a very long time, Brain didn't get a twinge of jealousy when he saw them together. It wasn't that he wanted Gillian for himself; she and Trigger were made for each other. It was more that he wanted what his teammate had. Someone who looked at him as if he were the sun in her sky.

"Yup," Aspen said with a nod. "For the last several years I've been attached to various Ranger units."

Oz whistled low. "Not an easy job," he observed.

Aspen smiled. "No, it's not."

Kinley leaned forward, and Brain saw Lefty's hand resting on the small of her back, keeping that small connection between them. "Forgive my ignorance, but you're a Ranger?" she asked.

Aspen shook her head. "No. I haven't been through Ranger School, but I *have* participated in training sessions with them."

Brain had already been impressed with the woman, but upon hearing that, he was even more so. He could tell by the looks on his teammates' faces that they were too. Gillian and Kinley probably weren't sure what Aspen meant, though. He decided to enlighten them.

"What she means is she probably *could* be a Ranger if she wanted. Their training sessions aren't as long as Ranger school, but they're just as intense. Days without food, crawling through forests and rivers trying to stay undetected. And I'm assuming, as their medic, you were tasked along the way with making sure your team stayed hydrated, that any blisters or other minor wounds were

5

taken care of, and generally had to keep them operating at one hundred percent, all while attempting to take care of yourself at the same time, yeah?"

Aspen blushed and simply shrugged. "All part of the job."

The more Brain got to know the attractive medic, the more he liked her. He could still remember how she'd trembled in his arms when he'd taken the kiss deeper, and how she'd looked at him afterward. Not in awe that he was a Delta operative. But as a woman looked at a man she wanted.

Knowing he wasn't exactly being nonchalant, Brain reached out and intertwined his fingers with hers. She looked at him and raised an eyebrow, but didn't pull away.

Taking that as a win, Brain simply smiled at her and reached out with his free hand to take a sip of the water he'd started drinking after finishing a beer. He wanted to be completely clearheaded tonight. Wanted to remember every second.

"Is it hard being a woman and working with such a traditionally male-dominated group like the Rangers?" Gillian asked.

Aspen sighed. "Yes and no. I mean, I take my share of ribbing, but for the most part, it's done in jest. There are, of course, those men who don't think I should be attached to the Rangers in any way, shape, or form, but when the shit hits the fan, bullets are flying, and people are dying, no one seems to care much about the fact I'm a woman."

"Who are you working with now?" Brain asked.

Aspen turned to him again, and when her brown eyes met his, he saw slight distress there. It was only for an instant because she hid it quickly, but even that quick glimpse made Brain want to seriously hurt anyone who dared make Aspen's life uncomfortable. He didn't know why he felt so protective of her, but he did.

"I'm attached to a team of about eight guys. Derek is best friends with the sergeant in charge of my team."

"Derek, the asshole who can't take a hint?" Brain asked.

Aspen winced. "Yeah. It was stupid to go out with him in the first place, especially considering how close he is to the guys I work with, but he was pretty insistent, and he'd stuck up for me when some of the other guys were giving me crap. In a moment of weakness, I said yes. But within two dates, I realized we weren't compatible."

"And he didn't realize the same thing?" Kinley asked. "I mean, generally the spark is either there or it isn't." She glanced at Lefty and gave him a small smile.

"I guess not," Aspen said with a shrug. "I tried to be clear that I wanted to keep him as a friend but anything more was off the table, and he didn't exactly take the hint...until tonight. Hopefully."

The more Brain thought about why she'd had to walk up to a complete stranger and beg for a kiss, the angrier he got. No woman should have to resort to that sort of thing just to get a guy off her back. No meant no, and this Derek was a grade-A asshole to keep harassing her after she'd said she just wanted to be friends.

Brain tuned back into the conversation around him when Aspen said, "And he was the kind of guy who always had to be right."

"Oh my God!" Gillian exclaimed. "I know exactly what you mean!"

Brain sat back listening to the women chat, trying to

rein in his anger. It was surprising; he'd never really had much of a temper before, but the thought of someone being a dick to Aspen ticked him off. She could very obviously take care of herself, but the feeling was still there.

"Like, if you say it'll take two hours to get somewhere, he has to disagree and say it'll take two hours and fifteen minutes," Gillian went on.

"Or if I suggested he cook something for twenty minutes, he'd tell me I was wrong and it's actually seventeen and a half minutes, otherwise it's overdone," Aspen agreed.

"Or a show's on at eight-thirty, not eight," Kinley chimed in.

"Or when I say a twenty-milligram slow IV push of ketamine over one minute is the proper protocol, he has to contradict me and say that fifty milligrams is correct, when I know for a fact that's only if it's being given intranasally," Aspen said with a laugh.

When everyone simply looked at her in confusion, she blushed, but laughed even harder. "Sorry, sorry, sorry. I forget that not everyone is as into narcotics as I am. I mean, not *into* them as in doing them recreationally, but as interested in them...uh... Shit. Um...or when I say that Mayor Larry Kline in the show *Stranger Things* was the Dread Pirate Roberts in *The Princess Bride*, and he tells me I'm wrong."

At that, everyone laughed.

Brain thought Aspen was fucking adorable. He made a mental note to try not to contradict her under any circumstances. He watched as she, Gillian, and Kinley laughed and joked together, and it made him feel good that they were getting along. Despite just meeting Aspen a few hours ago, he felt more comfortable with her than he had with any woman in a long time.

He still held her hand in his, and every now and then rubbed his thumb over the back of it, just to let her know he was still there. And every time, a small smile formed on her face, even if she didn't acknowledge him in any other way.

Looking up, Brain caught Trigger's eye. The other man gave him a small chin lift and lifted his glass in a subtle salute. Brain rolled his eyes and shook his head, but Trigger simply smiled.

It was hard to believe a few hours ago, Brain was trying to think of reasonable excuses to leave early, and now he dreaded every tick of the minute hand on the clock because it meant he was another minute closer to having to say goodbye to Aspen. He was enjoying getting to know her and watching her interact with the people who were closest to him.

After another hour or so, Lefty and Kinley were the first ones to call it a night. Trigger and Gillian weren't too far behind. Then Oz and Lucky headed out. And Doc. Until it was just Grover, Brain, and Aspen left.

"So…" Aspen said. "Grover? Brain?"

"My last name is Groves," Grover explained.

"So it has nothing to do with the little blue Muppet?" Aspen teased.

"No," Grover said with a shake of his head. "Do I really look like a Muppet? Or sound like one?"

She giggled. "No, but I know there's always a story behind nicknames. Besides, Grover is the coolest Muppet there is. He doesn't get enough press time or enough toys and shit made in his likeness. And you could be named Elmo, now *that* would be embarrassing."

They all chuckled.

"And you, Kane? Brain?"

He shrugged, not sure he wanted to tell her the reason behind his nickname. He wasn't exactly embarrassed about it, but for once in his life, he wanted to *not* be the nerd. Wanted to be a badass Delta Force soldier.

But of course, Grover was more than happy to explain.

"He's a fucking genius," Grover said, oblivious to the frown Brain was shooting his way. "He knows over two dozen languages. He's some kind of language savant. And I swear to God, he can hear someone say something once and he understands it. Comes in very handy in our line of work, I can tell you that."

Brain took another sip of water and refused to meet Aspen's gaze. Inevitably, when he met people and they learned what he could do, they either wanted a demonstration—meaning, they wanted him to rattle off all sorts of things in different languages—or they mentally backed off, thinking he was out of their league.

He tried to loosen his fingers from hers, but she tightened her grip, not letting go. In surprise, he finally looked over at her.

"That's cool," she said quietly.

Grover kept talking, oblivious to Brain's discomfort with the topic.

"He graduated from high school at age fifteen. Went to college right after that and got his first degree in two years. His parents were *pissed* that he joined the Army; they wanted him to be a rocket scientist or something."

"Grover?" Aspen said without looking away from Brain.

"Yeah?"

"Shut up."

Brain couldn't help it. He laughed.

Grover was silent for about twenty seconds, then he clued into the fact that his going on and on had made Brain uncomfortable. "I mean, Brain's smart, but he's also cool. And he's quite the ladies' man. He's loyal and down-to-earth too."

"I think it's about time for you to go, Grover," Brain said, shaking his head. "You're not helping."

"Right. Sorry. I'm leaving. I need to go over to my sister's place tomorrow. She's been avoiding me for some reason, and that shit needs to stop. So...I'll just go then. See you at PT tomorrow, Brain."

"Later," Brain told his teammate. Grover was clueless sometimes, but because he never meant anything maliciously, Brain and the rest of the team put up with his chatter.

After he left, Brain took a breath and looked at Aspen. "So," he said.

"So," she echoed.

"Grover's not exactly subtle," Brain told her.

Aspen chuckled. "No, he's not. But he means well."

"He does." Brain mentally smacked himself in the forehead. This wasn't exactly how he'd wanted their first one-on-one conversation to go. No matter what Grover had said, Brain wasn't a "ladies' man." He wasn't "cool." He was the brain. The smart guy. The one everyone turned to when they had a mystery that needed solving.

He was thirty years old, and he hadn't even lost his

virginity until he was twenty-four. He'd been out of his depth, socially; going to college so young meant most of the women avoided him like the plague. It wasn't until he'd joined the Army and had gotten some independence that he'd managed to figure out how to fit in with men his own age a little better.

"I'm embarrassed that I didn't ask earlier, but you and your friends...you aren't Rangers, are you? Because if you are, I totally put my foot in my mouth earlier."

Brain quickly shook his head. "No, we aren't Rangers."

"Thank God," she breathed.

Brain continued before thinking. "We're Delta."

Aspen went completely still and stared at him with wide eyes. "Please tell me you're kidding."

"Nope. And I know you know this, but please don't share that with anyone."

"Oh, I wouldn't. No way. And...oh, shit, I'm *such* a dork."

"No, you aren't," Brain told her immediately. She was anything but a dork.

"I am! You were going on and on about how hard Ranger training is, and I know you guys have been through much worse."

"It's not a competition," Brain told her.

She tilted her head as she studied him.

"What?" Brain asked.

"You aren't like most men in special forces I've met. Neither are your friends, for that matter."

"In what way?"

Aspen shrugged. "It's just that...you're so down-to-earth."

"You've been hanging around those asshole Rangers too long," Brain retorted.

She grinned. "They're not *all* assholes."

"Derek is," Brain told her.

Her grin widened. "True. Thank you for helping me earlier. I'm usually not so forward, but—"

"But he was being a dick, and you were desperate," Brain finished for her.

"Maybe not desperate," Aspen countered. Then she dipped her head and raised her eyes shyly. "Maybe I took one look at you and liked what I saw, and figured I could kill two birds with one stone."

It took a minute for her words to sink in, and when they did, Brain was shocked.

Women weren't attracted to him. Not like she was insinuating. He knew he wasn't hideous or anything. He had nice eyes...at least that's what others had told him. But he frequently forgot to comb his hair so it was usually in disarray. And he had a beard because he was too lazy to shave every day. It worked well when they were on a mission, but when they came home, he kept it simply because it was easier.

But to have this amazing, smart woman tag him from the moment he'd walked in the door was a heady feeling... and confusing at the same time.

"You're not used to compliments, are you?" she asked, uncannily accurately.

"I'm the brain," he said with a shrug, as if that explained everything.

Aspen actually rolled her eyes. But then she turned in her chair and looked him right in the eyes. "Yes, I wanted Derek off my back. I fucked up when I went out with him and now I'm paying for it. I have to see him all the time because he's very close with my platoon sergeant, our teams train together, and we actually participate in quite a few joint missions, but hopefully after tonight, he'll realize that we're just not compatible and things will go back to normal. But more importantly, I picked you to help me because I was attracted to you the second I saw you."

Brain noticed the blush on her cheeks, but she kept going.

"You walked in and looked like you wanted to be anywhere but here. And you might think you're 'only' the brain on your team, but it's more than obvious how much your friends admire you. If they only cared about you because of what you know, they wouldn't joke so easily with you. And Gillian and Kinley wouldn't have spoken so highly of you when we all went to the restroom.

"I don't know you, and I'm probably overstepping, but I've learned that life is too short to not say what I'm thinking...and I think you're pretty amazing, Kane, and I've only known you for a few hours. I haven't even heard you speak anything but English." She grinned. "You've already saved me from a very uncomfortable situation too, and the fact that you don't have a girlfriend is both confusing as hell and pretty damn lucky for me."

Her words echoed in Brain's mind, and he knew that he wanted—no, *needed*—to get to know this woman better. "Want to go out sometime?"

He promptly winced at the abruptness of his request.

But Aspen didn't laugh at him. "Yes," she said simply.

"Tomorrow?"

Now she *did* chuckle. "Yes," she said again.

Brain narrowed his eyes. "You aren't just saying yes

because of Derek, are you? Because as much as I like you, I'm not into pity dates."

Her grin faded. "Seriously?"

He nodded.

Aspen rolled her eyes. "Kane, I've sat next to you all night holding your hand. I just told you that I picked you out of all the men who'd entered this bar tonight. Hell, I offered you twenty bucks if you would kiss me." She leaned forward and poked him in the chest as she said her next words. "I haven't met a man who intrigues me like you do in a very long time. I spend every day of my life living and working with men, and frankly, it's almost turned me off the opposite sex altogether. But the second you bent me backward over your arm tonight, I was putty in your hands." Then she straightened. "Maybe this isn't a good idea," she mumbled.

Brain panicked. He couldn't let her pull back now. Somewhere deep inside, the confidence he'd seemed to be missing when it came to the opposite sex roared to the forefront. He wasn't letting the most interesting woman he'd met in ages get away so easily.

He reached out and grabbed the finger she'd been poking him with and shook his head. "Nope. You already said yes. Twice. I'm not letting you go back on your word now. Since we don't know each other, I'm happy to meet you somewhere if that will make you more comfortable, or you can trust me to pick you up tomorrow evening around six."

"Are you really Delta Force?" she asked.

Confused, Brain nodded. "I wouldn't lie about that."

She snorted. "Other people would. And I guess if the

Army and our government can trust you with their secrets, I can probably tell you where I live."

Brain relaxed a fraction.

"Can I have my finger back now?" Aspen asked.

Brain grinned. "Depends on if you're going to use it to poke me some more."

"Are you going to continue to say stupid shit?" she retorted.

"Probably," Brain said honestly. "I seem to do that a lot. I might be smart, but I do seem to have a bad habit of saying stupid shit around pretty women."

Aspen pulled on her hand and Brain immediately let it go. But instead of pulling away from him, she rested her palm on his chest and leaned closer.

"You smell so good," Brain blurted—then mentally chastised himself. He was supposed to be suave, not spewing out shit like that.

"Thanks," she said without seeming to miss a beat. "I don't wear perfume a lot because I roll around in the mud and work with guys all the time, but every now and then I break it out. It's gardenias. They remind me of Hawaii. I've only been there once, but I loved the scent of the flowers. And...shit...now I'm going on and on about something that you probably don't care about."

"I care," Brain told her immediately. He made a mental note about the gardenias.

"Anyway," Aspen said, leaning even farther into his personal space, "I was going to thank you for not thinking I was a crazy person tonight when I approached you."

"You're welcome," Brain told her, his eyes on her lips.

"I want to kiss you again," she whispered.

Inwardly, Brain was jumping up and down and

screaming *yes* at the top of his lungs, but he simply reached out and palmed the side of Aspen's face. She was near enough that all he had to do was lean forward a fraction of an inch and their lips would be touching...but for some reason, he wanted to wait.

"I want to get to know you," he told her. "And I want you to get to know me. I'm attracted to you, that's no secret. But I'm old enough to know that what I'm feeling for you is different. Special. And the last thing I want is to demean what I'm feeling by making out with you in the corner of a bar on the first night we meet."

Brain was afraid he'd proven himself the most idiotic male alive by turning her down, but when he saw her face soften as she nodded, he breathed a sigh of relief.

"You're very different," she said softly.

Brain shrugged. "I am," he agreed.

"I like different," she said, then straightened.

Brain let go of her reluctantly and stood when she did. She reached into her purse and pulled out a twenty-dollar bill and held it out to him. "I really do owe you."

Brain scowled at the money, and at her. "I'm not taking your money," he told her gruffly. "Put it away."

"I need to pay for my drinks at least," she argued.

Brain took the money then reached for her purse and stuffed it into an outside pocket. "Your drinks are already paid for. And you'll never pay for that kind of shit when you're with me."

She frowned. "Why not?"

"Because."

"Because you're a guy and I'm a girl?" she huffed.

"No. Because it's disrespectful. It has nothing to do

with gender or because I don't think you can't pay your own way."

"Then why?"

Brain hesitated. "You're going to think it's stupid."

"I'm not," Aspen told him.

"Fine, but you asked," he said. "It's because I want to spoil you. When I take a woman out, I don't want her to have to worry about *anything*. You need a ride? I'll take you. You prefer a taxi? I'll call one for you. You want to order the most expensive shit on the menu, fine. Do it. When I'm dating someone, I want them to know how special I think they are. And being special doesn't include worrying about paying the bill, the tip, dealing with assholes harassing them, or figuring out how they're going to get home. It's just how I'm wired."

He braced for her reaction. In the past, he'd had women flat-out tell him how crazy his idea of chivalry was, or that he was misogynistic. But it was how he felt, and he'd learned to make it clear up front so there wouldn't be issues later.

But Aspen wasn't laughing at him, or scowling. "If we're out together, and I see something that I want to buy for you, are you going to lose your mind?"

"No. It's your money, you can do what you want with it. But, as a caveat, don't think you can buy me a car or something and call it a 'gift.'"

Aspen burst out laughing. Threw her head back and guffawed so hard, Brain wrapped an arm around her waist to keep her from falling over. When she had herself under control, she looked him in the eye and nodded. "Deal. No buying you cars. Got it."

Brain smiled back at her. "Good. Tell me your number."

She didn't bat an eye at the abrupt change of topic. He also liked that she didn't ask if he was going to write it down or put it into his phone. She simply rattled it off as if she had no doubt he'd be able to remember it.

"I'll text you later so you'll have mine, and so you can send me your address," Brain told her.

"Sounds good."

They walked toward the door to the bar. Brain didn't feel the need to remove his arm from around her waist, and Aspen actually leaned into him as they walked. Her fingers curled into the belt loop at the back of his jeans and the small weight made Brain shiver in anticipation. None of the women he'd dated had ever done that, and it felt sorta like she was claiming him. He liked it. A hell of a lot.

As they exited the bar, Brain gave the bouncer a chin lift. When he looked at Aspen, she was smiling.

"What?" he asked.

"It's just that chin lift thing. It's such a guy thing to do."

Brain frowned. "And?"

"Nothing," she told him.

But he heard her mumble under her breath, "It's sexy as hell."

He smiled. He'd never really been called sexy. He liked that too.

Brain walked Aspen to her car, a very sensible white Hyundai Elantra GT. Looking around, he didn't see Derek or anyone else lurking about.

"Drive safe," he told her as he held the door open for

her. Aspen paused before she climbed inside and nodded. "You too," she told him.

"See you tomorrow night," Brain told her.

"I'm looking forward to it."

Having nothing else to say to prolong their evening, Brain closed her door and stood back. Before he'd thought about it, he'd given her a chin lift, and smiled when she grinned at him through the windshield. She lifted two fingers, waving at him before she pulled out of her parking space.

Looking down at his watch, Brain realized that he'd been at the bar with Aspen for hours. He hadn't stayed out this late, when not on a mission, in a very long time. There was something about her that made him forget he was the nerd. The smart guy. She made him feel...normal. For maybe the first time in his life.

After he got into his Challenger, he took the time to program her name and number into his phone. Then he sent a short text.

Brain: This is Brain. Looking forward to tomorrow. Let me know where to pick you up. Sleep well.

She didn't respond, but he didn't expect her to since she was driving. He threw his phone onto the passenger seat and headed for his house, smiling all the way.

CHAPTER TWO

Aspen Mesmer paced nervously around her apartment as she waited for Kane to pick her up. How she'd gotten through the day, she had no idea. She was both excited and nervous as hell about her date tonight.

After the debacle with Derek, she'd considered not dating any more military guys. She'd gone to the bar last night to have a drink because she didn't want to go home and be by herself. The day had been stressful and she'd been hoping for a nice relaxing drink before heading home. She'd just had the misfortune of Derek being at the same bar she chose. Why he was acting so attached after just two dates—a *month* ago—was a mystery to her. They just didn't have any chemistry.

Not like the chemistry she and Kane had. She'd noticed him the second he'd walked in the door. He was a bit scruffy-looking, but it was his eyes that had caught her attention first. His gaze had roamed the room, taking in everyone and everything. She should've known then that he was some kind of special forces soldier, but Derek had started whining about her not giving them a fair shot, and she'd started toward Kane without thought.

Asking a complete stranger to kiss her wasn't on top of the list of smart things she'd done in her life, but Kane hadn't let her down. At first it had been awkward, but then he'd taken control. Aspen wasn't a trusting person in general, but in his arms, she hadn't felt the least bit of fear that he'd drop her.

And the way he kissed? As if he'd been away for months and had just returned home? Damn. Her toes had curled in her Converse sneakers.

She'd also somewhat expected him to be as dumb as a box of rocks—it seemed all the most good-looking men were—but of course, she'd been wrong about that too. Way wrong.

Brain.

Apparently he was some sort of genius.

Smart. Hot. Muscular. Delta. And respectful and apparently a good friend and teammate to boot.

It had been a long time since she'd had an instant attraction to a guy, but who could blame her in this case? Kane Temple was everything any woman should want. He seemed a bit...innocent and old fashioned, which was a pleasant surprise. It had been Aspen's experience that a lot of special forces men were jaded and had a habit of sleeping with as many women as possible. Lord knew, most of the single Rangers she worked with were that way.

But Kane had refused to even kiss her at the end of the night. She hadn't been all that comfortable with his insistence on her not paying for anything, but after he'd explained why, she'd relented.

It all could've been a ruse she'd fallen for hook, line, and sinker. She really hoped not.

Time would tell.

She looked at her watch. He was supposed to be at her apartment in five minutes. They were going to dinner, then he'd bring her home. As far as first dates went, it was pretty tame, but Aspen was thankful. The last thing she wanted to do was hang with him all night if it turned out last night was a fluke, and he really was a douche.

But she hoped he wasn't. Hoped that the attraction she'd felt toward him at the bar carried over into tonight.

Aspen startled badly when a knock sounded on her door. She'd been watching out the window, but had apparently been so lost in her own head that he'd gotten past her. After verifying it was Kane, Aspen opened her door.

"Hey," she said somewhat shyly as she met his gaze.

For a second, they simply stared at each other in silence. Then Kane shook his head and smiled at her. "Hi."

Suddenly, Aspen felt like she was fifteen again and her very first boyfriend had come to pick her up. She didn't know what to say or do. All she could do was stare at Kane. He was wearing a dark olive-green button-up shirt and a pair of jeans. He'd trimmed his beard since the night before but his hair was still messy, as if he'd just run his fingers through it.

She didn't know much about his dating history, but she'd gotten the impression the night before that he hadn't had many long-term girlfriends. Which was crazy, because the man standing in front of her was fucking beautiful.

Aspen hadn't been sure what to wear, but had finally decided on a pair of jeans and a black tank top. It was still warm in the evenings and she wanted to be comfortable.

She wasn't a dress-and-heels kind of girl. If Kane didn't like her the way she was, it was better to find that out now rather than later down the line.

And any worry Aspen might've felt about the chemistry they had being a one-time thing was already blown out of the water. As they stood in her doorway staring at each other, she could tell that Kane was just as tongue-tied as she was.

"You look amazing," Kane said when the awkward silence got a little too long.

Aspen huffed out a self-deprecating breath. "I'm wearing a tank top and jeans, Kane. Not anything fancy."

He took a step forward, crossing her threshold, and Aspen took one step back before straightening her spine. She wasn't scared of Kane, but he made her feel off-center, which was unusual.

"You're supposed to say 'thank you,'" he told her. "You aren't very good at accepting compliments, are you?" he asked, almost mimicking her question from last night.

Aspen shrugged. "I don't get them very often, so...no."

"That's a fuckin' shame," Kane said. He hadn't taken his gaze from hers, and it felt good. He saw *her*, not a pair of boobs with a head, as it felt other men saw—like Derek. "You're the kind of woman who can wear a little black dress and heels and outshine the most beautiful cover model, but more importantly, change into a battle dress uniform and boots and still be the prettiest woman in the room."

Aspen had no idea what to say to that. She swallowed hard.

Kane was standing close, but he wasn't touching her.

Their eyes were almost level and his gaze was so intense, she had to drop her own. She could see his heartbeat in the hollow of his throat and could smell his clean scent. As if he'd just jumped out of the shower right before coming over. He wore no cologne, no artificial scents, and it made her want to pull him into her apartment and into her bedroom right that second.

It had been a long time since she'd wanted a man as badly as she wanted Kane.

"I see I'm going to have to compliment you more often," he said with a small smile. "To make it easier for you to simply say thank you. You ready to go?"

"Yeah, I just need to grab my purse. You want to come in?" Aspen asked.

Kane shook his head. "I'll just wait here."

Wondering why he didn't want to come inside, Aspen merely shrugged and turned her back on him to go get her purse. She returned in under a minute and saw that Kane was now standing just outside her apartment, in the hallway. She exited and locked the door and, as they walked down the hall, she asked, "You didn't want to see my apartment?"

He glanced at her with a look she couldn't interpret.

Then he blew her mind.

"I *do* want to see your apartment. I want to know everything about you. I want to know if you're the kind of woman who likes lots of pillows and blankets on her couch, or if you're more of a neatnik. I want to know if you have one of those single-cup coffeemakers, or if you're a pot-at-a-time kind of drinker. I want to flip through your movies and books and see what interests you.

"But, this is our first date. You don't know me, and the last thing I want is to make you uncomfortable in any way. And invading your personal space could not only be discomforting, but it's dangerous. You shouldn't invite anyone into your home before you really know them. What would've prevented me from closing and locking the door behind me and attacking you? I'll always keep you safe, even if you don't need me to. Because that's what a man does for the woman he's dating. He keeps her safe, doesn't let anyone else take advantage or disrespect her, and he tries to make her feel comfortable in his presence."

Aspen stopped in her tracks, right in the middle of the hallway of her apartment complex, and stared at Kane incredulously.

"Aspen?" he asked, his brows furrowed in obvious confusion.

"Are you for real? Or is this all a game?"

Kane looked even more confused. "A game?"

"Yeah. You're saying all these amazing things that are pretty much what every woman wants to hear. Are you hoping to butter me up so you can get in my pants later tonight when you bring me home?"

The second the words were out of her mouth, Aspen wished she could take them back. Kane's expression went from concern to resignation. He took a step away from her, and she felt cold all of a sudden.

"I'm not playing a game," he said in a low, even tone. "I am who I am. I spent a lot of time watching the adults around me when I was growing up. My dad's a nice guy, but he's not the most perceptive. He's never held a door open for my mom and often walked in front of us when we'd go from the car to a building. I was young when I started college, but I still saw how shitty a lot of men treated the women they were supposed to like. Then I joined the Army, and I've witnessed countless examples of women being treated like second-class citizens in countries all over the world. I've never wanted to be 'that guy.' I want to make sure any woman who goes out with me knows I respect her, and that she's important." He sighed. "I'm sorry if you think I was handing you a line. Maybe you were right; maybe this *wasn't* such a good idea."

The last sentence was muttered, and Aspen knew he was on the verge of walking away and leaving her standing in the middle of the hallway.

She reached out and clamped a hand on Kane's forearm. "I'm sorry," she said immediately. "I just...Derek was really nice on our first date. Attentive and funny. I didn't really feel any chemistry with him, but I thought maybe it might grow. So I agreed to go out a second time, and it was like he was a different man. He kept touching me in ways that made me uncomfortable. When he brought me home, he kissed me, then tried to grope me. He wasn't happy when I told him no, and honestly, he kind of scared me. I just...I'm leery. And you're saying all the things any woman would love to hear, and it all seems too good to be true."

"I'm not that asshole," Kane said, enunciating each word carefully. "I've known too many men exactly like him. If I say something, I mean it. And I won't lie, I'm attracted to you, Aspen, but I don't do one-night stands. I want to get to know a woman before I sleep with her. It's probably not very macho of me to admit it, but I want some sort of emotional connection with the woman I take to my bed. Physical attraction isn't enough for me. For the longest time, I was behind my classmates sexually. And when I did finally get interested in the opposite sex, I was too young for the girls around me. I'm not saying I want to be engaged before I'll sleep with someone, but fucking for the sake of fucking isn't what I'm after in relationships."

Aspen believed him. Honesty and sincerity was written all over his face. He wasn't just filling her head with pretty words, or using reversed psychology to get her to sleep with him. "Okay. I'm sorry I was rude."

"You weren't rude," Kane told her. "Just honest. But I'm letting you know right now, if I tell you something, you can absolutely believe that it's the truth."

Aspen nodded then leaned forward and rested her forehead on his shoulder. It was an intimate thing to do, considering they hadn't even left on their first date yet, but she needed to touch him. To let him know that she was really sorry.

They stood like that, her holding onto his forearm with both hands and her head on his shoulder, and him leaning into her, for at least a minute...before her stomach growled.

Kane chuckled. "You're hungry. I need to feed you."

"Worked through lunch," Aspen said with a shrug. "The teams are training hard right now just in case we're sent over to Afghanistan."

It was nice not having to explain what she meant. Kane knew because he was in the same circles as the Rangers. He probably knew more than they did, in fact.

"Yeah, things are getting ugly over there. There's a new guy who's stirring things up. The US is going to have to do something about him. Soon." Kane took hold of her hand and they started back down the hall as they talked.

Aspen nodded. "I understand the need to be prepared, but damn, running through countless scenarios in the back forty of the post isn't exactly my idea of a good time. It's freaking hot."

"It'll be hot in Afghanistan too," Kane said with a smile.

"I know," Aspen grumbled. "Now you sound like my platoon sergeant."

Kane held open the door to the apartment complex for her and, after she walked through, was right there by her side once more. He led her over to his black Dodge Challenger and held open the passenger door for her. Then he jogged around the front to get to the other side. He immediately started the engine, and the air conditioning, before he put on his seat belt. It was one more thing to like about him.

When he was belted in, he turned to her. "Where to?"

"What?"

"Where do you want to eat dinner?"

"You mean you haven't already decided?" Aspen asked in disbelief.

"Nope. I don't know what you like. Seafood? Mexican? Steak? Any decision I make is fraught with pitfalls. You might be a vegetarian, and if I chose a steak restaurant, this relationship would be over before it began. Or if I picked a seafood place, and you were allergic, there again, that wouldn't bode well for us. So the easiest and safest thing to do is to let you choose."

"But what if *I* make the wrong decision? That's a lot of pressure to put on a girl, Kane."

He smiled and, once again, Aspen decided that women were insane to not want this man. How the hell he was single was a complete mystery to her.

"You can't choose wrong. I eat anything. Literally. There's not one thing I won't eat."

"Nothing?" she asked, raising one eyebrow.

He laughed. "I can see I just threw down a challenge, didn't I?"

"There has to be *something* you don't like. No one likes every kind of food," Aspen told him.

"Fine. I don't like kimchi," Kane said with a shudder.

"Doesn't count," Aspen told him with a shake of her head. "No one likes fermented cabbage. Not if they're not from Korea and didn't grow up eating it."

Kane smiled at her. It was a gentle smile, filled with tenderness. Aspen knew she was crazy for reading so much into his expression, but she couldn't help it. When she was around him, he made her feel like the most important person in the world. It was heady, and she could definitely get used to it.

"What are you in the mood for, *cha-gee?*"

Aspen blinked at the foreign-sounding word. "What did you call me?"

She was surprised when Kane's cheeks flushed. "Sorry, it just popped out."

"And? What does it mean?"

"*Cha-gee* is 'darling' in Korean. Sometimes I find myself using a foreign word instead of the English one," Kane said.

"*Cha-gee,*" Aspen repeated, trying out the odd-sounding word.

"Food?" Kane asked.

She had the feeling he was trying to move on from what he perceived as an embarrassing slip of the tongue. "Tell you what, you can call me whatever foreign term of endearment you want, if you never make me choose where to eat after tonight. Don't you know women hate picking?"

He chuckled. "Deal."

Aspen took a deep breath and wracked her brain for where they should go. She was starving, and really, there was only one place she wanted to eat when she got this hungry. "Taqueria Mexico," she said.

"Taqueria Mexico Restaurant or Taqueria Mexico Lindo?" Kane asked immediately.

"You've heard of it?" Aspen asked.

"Uh, it's only the best Mexican food in Killeen," Kane said. "Now, do you prefer the restaurant on Rancier Avenue, or the smaller Lindo on Fort Hood Street?"

"Restaurant," Aspen told him.

Kane smiled and nodded. "Good choice."

It was insane how such a small compliment could make her feel so good. "And I have to warn you, I'm not one of those women who orders a salad and picks at it. I can put down a basket of chips and salsa all by myself, and then eat my entire dinner to boot."

Kane's smile didn't dim. "Good. Because I'm not going to let you order a salad then pick at my plate all night."

"Ha. No way. I ran five miles in the heat, then did burpees and crawled in the sand for what seemed like hours. I've earned every single calorie I'm going to consume tonight."

"I don't doubt it. But it doesn't matter to me if you've sat on your ass all day either. You are who you are, and so far, I'm liking exactly who that is, Aspen Mesmer."

His words stuck with her all the way to the restaurant. Aspen knew she wasn't super skinny. She had muscles from working out all the time, and she refused to starve herself to fit into a size four. She loved food. And carbs were her weakness. She had no problem wearing tank tops because her arms were damn impressive, if she did say so herself. She hadn't expected Kane to disparage her on their first night out, but hearing him say he liked her exactly as she was felt good.

They arrived at the hole-in-the-wall Mexican place, and he met her at the front of his car and reached for her hand. They walked inside and were quickly seated in a very colorful booth in the back corner of the busy dining room.

Surprising her, Kane sat at her side, instead of across from her. At her look, he asked, "Is this all right? I just figured we could hear each other better if I was sitting next to you. If it makes you uncomfortable, I can move. In fact, I'll just—"

Aspen grabbed his arm and shook her head. "Stay. It just surprised me for a second."

Kane slowly sat back down and shrugged. "I'm really not very good at the whole dating thing," he said a little self-consciously.

"You're doing more than all right so far," Aspen told him.

They were interrupted by the waiter coming by with a heaping basket of warm tortilla chips and a bowl of salsa. He took their drink orders and scurried away.

Kane scooted the salsa closer to her and nodded toward it. "Ladies first."

"Are you gonna get weird if I double dip?" Aspen asked.

He grinned. "Nope. Not at all. And the amount of

saliva that can be transferred by double dipping is actually very small. Hell, kissing exchanges more germs than sharing a bowl of salsa."

"Good to know," Aspen said with a grin of her own.

He wrinkled his nose. "There I go again. If I start spouting too much stupid shit, just smack me."

"Never. It's handy to have someone around who has all the answers."

"I thought you didn't like it when a guy always has to be right? You, Gillian, and Kinley had a discussion at length about that," Kane said.

"No," Aspen countered. "We don't like it when we're contradicted all the time and told we're wrong when we know we're right."

"Noted," Kane told her with another smile.

"I mean, it's obvious you're smarter than me, and I'm okay with that. But if I'm talking about the traffic, which route to take, or something medical, you'd better be damn sure you're right before you contradict me."

He was looking at her with an expression she couldn't interpret, and just as she was about to ask him what he was thinking, the waiter returned to take their orders. Luckily, Aspen didn't even have to look at the menu. She'd been there so many times she had it practically memorized. Kane didn't look at it either and ordered fajitas.

After the waiter left, their conversation slipped into the more typical things two people who wanted to get to know each other talked about. She told him that she was an only child and grew up in Minneapolis, Minnesota. She'd gone to college but had dropped out before finishing her Bachelor of Arts in English. She hadn't been sure what she wanted to do with her life after quitting school. She'd done a ride-along with the local police department when she'd considered law enforcement, and had been fascinated with the paramedics who'd shown up to provide life-saving measures to a couple who'd been injured in a motorcycle accident.

She'd been looking into becoming an EMT when she'd happened to meet an Army veteran. He'd been a combat medic in Vietnam and, after hearing his stories, she'd decided to enlist in the Army herself and follow in his footsteps.

"That couldn't have been an easy decision," Kane said between bites.

Aspen shrugged. "It wasn't a walk in the park, especially the special operations combat medic course. There were several times I didn't think I was going to make it, and not just because of the physical requirements."

"Let me guess...the good-ol'-boy network?"

Aspen nodded. "I know the Army has tried very hard to cut down on that kind of shit, but it's just more hidden now. The other women in my class and I went through hell trying to gain the respect of both our instructors and our fellow medics."

"And now look at you," Kane praised.

Aspen smiled. "I've worked my ass off," she admitted. "I know more than the average paramedic working on the streets does. I know the basics of dental medicine, I can perform extractions, studied large animal veterinary care, as well as the fundamentals of herbal medicine. Not only that, but I'm just as proficient with my weapon as anyone on the Ranger teams."

"And every day, you still have to prove yourself worthy of being there simply because you're female, don't you?"

Aspen had no idea how Kane had such uncanny insight. She nodded. "It's maddening and it pisses me off. I'm coming up on my reenlistment date, and I'm seriously wondering if I want to stay in, or if I want to get out and put my skills to use some other way. Somewhere they'd be appreciated more."

One thing Aspen really liked about Kane was how, when she spoke, he paid attention. He wasn't fiddling with his phone or looking around like he was bored. He studied her and was completely dialed into their conversation.

"You'd really get out?" he asked.

Aspen shrugged. "Honestly? I don't know. I really do like the Army. I like serving my country. But when soldiers with their shiny new Ranger tab find out that they have to serve alongside a woman, and they look down their noses at me, it gets old really fast."

Kane put his hand on her thigh. He didn't grope her, simply lay his heavy hand just above her knee, lending his support. "I'm sorry you have to go through that. It sucks."

She also appreciated that he didn't give excuses for the men she worked with.

"Thanks. But...what about you? I already know you graduated high school early and got your degree young too. Where'd you grow up? Do you have any siblings? Where are your parents?"

Aspen watched as his expression immediately closed off.

Her stomach clenched. She hadn't meant to ask anything that would upset him, but he obviously wasn't all fired up to talk about himself.

To his credit, he didn't blow her off completely.

"I'm an only child too. My parents were older when

they had me. My mom was forty-two and my dad was forty-eight. I guess they thought she couldn't get pregnant, then...surprise! They were both professors at Stanford and were thrilled beyond measure when I exceeded their expectations as far as being smart went. They hired private tutors for me when I was three or four, and from there, my entire life was about school."

"I bet they were proud of you," Aspen offered uncertainly.

"Oh, they were. Bragged about me to all their buddies. But when they pushed me to get my second master's degree after I got my first, I was done. I was a skinny, uncoordinated kid with no friends. I'd spent my entire life studying. I wanted to get outside and have some fun. They weren't happy when I told them I was done with school. That I was going to join the Army. They didn't talk to me for years after that."

"I'm sorry," Aspen said softly.

Kane shrugged. "It wasn't easy. I worked my ass off in basic and AIT. Even though I had a college degree, I wanted to be enlisted. I didn't want to be an officer. I wanted to get in the dirt with everyone else. I got a lot of crap, but I didn't care. For the first time in my life, I was doing what I wanted to do. I was happy. Tired as fuck, but happy."

"Did your parents forgive you?" Aspen asked.

"Forgive?" Kane shook his head. "I don't think so. But they're resigned to the fact that their genius kid wants nothing to do with academia. The funny thing is, I'm using what they taught me and what I learned while living under their roof far more now than I ever would have if I'd taken the path they'd wanted for me."

Aspen was fascinated. "Like?"

"Like the time we were in Africa. We were in the middle of the fucking jungle...lost, if you can believe that. And we stumbled into this village, and let's just say the natives weren't happy to see us at all. It took two days of me listening and watching, but I learned enough of their language to communicate. I reassured them that we were friends and weren't there to hurt them in any way. By the end of day three, we were all sitting around a fire in our underwear, participating in some damn traditional friend-ship ritual."

Aspen giggled. She was thrilled when Kane returned her smile.

"My friends weren't kidding last night when they said I know over two dozen languages. Something in my brain just picks them up really fast. I can't read all the languages that well, but I can speak and understand them. It's come in very handy over the years."

"I can imagine," Aspen told him.

The rest of the evening was spent talking about less intense topics. What genres of books they liked to read, favorite music, their latest choices in cars, and what they'd drive if money was no object. They talked so long, the manager of the restaurant eventually came over and informed them they were closing.

Aspen was shocked. Typically, she hated lingering over the table after eating. But she and Kane had talked for hours, yet it seemed as if she was just scratching the surface of getting to know him.

And one thing she *really* liked was that they hadn't talked about the Army the entire night. All Derek had seemed able to talk about was their jobs and politics.

Kane handed his credit card to the relieved waiter and within a minute, the man was back with the bill. Not ashamed to watch as he signed the check, Aspen noted that Kane gave their patient waiter a generous tip. That was just one more thing to like about him.

He stood and helped her up from the booth. When she was standing, he kept hold of her hand and walked her to the door. He stopped just outside to look around the parking lot. The restaurant was in a strip mall, so there wasn't a huge parking area, but he still took the time to survey it for any hidden dangers before heading toward his car.

Aspen didn't complain. She knew exactly what he was doing; she was trained to do the same thing herself. She may not have worked with a Delta Force team before—they didn't use combat medics, they relied on their own skills and training if the shit hit the fan—but she was trained to be observant.

Aspen rested her head on the seat, and they were both silent as Kane took her back to her apartment. He parked and turned off his engine when he arrived.

"Where do you live?" Aspen asked. She didn't want the evening to end, but she knew no matter how many questions she asked, it eventually would.

"I have a small house not too far from here."

"A house?" Aspen asked in surprise. "Not an apartment?"

"Nope. I wanted to feel settled. I've got a ninety-one-year-old widowed woman who lives on one side of me, and a family with three kids on the other. There are kids playing outside all the time, as well as older couples sitting on their porches when the heat of the day dissipates. It's...nice."

"It *sounds* like it," Aspen said, somewhat jealous. She'd always wanted a home. A real home. But her life in the Army hadn't really been conducive to that. Wracking her brain for something else to talk about, she gazed down at Kane's arm. It was on the armrest between them, and she blurted, "You have great veins."

He blinked, then chuckled. "Uh...thanks?"

Knowing she was blushing, Aspen ran a finger over the very prominent vein on his forearm. "It's just something I notice now. It's really hard to get an IV in some people, and when I see someone who has veins like yours, prominent, I can't help but think about how easy it would be to stick you."

At his choked laugh, she looked up and realized what she'd just said. "Stick with an IV. Like, get a needle in your veins. Shit...I'm shutting up now."

Kane smiled bigger. "You're fucking cute, *cha-gee*."

She wasn't sure how to respond to that. She'd never been called cute in her life. She was too tall. Too muscular. But somehow, when Kane called her cute in the same sentence he called her darling, it seemed like the best endearment ever.

"Can I call you tomorrow?" he asked.

"I'd like that," she told him.

"Good. Me too. Come on. It's late, and I'm sure you have to get up early for PT."

Feeling disappointed, but knowing their date had to end sometime, she nodded and got out of the car. Kane was there to meet her, and he took her hand and started walking toward her building.

"You don't have to walk me to my door."

"I know."

Aspen couldn't help but smile. She liked the feel of his hand in hers. A lot. Nervous about what would happen at her door, she kept quiet as they headed to her apartment. Once there, she unlocked it and then turned, staring awkwardly at Kane.

He smiled gently and brought his hand up to her face. He brushed her hair back behind her ear and his thumb caressed her cheek for a second before he dropped his hand. "I had a good time tonight, *querida*."

"Let me guess, Spanish?"

He smiled. "Yup."

"I did too," Aspen said.

"I'll talk to you tomorrow. Don't let the assholes get you down," he told her before taking a step away.

"No kiss?" Aspen blurted.

Kane shook his head. "If I touch those lips I've been staring at all night, I'll never leave."

His words were matter-of-fact. He wasn't flirting. Wasn't trying to get her to smile.

Aspen licked her lips and saw his pupils dilate as he watched. "But you *are* going to kiss me at some point, right?" she sassed.

"Oh, yeah," Kane breathed. "Count on it. Sleep well."

"You too," she told him.

"Go on. Get inside and lock the door. I'll head out when I know you're safely inside."

Aspen nodded and kept eye contact with him until the last second. She turned the deadbolt and latched the chain.

"Good night, Aspen," she heard him say, then his footsteps sounded as he headed back down the hall.

Taking a deep breath, she put her back to the door and slid down until she was sitting on her butt with her knees drawn up. For just a second, she held her breath—then she smiled, huge, and squealed like she was a teenager again.

Evidence was pointing to the fact that Kane was feeling the same chemistry she was. Thank God.

CHAPTER THREE

The next week and a half were crazy busy for both Brain and Aspen. They hadn't managed to get together again, but they had spoken on the phone at least once a day. One night they'd talked for over two hours, and another they'd only chatted for about ten minutes. And with every call, Brain felt even more comfortable with Aspen.

They'd finally been able to make plans to get together two nights from now, a full two weeks after their last date, and he couldn't wait. He was jittery and filled with anticipation about seeing her. Brain hadn't felt like this about a woman before, and it both thrilled and scared him to death at the same time.

The team had just gotten out of a morning-long meeting about the increasingly unstable situation in Afghanistan and were headed to lunch before returning to continue the discussion. Army brass were talking about the possibility of sending in troops to try to stabilize the area, and so far the Deltas weren't on the list of special forces teams to be sent, but that could change at any minute.

"Trigger?" Brain called as they all headed to the cafeteria on post.

"What's up?" his friend asked.

"Can I talk to you for a sec?"

"Of course. What's wrong?" Trigger asked.

"Nothing's wrong," he quickly assured him. "I just...I've been thinking about something a lot lately. How did you *know* Gillian was more than just another girlfriend?"

Trigger's shoulders relaxed as he realized Brain didn't want to talk about a matter of national security. He waved to the others, letting them know they'd catch up soon. Then he turned back to Brain with a shrug. "There was just something about her. It was impossible for me to *not* think about her constantly. When we went down to Venezuela to take out those plane hijackers, and Gillian was forced to be their negotiator, she was so calm. Capable. There was no doubt she was scared out of her mind, but she was doing her best not to let it show. I was intrigued from the start. It was actually painful to leave her behind when the job was done, and I thought about her every day after."

Brain nodded.

"Aspen?" Trigger asked.

"Yeah. I admire her. Not only for being a badass combat medic who can keep up with a Ranger team, but for doing it despite how much harder it is because of her gender. Not physically, but because of all the shit she has to go through to prove she's capable."

"And?"

"And what?" Brain asked.

"There has to be more to it. I mean, we've met a lot of women in male-dominated fields who are more than capable. What makes her different?"

Instead of answering right away, Brain thought about his friend's question for a moment. Why *was* Aspen different from other women he'd met? "She listens. I mean, *really* listens, and isn't just waiting for her chance to take over the conversation. She's also very nonjudgmental. I told her about my parents and how I grew up, and she didn't even blink."

"If we go back this afternoon and are told we're being sent on a mission in two hours, what would your first thought be?" Trigger asked.

Brain inhaled sharply.

"*That*," Trigger pounced. "What was that thought?"

"I'd want to call her. Tell her in person what was going on. Tell her that if she didn't hear from me for a while, it's not because I'm blowing her off."

Trigger nodded. "You're not thinking about calling your neighbor to take care of your plants and gather your mail. You're not running through scenarios that we could encounter on the mission. Your first thought is Aspen and making sure she's all right, and that she understands why you'll be out of pocket."

Brain nodded.

"*That's* how she's different from other women," Trigger told him firmly. "When your first thought is for her, whether she'll be all right while you're gone."

"I haven't known her very long," Brain argued.

"Doesn't matter. Just because you're thinking she's special doesn't mean you're going to get married tomorrow and have a dozen babies. My advice? Just go with it. Don't overanalyze it. You want to talk to her? Call. You want to see her? Make it happen. Don't pull the bullshit that us guys sometimes do in waiting a certain number of days before you call just so you don't look so eager."

"Yeah, that's not an issue," Brain muttered.

Trigger chuckled and clapped a hand on his friend's back.

"We've talked every night since we met," Brain admitted.

"Good. The best way to win a woman's heart is by being her friend first. Let her bitch about her day, don't offer to fix all her problems; generally, they just want someone to listen. But when it counts, stand up for her, and don't let anyone give her shit. She might be strong and tough, but it always feels good to have someone in your corner when shit hits the fan."

Brain nodded. He knew that better than anyone. He'd spent most of his childhood being alone. Kids his own age never wanted to play with him, and when he started high school and college, he was too young to have any true friends among his classmates. And while he didn't know if Aspen needed someone at her back, he'd be there if he could. "Thanks."

"Anytime. Now, I don't know about you, but I'm starving. Let's go eat," Trigger said.

"I'll be there in a second. Need to make a call first."

Trigger grinned. "I'm sure Gilly wouldn't mind getting to know Aspen better at some point."

Brain gave his friend a chin lift in response. He wanted Aspen to get to know both Gillian and Kinley better, as well, but at the moment, he was feeling a bit selfish. He wanted to learn what made her tick before his friends did.

He clicked on Aspen's number and brought his phone up to his ear. He wasn't sure if she'd answer or not, though he hoped she was able to get some lunch today and maybe was taking a break.

But the phone rang four times and went to voice mail. He hesitated, wondering if he was being stupid. If he should hang up and just talk to her tonight. But before he'd decided, the beep sounded in his ear. "Hi. It's me. Brain...er...Kane. We had a break for lunch and I thought I'd see if I could catch you. I don't really have a reason for calling...other than to let you know that I was thinking about you."

He winced. God, he sounded like the nerd he was. "Anyway, I hope today's going better than the past few. I'll call later tonight. Bye."

He clicked off the phone and closed his eyes in disgust. He'd sounded like a complete dweeb. Sighing, he pocketed his phone and started across the parking lot toward the chow hall. He liked Aspen. A lot. But he didn't have much experience when it came to relationships, and the last thing he wanted was to scare her away by hovering and seeming too desperate.

But that was the thing, he *felt* desperate to talk to her. To find out how she was doing. If she'd found out any more information about her team deploying. He wanted to know what she was planning on having for dinner and what kind of television shows she might watch this evening.

In short, he was hungry for every little scrap of information he could get about her.

Taking a deep breath, he did his best to temper his curiosity about Aspen. He was the brain, the one everyone turned to when they needed answers, and he needed to be sharp and focused when he went back into the meetings that afternoon, not letting his mind wander to Aspen. He had plenty of time to get to know her. He didn't need to learn everything in the first week.

With that somewhat soothing thought, Brain walked into the building determined to put Aspen out of his mind...at least for a few hours.

Aspen was exhausted. It was eight at night and she'd been up since five-thirty. Derek had been even more of an ass than usual the last few days, and she couldn't decide if he was just being petty about the fact she didn't want to go out with him anymore, and taking it out on both their teams, or if he was nervous about escalating tensions in the Middle East and the potential for an upcoming mission.

Regardless of the reasons, the last few days had been brutal. Her Ranger team, along with two others that included Derek's, had been training in the "towns" built on Fort Hood's desolate back country. They'd been crawling in the dirt and baking in the sun. As the combat medic to her team, Aspen wasn't exactly required to complete the same training the men were, but she felt obligated. If they were in the middle of nowhere in Afghanistan, she'd have to follow alongside her fellow soldiers, treating any injuries that might happen and making sure they stayed hydrated.

And if she didn't want to be treated differently because she was a woman, she felt as if she needed to sweat and suffer right along with her platoon-mates.

Tonight, they'd done an exercise where they'd had to attempt to sneak up on a Taliban "stronghold" undetected. It was somewhat of a bullshit mission, because of course the "bad guys" knew they were out there trying to sneak in, and therefore hyper-alert. In a real-life situation, the terrorists wouldn't know they were coming. But, they had to play the game. They'd been caught over and over again, and had been screamed at by everyone from the platoon sergeants to the officers overseeing the training. It was demoralizing and frustrating, and Aspen was more than ready to collapse into bed and sleep for twenty-four hours straight.

Except she had to get up at five-thirty the next morning and head back to post to do it all over again tomorrow.

She stood in the small galley kitchen in her apartment, staring into her refrigerator blankly. She needed to eat something but had no idea what she was in the mood for. She had no energy to cook anything and, if she was honest with herself, the cool air from the fridge felt better than the thought of food anyway.

The sound of a knock on her door startled Aspen out of her semi-dazed state. She turned to answer it when her phone rang. Not looking at the display, she clicked on the green button at the same time she looked through the peephole in her door.

"Hey, it's Brain."

"Hi, Kane," Aspen told him tiredly, frowning at the man standing at her door wearing some sort of uniform and carrying a brown paper bag. "Can you hold on a sec? There's a guy at my door who I think is lost."

"He's not lost," Kane told her. "I sent him."

Confused, Aspen opened the door.

"Aspen Mesmer?" he asked.

"That's me."

"Here ya go. Enjoy." The delivery man held out the bag, and as soon as she took it from him, he turned and headed down the hall.

"What in the world?" she mumbled.

"I got worried when you weren't answering your phone earlier tonight, so I called a friend on post and he told me your platoon hadn't returned from your training exercise yet. I asked him to let me know when you were back, and I ordered dinner for you. You told me before that since I made you pick where we ate that first night, I had to choose the rest of the time, so...that's what I did. I hope it's okay."

"You got me dinner?" Aspen asked. She already knew the answer, but her brain wasn't firing on all cylinders at the moment. Her stomach growled when the scent of the food rose from the bag, filling the air and making her realize exactly how ravenous she was.

"Yeah. I don't know if you'll like it or not, but I thought that you probably need protein. After being in the heat all day, you need to replace the nutrients you lost. I ordered from Hawaiian Grill. I ordered the laulau plate, which is pork wrapped in taro leaves and steamed for several hours until it's so tender, it just falls apart on your fork. It's delicious. But in case you're not a pork fan, I also got you a hamburger steak; a patty served with their home-made teriyaki sauce. It's fantastic. There's also an order of chicken long rice made Hawaiian style on the side."

Aspen had put the bag down on the counter and unpacked it as Kane was explaining what he'd ordered.

The servings were huge, and she knew there was no way she could eat everything. But she was so grateful for the gesture, and that she didn't have to cook anything for herself, she was speechless for a moment.

"Aspen? I hope I didn't overstep. I've been where you are. So tired from training that I couldn't muster up the energy to cook myself anything. But that only made the next day more difficult and painful. From the meetings I had today, I'm guessing that your training isn't going to get easier anytime soon, so...I thought I'd do what I could to make your life a little simpler."

Aspen felt her eyes tear up, and she closed them. Clutching her phone in her hand with a death grip, she whispered, "Thank you."

"It's okay then?" Kane asked. "Not everyone likes Hawaiian food."

"I have no idea if I do or not, but I can guarantee right now I'm going to eat as much of this delicious-smelling meat as possible then pass out in a heap of exhaustion and food coma," she told him.

"Good. And I swear I'm not a stalker or anything. I was just worried about you when I couldn't get ahold of you all day. And that message I left around lunch...sorry about that too."

She hadn't even bothered to look at the notifications on her phone. "You left me a message?" Aspen asked.

"Oh...um...yeah. You can just delete it."

Curious now, wondering why Kane seemed so uncomfortable with the message he'd left, she asked, "What did you say?"

"Nothing. I had a break for lunch and thought maybe I could catch you."

"You know that as soon as we hang up I'm going to listen to it, right?" she asked. "You can't tell a woman not to listen to a voice mail and expect her to just delete it," she teased. "Were you a dick? Did you yell at me because I wasn't there to answer?"

"No!" Kane exclaimed. "God, I'd never do that! Has someone done that to you before? Fuck them."

She loved how he immediately got upset on her behalf. "I was kidding, Kane!"

He sighed. "I just realized after I hung up that I sounded ridiculous. Like a fourteen-year-old boy who was desperate for attention from the girl he had a crush on."

Aspen swallowed hard. "Do you have a crush on me?"

He didn't even hesitate. "Yes."

"And you think I'm going to be upset that you called me in the middle of the day and left me a message?"

His answer wasn't as quick this time. "I don't know."

"I'm not," Aspen told him. "Thank you for calling. I didn't have even five minutes to myself today. When we did take a break, I had to go around to my guys and make sure they were staying hydrated and weren't going to crash on me. Then I had just enough time to shove a sandwich down my throat before we were off and running again."

"You need to remember to take care of yourself too," Kane told her firmly. "You won't do any good for your team if you fall on your face. Believe me, I've learned that the hard way."

Aspen loved that he was so concerned about her. She liked the guys she worked with, but not one had even thought to make sure she was taking care of herself.

"And if it was up to me, I'd make sure your team realized that *you* are one of the most important people at their sides. Taking care of their medic should be their top priority, because I guarantee if they ever found themselves in the middle of a firefight and got shot, they'd be damn sad if you weren't around."

Aspen chuckled. She knew she was punchy from being tired and hungry, but she couldn't stop herself. "They'll be sad?" she asked.

"Sad. Pissed. Dead. Whatever," Kane said without a trace of humor.

"It's okay. I'm fine," she told him quietly. "Thank you for dinner."

"You're welcome. Are we still on for the night after next?" he asked.

"As long as Derek and the other platoon sergeants don't think we need another evening training session," she told him. "What did you have in mind?"

"It's been a long week for you. What do you think of staying in? If you come over to my place, I can grill us some steaks and we can hang out and watch a movie or something. I'm a typical guy, and I have a huge-ass TV and a ton of movies. Or we can pick something from Netflix. Whatever you want."

"Staying in sounds great," Aspen told him.

"Good. I should be done on post around four, barring any major disasters. I'll stop by the store on the way home, and then I need to mow my neighbor's lawn. I've been putting it off and it looks like a jungle, so I need to get on that. How about if we plan on you coming over around six-thirty? I know that's a little late for dinner, but it won't take long to grill steaks, and I can steam some veggies pretty quickly too."

"That sounds perfect," Aspen said. And it did. "Kane?"

"Yeah, *liebling*?"

She chuckled and forgot what she was going to say for a second. "What language was that?"

"German."

"Right. Anyway, thank you for remembering me today."

"You don't have to thank me for that," he told her. "It seems as if I can't *stop* myself from thinking about you. It's a little disconcerting, if you want to know the truth. But I talked to Trigger today, and he said he was the same way with Gillian, which made me feel a little better."

Aspen sucked in a breath. "You talked about me to your teammate?"

"Yeah. Not about anything too personal. Just this unusual need to know how you're doing and check on you constantly. He and Gillian are going to get married soon, and they're tight. *Really* tight. I figured he or Lefty were the best people to get advice from since they're in serious relationships. I haven't felt like this...ever...and needed to know if it was normal."

She liked that. "It's not."

"Not what, normal?" he asked.

"Yeah. I haven't felt like this either. I thought about you a lot today too. When I was so tired that I didn't think I could crawl another inch, I thought about you standing nearby cheering me on. It helped. A lot."

"Good. But you don't need me to cheer you on. You're badass and amazing just as you are, Aspen."

"Thanks," she whispered.

"Go eat," he ordered. "Before it gets too cold. Although, I have to admit that pork is amazing even when it's no longer hot."

"I'll talk to you tomorrow?" Aspen asked.

"Yeah. If I can't get ahold of you, I'll leave another dorky message...like the one you'll hear when you listen to what I left earlier," he said with a chuckle.

"I'm sure it's not dorky," Aspen protested.

"And I'm sure it is. But fuck it, I guess I'm okay with being dorky because there's no other way I *can* be. I'm the brain, now and always. Sleep well, *liebling*."

"I will. You too."

"Good night."

"Night."

Aspen clicked off the phone and instead of reaching for the food, she immediately clicked on the voice mail message icon she'd missed before.

"Hi. It's me. Brain...er...Kane. We had a break for lunch and I thought I'd see if I could catch you. I don't really have a reason for calling...other than to let you know that I was thinking about you. Anyway, I hope your day's going better than the past few. I'll call later tonight. Bye."

She played it twice more, smiling huge as she listened. The message *was* a bit dorky, but it was obvious it came from Kane's heart. He'd called just because he was thinking about her. How could she not love that?

Deciding she was never deleting his message, ever, she finally put her phone down and grabbed a fork from her silverware drawer. Not even bothering to get a plate, she picked up the pork dish and took a huge bite, groaning in ecstasy at the Hawaiian spices that exploded across her taste buds.

Making up her mind right then and there that Kane could always decide where and what they were eating, she devoured the rest of her dinner standing at her counter, moaning in delight with every forkful.

Later that night, lying in bed, Aspen played the message Kane left for her once more before putting her phone on her nightstand and turning onto her side. She never would've thought a plea for a kiss to try to ditch Derek would lead to this...her lying in bed, daydreaming about a fellow soldier. A man she couldn't seem to get out of her head.

She wasn't ready to run off to Vegas and marry him, but Aspen couldn't deny that she wanted to see where their relationship might go. They were both in the military, which wasn't conducive to long-term relationships. And he was in special forces, which also wasn't ideal. But he was genuinely nice, funny, smart, and yes, awkward. She couldn't wait to see how their next date would go.

CHAPTER FOUR

Brain was running behind. They'd had a briefing that ran long, so he'd rushed through the grocery store. At home, he had changed into a pair of shorts after throwing the steaks into the fridge. He didn't bother with a T-shirt, knowing he was about to sweat about four gallons while he mowed his neighbor's lawn.

It was still hot outside, and Aspen would arrive within an hour. He figured he had just enough time to get the grass cut, shower, and prep the steaks before she arrived. Of course, he didn't count on Winnie Morrison—his ninety-one-year-old widowed neighbor who he tried to check on at least every other day—wanting to talk so long.

When he was finally able to begin tackling her lawn, twenty minutes had gone by. It wasn't that Brain didn't want to talk; Winnie was funny and very entertaining. He was just aware that time was ticking by and Aspen would be arriving soon. But he refused to do a rush job on the lawn; seeing uneven grass would just annoy him, and it wasn't fair to Winnie.

He was only halfway done when he saw Aspen pull into his driveway. He cut off the mower and ran an arm across his sweaty brow as he headed toward her. He was smiling, but by the time he got close, he was frowning.

Aspen looked awful. She was pale, and he could see her hands shaking.

"What's wrong?" he asked as soon as he got close.

"Gee, that's not exactly the greeting I'd expected," she quipped.

"Aspen, what's wrong?" Brain repeated, not sidetracked by her weak attempt at humor.

She sighed. "I'm just tired."

Brain thought it was more than that, but he didn't want to stand out in the sun arguing about it. He wanted to hug her, but he was covered in sweat and he didn't think she'd appreciate it. So he took her by the elbow and steered her toward his front door. "Come on," he said.

"Am I early?" she asked, her brows furrowing.

"No. I'm sorry, I'm running behind. I promised Winnie I'd get her lawn mowed but work ran late. Will you be all right hanging out while I finish up out here?"

She stopped in her tracks, and Brain had no choice but to stop as well.

"You're going to let me sit around your house when you're not there?"

Brain snorted a laugh. "Are you going to steal my shit?"

"No!" she exclaimed.

"Go through my bathroom cabinets?"

"Of course not."

"Not that I care if you do, all you'll find is the normal aspirin, bandages, and maybe some anti-fungus lotion or something. Aspen, I don't care if you're in my house without me there. This might only be our second official date, but I've been talking to you for almost two weeks. I'd like to think I'm starting to know you pretty well. Not to mention, you're exhausted. I'm willing to bet sitting in the air conditioning sounds pretty damn good right about now. It'll take me another twenty minutes or so to finish up out here, then I'll be in. I'll shower and get dinner started. All you have to do is relax."

Brain was alarmed when her eyes immediately swam with tears.

"Shit. Aspen?"

"I'm okay," she told him then took a deep breath. "It's just been a hell of a week."

Not able to help himself, Brain raised a hand and brushed a strand of her light brown hair off her cheek and behind her ear...and noticed she wasn't sweating, even though it was at least ninety degrees outside. He frowned. "You're dehydrated," he told her.

"I know."

"And probably have a bit of heat exhaustion."

"I know that too," she said wearily.

Kicking himself for keeping her outside, he took hold of her arm again and headed for his door. He'd planned to let her in then go right back to his mowing, but there was no way he could leave her knowing that she wasn't just tired, she was ill.

He brought her straight to his kitchen and pointed to a stool at the bar-height counter. "Sit."

She did as he requested, and Brain opened a cabinet and got out a large metal cup. He put some ice cubes in, then filled it to the brim with filtered water from a jug in his fridge. He put it in front of her and ordered, "Drink."

She nodded and brought it to her lips. Brain then grabbed a honeydew melon he'd bought to cut up for dessert and quickly chopped it into bite-size pieces. He put them in a bowl and scooted it across the counter toward Aspen.

"Nibble on those too. The sugar will go a long way toward making you feel better. Finish up that entire cup of water, then refill it." Brain knew he was being high-handed, but he hated seeing her this way. He walked around the counter and once more took hold of her elbow. "Come on, grab your water, I'll get the fruit. You'll be more comfortable on the couch while you wait for me."

Aspen sighed, but she nodded and got up. They walked over to his couch, and Brain hovered over her as she sat. He grabbed his remote control and briefly went over which buttons did what.

"Go, Kane. I'm fine."

He wanted to argue. Tell her she wasn't fine, and that he wasn't happy someone hadn't noticed her physical state. Yes, she was an adult, and a medic, and should've taken care of herself, but he still didn't like that she was in rough shape. He finally nodded and headed back outside. If he stayed with her, he'd probably say something he'd regret later.

He knew Aspen's platoon had been training hard. Rumor had it the Rangers would be heading over to Afghanistan soon. He hated that, but understood it was part of her job, just as deploying was part of his.

But he definitely didn't like that her platoon sergeants and officers in charge of her unit weren't taking care of their soldiers. Yes, they needed to acclimate to the heat, as

Afghanistan didn't exactly have a temperate climate, but running their soldiers ragged wasn't smart.

And Brain hated to admit it, but the fact that Aspen was a woman was at the forefront of his mind as well. It was obvious she was tough enough to make it through Ranger training and the combat medics course, but she was still physically weaker than most men. She wouldn't want to hear him say that though, so his best course of action was to retreat until he could get his anger under control.

He wanted to talk to Trigger and see if he could put a bug in someone's ear about what was going on with the Ranger units. He didn't like to interfere, but if Aspen was on the verge of heat exhaustion, the men she worked with probably were too. And that was dangerous and stupid on the parts of the officers.

Brain wasn't sure he was any calmer by the time he'd finished mowing Winnie's lawn, but the twenty minutes of resting and getting some fluids had hopefully helped regulate Aspen's body.

He waved at Winnie, who was watching from inside her house. Brain had to grin at the enthusiastic way she waved back. She'd admitted to him once that while she might be over three times his age, that didn't mean she didn't like ogling him.

His mind quickly turned back to Aspen as he went inside and headed for the living room, where he'd left her. He'd expected to see her sitting on the couch, but instead she was standing at the sliding glass doors that led outside. He'd thought about fencing in his yard, but hadn't gotten around to it yet. Besides, it was easier to look over at Winnie's house to check on her without a fence.

Brain glanced at the cup of water and noticed that it was mostly full. She must've finished the first cup and refilled it. The bowl of fruit was half eaten as well. "Aspen?"

She turned, and he could see from the way her shoulders slumped and the dark circles under her eyes that their plans for the night had changed. He walked over to her and held out his hand. She immediately reached out and grabbed hold of him. Without a word, he turned and walked toward the stairs, grabbing her cup of water as he went by.

His house wasn't huge, only about fifteen hundred square feet, but he'd done some remodeling on his master bedroom and it was his favorite room in the house. She followed him without protest. He opened his bedroom door, and she still didn't say a word. He towed her over to his bed and gestured for her to sit. She did, then looked up at him.

Brain put her cup on the small table next to the bed and went over to the leather chair in the corner. He had a quilt lying over it that he'd bought a few years ago. He'd seen it in a store, and imagined it was like something a mom or grandmother would make. He couldn't resist buying it. Sometimes when he couldn't sleep, he'd sit in the chair and cover himself with the quilt and try to think about the good things in his life, rather than the ugly memories that occasionally kept him awake.

He brought the quilt back to the bed. "Lay down, *tesoro*."

At the questioning tilt of her head, he smiled. "Italian. Lay down."

She did without question, which told Brain how tired

she really was. He leaned over and removed her sneakers, then covered her up with the blanket, tucking it around her. "I'm gonna shower. Just rest, Aspen."

"I'm okay, Kane," she told him.

"I know you are," he lied.

"I feel better after drinking all that water and eating the fruit."

"Good."

She eyed him sleepily for a long moment. "You're really good-looking."

Brain chuckled. "Thanks?"

"Seriously. When I'm ninety years old, I want someone like you to mow my grass in nothing but a pair of shorts too."

Still smiling, Brain leaned over and kissed her temple. "Rest, Aspen."

"'Kay. Kane?"

He'd just started heading for the bathroom, but at the sound of his name on her lips, he turned back. "Yeah?"

"Why are men such assholes?"

Every muscle in his body clenched, but he forced himself to sound as calm as possible. "We're not all assholes."

She sighed. "I know. But the assholes sometimes block out everyone else."

Brain couldn't help himself. He walked back to the bed and sat. Aspen was on her side with her legs curled up, and he leaned over her, putting a hand on either side of her shoulders. "I wish I could tell you I've never been a dick, but I'd be lying. When I first joined the Army, I didn't think women should be in combat units. I wasn't sure they should be flying helicopters in hostile territory either. Not because I didn't think they were strong enough, but because it just seemed inherently wrong for them to be putting themselves in danger. Over the years, I've come to see the error in my thinking."

"How?"

"It started when a woman saved my life. And the lives of my teammates, as well. We were pinned down in a town in Africa. I can't say where or what was going on, but suffice it to say, we were fucked. The more time that went by, the worse the situation got. People appeared out of nowhere with more and more weapons, and it was only a matter of time before we'd be overrun. There were only seven of us against hundreds of townspeople who weren't happy we were there."

Aspen's eyes widened. "What happened? How'd you get out of there?"

"A helicopter screamed in from the west. One second we were on our own, and the next, the most beautiful sound we'd ever heard reached our ears. The pilot flew like no one I'd ever seen before. Skimming the tops of the buildings, scaring the shit out of the people. That chopper landed in the middle of a neighborhood with—I swear I'm not lying—about one foot of clearance on either side of the blades. The door opened, and the seven of us all leaped in. We were lying in a tangle of arms and legs but the pilot didn't wait for the door to shut. She'd seen someone holding an RPG pointing right at us."

"She?"

"Yeah. She. The guys in the back were attempting to shut the door, and my team was useless because we were all tangled in a heap. The pilot raised the chopper, turned it, and using her left hand, aimed a pistol out the small window next to her and shot the guy holding the rocket launcher right between the eyes. He fell back, and she calmly put down her pistol, grabbed the controls, and got us the hell out of there. I swear to God she didn't even break a sweat.

"When we landed—I'll never forget this—she turned to us, grinned, and said, 'That was fun.' I've been close to death several times over my career, but that was the closest call I've had. And that pilot thought it was 'fun.'" Brain shook his head in disbelief.

"Do you know where she is now?" Aspen asked.

"She's working for a commercial airline. Probably making damn good money, but most likely bored out of her mind," Brain told her. "I'm sorry the guys you're working with can't see what an asset you are to them."

"It's not all of them," Aspen admitted.

"Derek," Brain said from between clenched teeth.

"He's always been hard on the teams. I guess I must have excused his behavior before going out with him because I was enamored of his good looks or something. But now that he thinks I dissed him, he's *really* making our lives miserable."

"You should say something," Brain suggested.

"To who?" Aspen asked. She didn't sound mad, just defeated, which angered Brain. "I have no proof it's because of me. You can't know what it's like being a woman in the special forces. And I know I'm not a *real* Ranger but—"

"Don't," Brain interrupted. "Don't belittle yourself. You *are* a real Ranger. You might not wear the Ranger tab on your uniform, but you're right there alongside them on missions. You go through the same shit they do. You've been through the training."

"You're right," Aspen said a little more confidently. "Anyway, I can't tell on Derek as if we're on the playground or something. Shut up and follow orders is the name of the game. I'll be looked at as if I just can't hack it. It's not worth the trouble I'll have to go through. It's easier to just endure his bullshit."

Brain wanted to protest. Wanted to tell her she should go to the major in her unit and let him know what was going on, but he knew she was right. The first thing someone would think was that she was complaining because she couldn't handle the training. And that pissed him off.

"I'm okay," Aspen told him softly.

"You want to talk about today? This week?" Brain asked.

"Yeah, but not right this second. You need to shower. You stink." She grinned. "And I'm hungry."

Brain smiled. He liked that she wasn't shutting him out. She might not want to talk right this second, but she would. It was enough. "Okay, *tesoro*. Rest your eyeballs while I shower."

"Rest my eyeballs," she said with a small laugh. "I don't think I've heard that saying before."

"My mom used to tell me that when I stayed up too late studying. She'd come into my room and tell me it was time to rest my eyeballs, that the math would be there in the morning for me to study."

Aspen smiled at his memory.

"Are you really okay?" he asked softly.

For the first time since she'd arrived, some of the

tension around her mouth eased and she nodded. "I am now."

"Good."

"Kane?"

He shook his head in exasperation. "I'm never gonna get clean if you keep asking me shit," he told her.

Her lips twitched, but she went on. "I'm sorry to be a downer. I've been looking forward to seeing you again since you dropped me off at my apartment last time."

Something inside Brain settled. He felt as if he'd known Aspen for ages. They hadn't kissed, except for that first time at the bar, but he knew her better than most of the women he'd dated over the years. Talking on the phone had forced them to get to know each other without a physical attraction getting in the way. "Me too. And you're not a downer. Tonight was always going to be about relaxing."

"Me sleeping in your bed probably wasn't what you had planned," she said.

Brain couldn't help it, he raised an eyebrow suggestively.

Aspen giggled. "Okay, maybe it was."

"It wasn't. Seriously. I'm enjoying getting to know you, Aspen. The good *and* the bad. Relationships aren't always sunshine and roses, and I never want you to think that you can't share your true feelings, whatever they are. If you're pissed, be pissed. If you're upset, be upset. If you're happy, be happy. Got it?"

"Got it," she said. "Is it all right if I take a short nap while you're showering?"

"Of course."

"It's just that I haven't been sleeping well, and today was hard."

Brain put his finger over her lips. "You don't have to explain to me. I'm honored you trust me enough to let down your guard and sleep."

"You don't scare me, Kane."

He knew she was teasing, but *he* wasn't when he said, "Good." Then he leaned down and kissed her temple once more and stood. He headed for the bathroom without looking back. He knew if he did, he might not leave her side again.

Ten minutes later, Brain was showered and had put on a pair of sweats and a T-shirt. His feet were bare and he hadn't bothered to shave or brush his hair. He wanted Aspen to feel as comfortable as possible, and he figured if he looked comfy, she might relax even more.

When he walked out of his bathroom, he stopped in his tracks when he looked at his bed.

Aspen was curled up under his quilt...and he'd never seen anything so beautiful in his life. Her cheeks were flushed, which he was glad for after seeing her so pale earlier. He had a sudden urge to join her on the bed, but forced his feet to move toward the door. She probably wanted him to wake her up when he was done with the shower, but there was no way in hell he was doing that. If she needed to spend the entire evening sleeping, then that's what he'd let her do.

They'd have other evenings together. Brain knew better than most how being tired could suck the life out of you. She'd been working her ass off for the last few weeks to get ready for the possibility of deploying to Afghanistan with her platoon. He was more than happy to let her sleep.

He shut the bedroom door almost all the way, leaving it open a few inches, then he made his way downstairs. Aspen had said she was hungry, so he'd make something that could easily be warmed up whenever she woke. He could still use the meat he'd bought, but not as a typical steak.

Two hours later, the green chili stew he'd thrown together was simmering in the Crock-Pot and he was sitting on his couch with his feet on the coffee table in front of him, watching a football game on his big-screen TV. The sound was turned down low and he was nursing a glass of wine he'd poured himself an hour ago.

He heard something behind him and turned to see Aspen standing at the bottom of his stairs. She had his quilt around her shoulders and her hair was flattened on one side. She had the cup of water in her hand and her eyes were glazed over; she looked as though she was sleep-walking.

He immediately stood and held out an arm. "Come 'ere, *chérie*."

"French," she mumbled as she walked toward him. "I know that one."

He grabbed the cup from her and put his arm around her shoulders and hugged her as she arrived at his side. Surprisingly, she turned and leaned into his chest, giving him her weight. Brain put his arms around her waist and held her as she burrowed her nose into his neck. Because of their similar heights, she fit against him perfectly.

"Feel better?" he asked.

She shook her head. "No. I've never been a napper. I wake up more tired than I was when I laid down."

"And grumpier too," he joked.

She simply snorted.

"Hungry?" he asked.

She shook her head, but said, "Yes."

Brain couldn't help it, he chuckled again. "Right. How about you sit while I dish you up some soup."

Aspen lifted her head and took a deep breath. "It smells amazing."

Brain shrugged. "It's nothing fancy. Green chili stew. I still grilled the steaks I bought then cut them up for the soup. Threw in some canned tomatoes and green chilies. Some beef broth, water, and some carrots rounding it out. It's simple but filling. And it'll clear out your sinuses," he warned. "I figured after you ate that hot salsa when we went out the other night that you could handle it."

"I can handle it," Aspen echoed, looking him in the eye.

Brain wanted to kiss her right then and there, but he forced himself to let go and take a step back. "I'll get you more water too," he told her, holding up the cup he still had in his hand. "Getting overheated and exhausted isn't anything to mess with."

"I know. And thank you," she told him as she sat, pulling the quilt closer around her as she did so.

Brain dished up their meal and returned to her side within minutes. They ate without talking, watching the game on TV and enjoying the simple fare. After she finished, Brain asked if she wanted more.

"No, I'm good," Aspen said. "Thank you. It was delicious."

"Any time," Brain responded, reaching for her bowl. Before heading into the kitchen to put their dishes in the sink, he picked up her cup of water and handed it to her without a word.

Aspen chuckled and dutifully took a sip. "Bossy," she muttered under her breath.

Brain smiled. It wasn't that he was bossy, he just wanted to take care of her. He wasn't sure she'd had much pampering recently, and he was happy to oblige.

He returned to his small living area and sat next to Aspen. She immediately turned and leaned into him. Brain lifted his arm and put it around her shoulders as she snuggled into his side. He was happy to sit there all night without saying a word. He was that comfortable around Aspen. He wasn't going to force her to talk about what had happened that day to make her show up looking completely exhausted and out of sorts. If she wanted to share, he'd listen. Otherwise, he'd just be there for her.

Aspen felt a hundred times better than she had when she'd shown up on Kane's doorstep, which was telling, since she still felt like shit. She'd known she was dehydrated and on the verge of collapse, and the two-hour nap she'd taken in Kane's bed, surrounded by the smell of clean cotton sheets —and Kane himself—had been the best sleep she'd gotten in a week.

Ever since they'd begun their training for whatever hell awaited them in Afghanistan, her sergeant and Derek, who was in charge of the other platoon, had pushed them almost beyond their limits. It was more than obvious they'd be heading across the world soon, but of course they didn't have any real details about what they'd be doing yet. So they were training for the worst.

But in her professional opinion, the platoon sergeants were being idiots. They weren't taking care of the men under their command and were instead driving them into the ground. And while she couldn't prove it, Aspen suspected Derek was the real driving force behind the over-the-top training.

Sergeant Vandine, her platoon sergeant, was normally pretty laid-back. But with Derek egging him on, he'd become a hard-ass. She'd dealt with his attitude plenty over the last week, but so had all the other Rangers. When she'd tried to talk to him today, he'd pulled rank and told her if she couldn't handle what it took to be their combat medic, he'd ask for her to be replaced. That had hurt. *A lot.* Especially since she'd just been looking after the physical well-being of the men in her platoon.

She hadn't known what to expect from Kane when she'd shown up at his house. She'd pretty much been planning on telling him she was too tired to do anything, but the sight of him without a shirt on, his body shining with sweat, had literally left her speechless. He'd realized right away that she was dehydrated and had immediately done his best to fix it...which was more than the men who were supposed to be her teammates.

She'd drank the water and eaten some of the fruit, feeling better, and had watched him mow his elderly neighbor's lawn. He'd already worked all day—she knew he was putting in some long hours—and yet he'd still gone out of his way to do something nice for his neighbor. Then he'd tucked her into his bed and left her there to sleep.

Not for one second had she been worried he'd take

advantage of her while she was asleep and vulnerable. She may not have known him long, but she felt safer with him than with her team. Which was depressing as hell, since she'd known them for over two years.

She'd always admired the camaraderie of the special forces teams, and had been thrilled when she'd made the cut to be a combat medic attached to the Rangers. But the reality had been very different from what she'd thought it would be. Then, as now, she was an outsider, simply because of her gender. It made her more sad than anything else.

She'd woken up groggy, confused, and hungry. The smell of something delicious permeated the air and she'd moved without thought, following it down the stairs.

Aspen had never dated a man as selfless as Kane. Now that she thought about it, she'd talked more about herself during their phone calls than he did. He was always asking how she was doing and wanting to know how *her* day was and about her childhood. He was comforting to talk to, and she never felt as if they talked for as long as they did. One night they'd talked for three and a half hours, and it still felt as if it had been only fifteen minutes or so.

Now she sat tucked against his side, her belly full, no longer dehydrated, not quite as exhausted as she'd been when she arrived, and she couldn't think of anywhere she'd rather be.

She glanced up at Kane, and saw he looked completely relaxed as he watched the game on TV. Looking over at the glass of wine he'd been drinking when she came downstairs, she couldn't stop the question from escaping her lips. "Wine?"

He looked down at her and shrugged. "My parents are

wine connoisseurs, and I started drinking it with them around age fourteen. I can drink beer, but prefer wine now, actually. What about you?"

Aspen wrinkled her nose. "I'm a mixed-drink kind of girl. Give me a nice Sex on the Beach or a Malibu Sunset and I'm good to go."

"I'll remember that," Kane said.

And Aspen knew he would.

She was silent for a bit longer, then blurted, "Are you close with your team?"

As if he understood that she wasn't just making idle conversation, Kane clicked the mute button on the TV and turned toward her a little, giving her his complete attention. "Yes."

"No, I mean, are you *close?*" Aspen asked.

"I would gladly give my life for any of my teammates if it came to it," Kane said solemnly. "And more than that, I'd do the same for Gillian or Kinley, simply because I know how much Trigger and Lefty love them. My team is the family I never had growing up. They don't always understand me, but I know with one hundred percent certainty that they have my back. Whether that's on the battlefield, or in a Walmart parking lot at Christmas as we fight for the last shopping cart."

Aspen smiled a bit at that last part, but didn't respond.

"What happened today?" Kane asked softly.

"I think I told you before...I decided to join the Army and be a combat medic because of the camaraderie of the teams."

Kane nodded.

"I knew that it wouldn't be easy, me being a woman, but I truly thought I could overcome any prejudice. That my team would see how good I was at my job and would have my back like you have your team's, and vice versa."

She fell silent, trying to decide how to continue. One thing she liked about Kane was that he didn't ever interrupt her when she was thinking. Or try to fill an awkward silence.

"Today started out like the rest of the days this past week. We spent some time inside going over the latest intel from overseas and what our role might be if we're deployed. Except I think we all know it's not a matter of if, but when. We headed out to the trucks at about ten and drove to the little town that's erected north of the main post. We went through scenario after scenario for hours. It was hot, and we hadn't had a break for lunch. Derek and Sergeant Vandine kept pushing us, and of course the teams just went along with whatever they said.

"It was around three-thirty, and two of the guys on my team had run out of water and they didn't look good at all. Hell, none of us were faring very well, lying in the dirt in the sun, and I said something about it to Sergeant Vandine. I suggested that we needed a break, that we were on the verge of heat exhaustion. I thought for a second he was going to agree with me, but then he saw Derek was listening and so he lambasted me in front of everyone.

"He told me that he wasn't surprised I'd wussed out. Said that I was a weak link on the team who was going to get everyone killed when we went to Afghanistan. I waited for Sergeant Vandine to stick up for me, to tell him to back off...but he didn't." Aspen looked down at her hands and picked at a hangnail.

Kane covered her hands with his own and said, "What did the guys on your team do?"

Aspen looked up at him. His voice sounded calm, but there was an undercurrent that she couldn't read. "Nothing."

"What do you mean, nothing?" Kane asked, no longer calm.

She shrugged. "Nothing. They just kinda listened in, but didn't say anything. But it's okay. I mean, they didn't ask me to speak up, and the last thing they needed was Derek's wrath coming down on them."

"No," Kane said flatly. "Fuck no. First, you're the *medic*. You have the team's best interests at heart. If you say they need a break, they need a break. You're not some greenhorn straight out of basic training. You know what being a Ranger is about. Hell, you went through the same training they did. Second, a good leader wouldn't push his or her team to the edge of collapse. It's stupid, and it's inviting an ambush or the risk of his troops being taken captive. Third—and this is the most important—a team sticks up for a teammate when they're right. And you were right."

Aspen closed her eyes and sagged into Kane's side. Her eyes teared up again, and she did her best to keep from crying. Some super-soldier she was, crying for God's sake. If Derek could see her now, she'd just prove him right, that she couldn't cut it as a special forces combat medic.

"Stop it," Kane ordered.

Surprised, Aspen looked up at him. "Stop what?"

"Stop thinking about that asshole and what *he* might think. You aren't a robot. Neither are the others on your team. You were trying to do the job your platoon sergeant wasn't. Namely, looking out for the best interests of the men at your side. That's what a good leader is all about,

Aspen. Making the hard decisions even when it's obvious they won't be readily accepted."

That did it. The tears spilled over and coursed down her cheeks. "I'm sorry," she choked out, twisting her neck to wipe her face on her shoulder.

Kane's hand went to her chin and he turned her back toward him. "Don't ever be sorry for showing emotion, *elskling*. People think soldiers are machines, when in reality we probably feel more than the average person. We see more. Experience more heartbreak and fear. We feel guilty about the things we have to do, and horror movies have nothing on what we've seen in real life. Go ahead and cry —but don't cry over that asshole or how he treated you. He's not worth even one of your tears."

Feeling as if she'd finally found someone who truly understood her, Aspen cried harder. She soaked Kane's shirt, but he didn't seem bothered in the least. He stroked her hair and held her close as she released the emotions that had been building up within her for the last week. Sadness, frustration, and anger at the refusal of the platoon sergeants to see what was right in front of their faces.

"And as for your team not having your back...I'm sorry," Kane said after she'd stopped crying. "It sucks because from everything I know about you, I'm certain you're a damn good medic and they should be thanking their lucky stars you're in their platoon."

"I could suck," Aspen told him.

"You don't," he said with such conviction, Aspen couldn't help but tear up again. "I don't know the men you work with, but I'm going to try to give them the benefit of the doubt. They were suffering from heat exhaustion, like you were. They're probably nervous about being deployed and it's very stressful to train for a situation you know will most likely be nothing like what you expect. Peer pressure is also a very hard thing to overcome. I bet some of them came up to you when you got back to base and thanked you for saying something, didn't they?"

Aspen nodded. "Yeah. It seemed as if they felt bad about not sticking up for me."

"Right. There you go," Kane said.

She looked at the man who was holding her and saw that his jaw was still tight. "*You* would've said something."

He immediately nodded.

"And so would your team."

He nodded again.

Aspen snuggled closer, pushing one arm behind his back and throwing the other around his belly. Her knees were pulled up and resting on his thigh. She was practically sitting in his lap, but she didn't care. She was comfortable and more relaxed than she'd been all week. "That's what I want. It's why I joined the Army."

"And you're not getting it," Kane concluded.

"No. And it makes me really sad."

"Do you think you'd get it in another job?" he asked.

Aspen shrugged. "I don't know. Maybe, maybe not, but at least now I can lower my expectations."

"I hate that for you," Kane said.

Before Aspen could comment, he continued.

"I'm not a fortune teller. I have no idea what will happen tomorrow, or next week, or next month. But one thing I *do* know, if this thing between us works out...if we keep seeing each other and get closer, you'll have that with me and my team."

Aspen looked at him in surprise.

"I mean it," he said, his hazel eyes piercing in their intensity. "Gillian and Kinley are amazing, and I think you'll click with them. And if you need anything, anything at all, all you have to do is call Trigger. Or Lefty, Oz, Lucky, Doc, or Grover. They'll come, no questions asked."

"Team Brain, huh?" she asked, needing to make a joke otherwise she was going to start bawling all over again.

"Hell yeah," Kane told her.

"*Elskling?*" she asked, remembering what he'd called her earlier.

Kane's gaze dropped from hers. "Norwegian."

"Don't be embarrassed," she told him. "I like it."

"Only a nerd knows how to say 'darling' in two dozen languages," he retorted.

"Well, I know the drip rate for two hundred milliliters of lactated Ringer's IV solution is fifty drops per minute for one hour, so if you're a nerd, then I am too. Us nerds have to stick together."

Aspen loved the smile that formed on Kane's lips. He really was beautiful, inside and out. But she didn't think she'd tell him that. Macho Delta Force operatives probably wouldn't like to be called beautiful.

"You working tomorrow?" he asked after a while.

"No. We actually have the day off, but we have to go in on Sunday. There's supposed to be another meeting about our possible deployment."

Kane wrinkled his nose, and Aspen couldn't help but laugh. "I know. But the good thing is that it won't be a six-month rotation or anything. They're saying two months. They're hoping that'll be enough time for the Rangers to track down the guy causing the latest problems. Cut the head off the snake and all that."

"That's good," Kane said. "You gonna write?"

"To you?" Aspen teased.

"No, my neighbor, Winnie," Kane teased right back.

"I might if I had her email."

"She doesn't have email," Kane told her. "Maybe I should give you mine, and I can pass on messages to her."

"Sounds good," Aspen said with a smile. She loved this. Loved kidding around with Kane. Loved being serious with him. She just flat-out enjoyed everything about him.

"Since you don't have to work tomorrow, want to watch a movie?"

"You'd give up football to watch a movie with me?" she asked.

"Of course...I can tape the game."

Aspen burst out laughing. "On one condition."

"Name it," Kane told her.

"I get to pick the movie."

He groaned comically. "Fine, but you drive a hard bargain. I can't promise not to start snoring in your ear if you pick something completely awful."

"Would I pick something awful?" Aspen asked, pretending to be offended.

In response, Kane reached over and grabbed the remote off the coffee table in front of them and handed it to her without a word.

* * *

Brain held Aspen close and closed his eyes. She'd fallen asleep about halfway through *Real Genius*. He'd always loved the eighties movie, especially since it featured a group of super-smart teens.

He was still pissed way the hell off at Aspen's team. How dare they let her take all the flack from that dimwit Derek. He wasn't even their sergeant, and yet the assholes *still* didn't stick up for her.

He hadn't lied; he had the utmost respect for medics, and he'd bet a million bucks that the Rangers wouldn't be so quick to dismiss her simply because she was a woman when they were lying on the ground with their legs blown off from an improvised explosive device. No, they'd be crying out for Aspen to save them, not caring what danger it put her in.

Taking a deep breath and trying to control his ire, Brain glanced at Aspen. She'd scooted down and was currently using his thigh as a pillow. He'd been running his fingers through her hair for the last hour and had no desire to stop or move. He was glad she was getting some sleep. She obviously needed it.

He hated that she'd probably be deployed soon, but he understood it was part of her job, as it was his. There would come a time when he'd be called up for a mission, and he'd have to leave her behind.

Stopping his thoughts in his tracks, Brain shook his head. He was getting way ahead of himself. They'd just started dating...at least he *thought* they were dating. They'd only hung out twice, but because of how much they'd spoken on the phone, he felt as if they were getting pretty close.

She just seemed to get him. Maybe it was because she was in the Army as well. Maybe it was just who she was.

Whatever it was that made their connection seem so intense...Brain liked it. He liked *her*.

Closing his eyes and listening to the scene in the movie where the laser focused on Jerry's house and the hundreds of pounds of popcorn began popping, Brain did his best to relax. He couldn't control the future, but he could enjoy the present.

He'd just close his eyes for a few minutes. Then when the movie was over, he'd wake Aspen, get some coffee into her so she'd be safe to drive home, then he'd follow her to make sure she got there all right. He loved having her at his place, but she'd probably want to go home to her own bed soon.

The last thing Brain remembered thinking before he fell asleep was how much he'd liked seeing Aspen sleeping in *his* bed.

CHAPTER FIVE

Aspen woke up slowly. She was so comfortable that she didn't want to move. In fact, even thinking about moving was extremely abhorrent. She was sore all over from a week of training, and opening her eyes, getting up, showering, and going into work was the last thing she wanted to do. Eventually she realized that she didn't have to work today, but she still didn't want to get up.

It wasn't until her pillow moved that it finally clicked where she was and why she was so comfy.

Kane.

Her eyes popped open and she tilted her head back, staring right into Kane's hazel eyes.

"Hey," he said, his voice low and raspy from disuse.

"Hey," she repeated.

"Sleep all right?"

Aspen nodded. "Amazingly so. But don't ask me to move too fast this morning."

He smiled. "Sore?"

"All over," she admitted.

"I didn't mean to fall asleep," he told her.

Aspen was pleased that he didn't beat around the bush. She was surprised, but not upset, to realize she and Kane were still on his couch and had obviously been there all night. "It's okay," she said.

"Seriously. I had grand plans of waking you up, getting some coffee into you so you'd be safe driving home, then following you to your apartment to make sure you got there all right."

Aspen stared at him for a second without commenting.

"What?" he asked.

"You were going to follow me home?"

"Of course. Why does that surprise you?"

"Well, because I don't live that far away, and I know you were tired too."

"There's no way I was going to wave to you from my doorstep and send you off by yourself. Nothing good happens after midnight, and while Killeen isn't exactly the murder capital of the world, that doesn't mean that bad things don't happen. And nothing's going to happen to you on my watch, not if I can help it."

Aspen was literally speechless. She couldn't help recalling her second date with Derek; she'd needed to use the restroom after dinner, when they were leaving. Derek had joked that since she was "practically" a Ranger, he was sure she could manage to get home all right. She'd laughed at the time, but when she'd come out of the bathroom, he'd already left. The parking lot had been dark, and while it was only around ten at night, it had still struck her as rude.

While both men were handsome, the differences between Kane and Derek were like night and day. While

Derek was good-looking on the outside—and he knew it—inside, he was conceited and selfish. Kane, on the other hand, was a little awkward and unsure of his appeal, but he was generous and genuinely concerned about others' welfare. Time would tell what his faults were, but Aspen was beginning to think any faults he had would be overshadowed by his good features.

"Are you mad?" Kane asked, bringing Aspen out of her internal musings.

"Mad that you didn't disrupt my sleep and let me get a full night's rest after a completely hellish week? Or maybe upset that I had to lie practically on top of you on your insanely comfortable couch all night? Um...no." She grinned as she said the last.

"Well, sleeping with you on our second date wasn't exactly in my plans," Kane teased.

For a second, Aspen could only blink in surprise, then she laughed. "We did, didn't we?" she asked.

"And without even a kiss," Kane continued to tease.

"I'm sure that can be remedied...but not until I've brushed my teeth and don't have morning breath," Aspen told him. She liked the look of both lust and tenderness on his face.

She was lying on her side next to him, her back to the couch as he rested on his own. One of his arms was around her and the other rested on top of her hand, which was on his chest. They were snuggled together cozily, and she had no desire to move anytime soon. She had no recollection of how they'd ended up in the position they were in, but she definitely had no complaints.

"What's on your plate for today?" Kane asked. "I know

you said you had the day off, but wasn't sure if you had plans."

"Just errands," Aspen said with a wrinkle of her nose. "I need to go to the grocery store, but I don't want to get too much in case we're deployed, as everyone thinks we will be. I've got a few bulbs out in my apartment that I need to replace, and I planned on sitting around doing absolutely nothing for a few hours too. Why?"

For the first time, Kane's eyes drifted from hers, as if he wasn't sure about what he was going to say. It was interesting how confident he was in some areas, but tongue tied in others. "The guys were all going to come over here today. Gillian, Kinley, and hopefully Devyn too. I thought you might want to hang with us for a while after you do your errands."

"Who's Devyn?"

"Grover's sister. She recently moved here from Missouri. We're all pretty sure Lucky has his eye on her, but Grover's clueless about it so we're all just watching to see when the fireworks will start," Kane told her.

Aspen wanted to. She *really* wanted to. All the talk the night before about how let down she was that working with the Rangers hadn't gained her the team she so desperately wanted made her both hesitant and eager to accept his invitation. Hesitant because watching Kane with his team would bring home exactly what she didn't have, and eager because maybe, just maybe, she could find what she was looking for outside work.

"It's okay if you say no, I know how precious a day off can be, especially when you're training for a mission."

"I want to," Aspen blurted.

The smile that crossed Kane's face was beautiful. "Good," he said.

"What time?"

"Around four?" he said. "I'll go get some burgers and stuff and we'll hang out for a bit until it's time to eat. Don't be surprised if Winnie wanders over. She loves when I have cookouts because she gets to come and 'ogle the hot Army dudes.' Her words, not mine."

"I think I'm going to like your neighbor," Aspen said with a laugh.

"Everyone does," Kane said easily. "I think Gillian and Kinley have adopted her. They look after her when we head out on missions, which makes me feel better."

"What should I bring?"

"Nothing," Kane said immediately.

"Nope. Not happening. You either tell me what I should bring, or I'll go overboard and probably embarrass myself by bringing over way too much food," Aspen told him huffily.

He smiled. "Okay, since you're going to the grocery store anyway, how about if you bring some sort of salad. I'm not saying anyone other than the women will eat it, because you know, us manly men have to eat our meat and all, but..."

Aspen rolled her eyes. "Fine. I'll make potato salad. Even manly men like you and your friends can't turn that down...I mean, meat and potatoes go together like peanut butter and jelly."

"Homemade?" Kane asked.

"Of course. Store-bought stuff is gross."

"Mayonnaise or mustard based?"

Aspen eyed him. "Is this a deal breaker?"

"It could be," he teased. "Stop stalling, which one?"

"Mustard, of course," Aspen said.

Kane breathed out an exaggerated sigh of relief. "Thank God."

Aspen chuckled. "You're a nut."

"Nope, just picky about my potato salad," he told her. Then the smile fell from his face. "Thank you for not being weird about this morning. I really didn't mean for this to happen." He gestured to the both of them lying on the couch with his head.

"It's fine. Honestly, I'm glad you didn't wake me up. I haven't been sleeping all that well, and I feel better this morning than I have in quite a while. You did me a favor."

"Can't say it was that much of a hardship," Kane told her. "When I woke up with a crick in my neck around two, I moved us into this position. You were out like a light and barely even protested when I hauled you against me."

Aspen shrugged. "When I'm out, I'm out, but it doesn't happen every night. Sometimes I toss and turn. Too many memories rolling through my brain."

"I know about that," Kane said, and Aspen figured he did. They hadn't talked about the missions they'd been on, they both knew talking about specifics was out of the question, but she wasn't naïve enough to think he hadn't seen some pretty horrific things in his time as a special forces operative.

"I think I might have an extra toothbrush in my bath-room," he told her, lightening the mood.

"You have so many women staying the night that you need to have spares?" Aspen asked before she thought about her words.

But Kane didn't miss a beat. "Hell no. I think I got an

extra at the dentist last time I was there and never bothered to change out my old one. I know, I know, I should, but I'm not a fan of change, and besides, there didn't seem to be a need."

He was babbling a bit, which Aspen thought was cute. "I know," she told him, patting his chest. "I'm sorry, that was rude of me to say. You're an adult and we just met."

"It's been over six months since I've been on a date with anyone," Kane informed her. "And at least two years since I've *been* with a woman."

His cheeks flushed as he admitted that last part, and Aspen couldn't help but be shocked. "What is wrong with the women around here?" she asked.

He stared at her for a moment before saying, "You don't see me the same way as everyone else."

"Well, that's just stupid," Aspen declared, feeling somewhat annoyed. "You're gorgeous, Kane. I mean, could your eyes be any more beautiful? And your hair is always adorably mussed, which makes me want to smooth it down, which is silly because you're a grown-ass man. And when you smile at me, my knees go weak."

"And then I open my mouth and say something over-the-top geeky, which makes other women's eyes glaze over, and they realize that they'd have to put up with *me* in order to have the privilege of looking at my physical attributes up close and personal."

"Oh, for God's sake," Aspen said, downright pissed now. She sat up and glared at him. "For the record, your smartness doesn't turn me off. I'm sure if we compared SAT scores, yours would probably blow mine out of the water, but who cares? Anytime you want to babble at me in Zulu, you go right ahead, it's not going to bother me."

"*Sithandwa*," Kane said.

"Bless you."

He smiled. "That was darling in Zulu," he informed her.

"Shit, really?" Aspen asked, sidetracked from her rant for a moment. "I was totally kidding about you knowing Zulu. Hell, I don't even know what part of Africa the language is spoken."

"Mostly South Africa. The Zulu are a Bantu ethnic group, and the largest in that region at around ten to twelve million people," Kane said.

Aspen smiled. She put her hand on his cheek. "My point is, I think it's cool how smart you are, Kane. I find it amazing that you moved through school so fast. I'm impressed that you joined the Army as an enlisted man, and it's more than obvious your teammates think the world of you. All evidence is pointing to the fact that you're not only smart, you're a good man to boot, which in my eyes is more important."

Kane studied her for a long moment, a gamut of emotions rolling through his eyes and on his face. "Thank you," he whispered.

"You're welcome," Aspen whispered back, feeling the air crackle with anticipation and the chemistry between them.

"The toothbrush should be in one of the drawers to the left of the sink," he said.

"You don't care if I go through your drawers?"

"You're welcome in my drawers anytime."

Aspen couldn't help but laugh at the badly veiled innuendo. "How about we start with a few kisses first?"

"Deal," he said, then sat up, taking her with him.

Aspen shouldn't have been amazed at his strength, but she still was. He moved her as if she was a petite five foot four, rather than the five-nine she really was. Even at almost the same height, he had no problem lifting her over him and helping her stand.

She groaned. "God, I'm so sore."

"When you get home, you should take a long hot bath," Kane said. "Then do some stretches. It'll help."

"A bath sounds amazing," Aspen said on a sigh.

He stared at her, and she could practically read his mind. "I'm not getting naked in your tub," she quipped. "That might be pushing the second-date thing a little. I mean, I know we slept together and all, but rubbing my naked ass in your tub before I know when the last time you've cleaned it is going a bit far."

As she hoped, he laughed. "Fair enough. And I'll admit that I have no idea when the last time that tub was scrubbed, but I'll get on that today, just in case. You know, for future sleepovers."

"You do that," Aspen said with a smile. She chalked "not cleaning his tub enough" in the con column she was mentally keeping, but had to add, "willing to scrub when asked" in the pro column.

"I'll start the coffee while you go and brush your teeth," Kane told her.

"I hope you have sugar and creamer," Aspen muttered. "I like it sweet."

"Noted," Kane said. "You told me that about your alcoholic drinks too."

Aspen shrugged. "What can I say, I have a sweet tooth."

"Also noted. Go on, your sweet coffee will be waiting when you come back downstairs."

"Kane?"

"Yeah?"

"Thanks."

"For what?" he asked with a tilt of his head.

"For being so amazing. For not taking advantage. For letting me pick the movie, and for not being an asshole."

"I can be one," he said candidly.

"I'm sure you can, just as I can be a bitch. But I doubt you'd do it on purpose, and never to one of your friends."

"True."

"I feel safe with you, and I can't say that about a lot of people."

"That's a shame," he told her with a small frown. "You should be able to say that about the men you work alongside of."

Aspen shrugged.

"You'll always be safe with me," Kane vowed.

"Thanks," she whispered, then backed away from him before she did something she might regret later, like grab him and shove her hand down his pants to see if the erection she'd felt against her leg earlier was as big as it felt.

They kept eye contact until she reached the stairs and turned to head up them. She thought Kane groaned, but then decided she was hearing things.

She had to get her shit together. She was falling for Kane hard and fast, and frankly, it scared her. This wasn't like her. She was cautious and never fell headlong into relationships. But there was just something about him that made her feel giddy and want to throw caution to the wind.

Doing her best to turn her thoughts to the errands she needed to get accomplished before she headed back here to spend the evening with Kane and his friends, Aspen found the spare toothbrush Kane had told her should be in the bathroom.

Thirty minutes later, she was standing next to the driver's-side door of her car in his driveway, feeling nervous.

"So...four o'clock, right?" she asked.

"Yeah."

"Anything you want me to bring other than the potato salad?"

"Just you," Kane said. Then he brought his hand up to her face and brushed his thumb along her cheekbone. "I'm sorry you had a hard day yesterday. Thank you for letting me try to make it better."

"You didn't try, you *did*," Aspen said.

"Good." He took a step closer. "May I kiss you?" he asked softly.

Staring into his eyes, Aspen nodded.

But Kane didn't immediately lower his head. His eyes ran all over her face, as if he was trying to memorize her features. Then he ran his thumb over her bottom lip.

"Kane?" she asked hesitantly.

"Hmmm?"

Aspen licked her lips and saw his pupils dilate. "Are you gonna kiss me or what?"

Instead of answering, he dropped his head. His lips brushed over hers in a chaste caress. Once, twice. Then he moved one hand to the small of her back and pulled her into him, and his other hand went to her nape. Aspen felt surrounded by him as his mouth suddenly captured hers in a fierce and intense kiss.

She'd only ever felt tingles in her fingers and toes because of a kiss once before—when Kane had kissed her in the bar. Her lips parted, and then he was there, licking, sucking, nibbling. This wasn't a mere kiss, it was a claiming —and Aspen was more than happy to be claimed.

One hand clamped onto his biceps and the other gripped his shirt at his side as she took what Kane was giving her. The stubble on his face lightly scratched her skin, only enhancing the overwhelming experience.

It wasn't until they heard a catcall coming from next door that Kane lifted his head. He didn't remove his hands from her though, merely turned his head, then chuckled low in his throat.

Aspen turned to look as well and smiled when she saw Winnie standing on her front porch, her newspaper in hand, waving at them. Kane gave her a chin lift, then turned to look down at Aspen once more.

"I know I need to let you go, but I really don't want to," he admitted softly.

And right then and there, Aspen knew she was a goner. "You've got stuff to do," she reminded him.

"I know."

"So do I."

"I know that too," Kane said, but didn't release her.

Aspen smiled and ran her hand up and down his arm. "I'll see you this afternoon."

Kane took a deep breath and let it out slowly, then he straightened and lowered his hands, running one through his hair, making it stand up even more than it was already.

He licked his lips, and Aspen wanted to jump him right then and there. But she refrained...barely.

"Let me know when you get home?" he asked.

"It's only a short drive," she protested.

"Please?"

How could she deny him when he asked so nicely? "Okay."

"This isn't me being controlling," he told her. "I just want to make sure you're safe."

"I know." And she did. It felt good to know he was concerned about her. "I'll text when I get there."

"Okay. I'll see you later."

Aspen nodded. Kane reached around her and opened her door. She noticed that even after she sat, started the car, and backed out of his drive, Kane remained there, watching her. She felt a little self-conscious about it; no other boyfriend had ever focused on her so intently.

When she got to the end of his street and looked in her rearview mirror, she saw Kane had walked next door and was talking to Winnie. He was the most considerate man she'd ever met...and somehow that scared the shit out of her. He couldn't be that perfect, could he? Eventually she'd find some character flaw, and she prayed it wouldn't ruin everything else she'd learned. She didn't want or need a perfect man, but so far, Kane was everything she'd dreamed about as a little girl.

Time would tell if he was going out of his way to be overly nice, but she had a feeling he wasn't. That Kane Temple was exactly who he seemed to be. A nice guy who'd been overlooked by women wanting an edgier, more dangerous man. But that wasn't what Aspen wanted. She lived a dangerous enough life as it was. She wanted someone who would be at her side through thick and thin, and it seemed, so far, that Kane just might be that man.

Her thoughts once more scaring the shit out of her, Aspen decided she should take a step back. She was getting in too deep, too fast. She'd still go over to his house this afternoon, but she'd fortify her mental shields first. She needed to slow down, get to know Kane a lot better. Then she could decide if she wanted to take things further.

Her decision made, even if it was an uncomfortable one and not something Aspen wanted to do, she parked at her apartment complex and took a deep breath. Kane's clean scent clung to her clothes, already making her waiver. "Please let him be exactly who he seems to be," she whispered, before getting out of her car and heading up to her apartment.

CHAPTER SIX

It was four-fifteen, and Brain was standing in his kitchen talking to Oz. The others were either outside or sitting in his living room. His house was packed, but he loved having his friends over.

"Is Aspen coming?" Oz asked.

"She said she was," Brain replied.

"Everything going okay with her?"

Brain nodded. "Yeah. Almost *too* good."

"What do you mean?"

"Just that. She's hardworking, nice, funny, smart...she seems too good to be true," Brain told his friend. "I haven't been the best judge of character in the past and the last thing I want is to fall for her, only to have her change once we're together."

"I can understand that. You haven't hung out with her much though, right?" Oz asked.

"No. Just twice. But we've talked on the phone and texted a lot. I feel as if I already know her better than anyone else I've ever dated," Brain said.

"I don't want this to come out wrong but...you want me to watch her when she arrives? Not spy on her, but give you my opinion on how she interacts with the others? Sometimes it's easier to see someone's true nature when you aren't lusting to get into her pants."

Brain knew he was blushing but did his best to ignore his discomfort. "I mean, I'm always open to your opinion, but I absolutely don't want you spying on her. It would make her uncomfortable."

"You know she wouldn't even know what I was doing," Oz said.

"I know, but still, no. I like her, Oz. A lot. And I think that's what's making me uneasy."

"I'm happy for you," his friend said, clapping him on the shoulder.

"Thanks."

"Just remember that she's not perfect. No one is. If you look too hard for her faults, you might overlook all her good qualities."

"Not a chance of that," Brain said with a small chuckle. "Her goodness shines so bright it's impossible to see anything else. Which is a part of my worry."

"What can't you see?" Kinley asked as she came into the kitchen, Lefty at her heels.

"Anything when someone as beautiful as you is around," Oz quipped.

Kinley blushed but rolled her eyes.

"You hittin' on my girl?" Lefty asked, throwing an arm diagonally across Kinley's chest and pulling her back into him.

"Nope, wouldn't dream of it," Oz said with a smile.

Then he gave Brain a chin lift and squeezed past the couple into the other room.

"When's Aspen getting here?" Kinley asked.

"I might get a complex with everyone asking about Aspen," Brain joked.

Kinley frowned and shook her head. "No, I'm always happy to see you, Brain."

"I know you are," he told her. "I was kidding. And I'm hoping any time now. She had some stuff she needed to get done today, so she might be running late."

"Have you called or texted her?" Kinley asked.

Brain shook his head. "I didn't want to bug her."

Kinley rolled her eyes again and pulled out her phone. "What's her number?"

Brain hesitated. He wasn't sure he should give it out without Aspen's approval, but at the impatient look in Kinley's eyes, he caved and rattled it off.

Kinley's fingers moved quickly over the keyboard on her phone and she nodded. "There."

It was seconds later when her phone vibrated in her hand. Lefty read the text she'd just received out loud from over Kinley's shoulder. "I'm about to leave. Running late, as usual. Sorry."

"Don't be upset, Brain," Kinley said, always wanting to be a peacekeeper. "I'm sure she's not always late."

Brain couldn't help but laugh. He'd just been bitching to Oz that he hadn't found any flaws in Aspen, and now he knew at least one. She hadn't been late last night when she'd come to his house, but that was probably because she'd come straight from work. He thought back to their phone calls over the last week and a half and realized that, most of the time, if they'd planned in advance, she *had* called later than they'd scheduled.

But he could deal with her being late. He pulled out his own phone and shot off a quick text.

"You aren't yelling at her for running late, are you?" Kinley asked.

"What? No," Brain said firmly. "I just told her to take her time, to not get in an accident or a ticket racing over here."

"Good," Kinley said. "I like her. I don't want you doing anything to make her break up with you."

Brain rolled his eyes. "I think that ship's sailed," he told her honestly. "I'm overbearing and overprotective. I fell asleep on her last night, and even when I woke up at two in the morning, I didn't apologize and get her home, I let her sleep on top of me instead. I also bad-mouthed her team and made her cry. I'm not sure I'm batting a thousand here."

Kinley simply shook her head. "Overprotective isn't a bad thing," she argued, looking back at the man holding her. "And believe me, waking up on top of the guy you like isn't a hardship. Cut yourself some slack," she ordered. "But also, don't be a dick so she wants to stick around, okay?"

Both Brain and Lefty chuckled. "Got it. I'll do my best."

"Good. Let me know when she gets here," Kinley told him.

"Uh, the house isn't that big, I think you'll know," Brain told her.

"I might be outside," Kinley said, then turned, towing Lefty out of the kitchen behind her.

At one point, Brain might've rolled his eyes at his teammate and accused him of being pussy-whipped over his girlfriend, but he had a feeling if Aspen was the one towing *him* around, he wouldn't complain one whit about it. He'd follow her wherever she wanted to go.

The get-togethers at his house were once all about him and his teammates eating burgers and talking shop until late in the night, but now that Kinley, Gillian, and Devyn had joined them, they had all kinds of side dishes with their burgers, and he'd even bought a blender to make margaritas for the women when they wanted them. Winnie came over more often than not, joining in the fun. And typically, after Trigger and Lefty took off with their girlfriends earlier than usual, everyone else slipped away soon after.

The changes were fine with Brain. He loved seeing his teammates happy, and having the women join their group made them talk about work less and simply enjoy being together. Brain hadn't had that before he'd joined the Army. If he was invited to get-togethers, they were study groups, and he'd always left before any alcohol had come out. He loved being a part of this group. That was one of the reasons he always invited people over to his house, so he could be in the thick of things.

He'd just finished making another batch of margaritas when he heard a knock on the door. Knowing enough time had passed for Aspen to arrive, he intercepted Doc and opened the front door himself.

Aspen was standing on his doorstep, looking delightfully mussed.

"I'm sorry I'm late. I actually fell asleep, if you can believe that. I did all my errands, but my legs were sore from training and I sat on my couch for a small break and woke up three hours later. I had to finish the potato salad, even though it probably didn't sit in the fridge long enough, and then get changed."

Brain didn't comment, simply reached out and pulled her into his house. He kissed her hard, but way too briefly for his peace of mind. "I'm just glad you came," he told her.

"Me too," she whispered.

"And, I'm glad to know you aren't perfect."

"What? Who said that? I'm far from perfect, Kane."

He shook his head. "I can handle you being late. Especially if it's because you napped. You obviously needed it."

"I'm not always late," she protested.

He raised an eyebrow.

"Okay, maybe I *do* tend to be late more often than not, but it's not on purpose," she protested. "And what about you? You're pretty damn perfect yourself. What are *your* flaws, so I don't feel so disgruntled that you already know about my tendency to be late?"

Brain opened his mouth to say that he had plenty of flaws, but Gillian spoke up from behind him before he could.

"Brain doubts himself way too much," she said.

"And his feet stink!" Trigger said with a grin. "Seriously, when we're on a mission and he takes off his boots, we all nearly pass out."

Brain flushed and turned to his friend, glaring at him. "Shut the fuck up."

But amazingly, he heard Aspen giggling. He turned back to her. She stepped toward him and hooked her arm in his. "I'll work on you doubting yourself, and I can handle stinky feet."

"I thought you were never going to get here," Gillian told Aspen, breaking the intimate bubble between her and Brain. "Brain made margaritas, and somehow they taste so much better tonight than in the past. You have to try one."

"That's because I made them extra sweet," Brain said, not taking his eyes from Aspen's. He saw the moment his words registered.

"Thank you," she mouthed, before she let Gillian drag her off toward the kitchen to drop off the bowl of potato salad she was holding and to get a drink.

"Gillian's been talking about seeing Aspen again all afternoon," Trigger told him. "She really likes her."

"Good. Aspen could use some friends," Brain said, watching Aspen laugh at something Gillian said. Before long, his small kitchen was packed full when Kinley and Devyn joined the other women. They all topped off their cups and made a toast.

"Feels good, doesn't it?" Trigger said.

"What?" Brain asked, tearing his eyes from Aspen to look at his friend.

"Wanting happiness for someone else more than you want it for yourself."

Brain thought about Trigger's words for a second, then he nodded. That was exactly how he felt. What he wanted didn't seem to matter as much when Aspen was around. He only wanted her to fit in, to find the camaraderie she'd been looking for her entire life.

"Come on," Trigger said, throwing his arm over Brain's shoulders. "I'm hungry. You've got burgers to grill. She's fine. The girls'll take care of her."

Brain nodded. He knew his friend was right. Aspen was in good hands.

Two hours later, while Brain and Aspen washed dishes, everyone else sat around his living room. They were laughing and talking after stuffing themselves with burgers, the best potato salad Brain had ever eaten, as well as the other side dishes everyone had brought over. Winnie was sitting contently in a rocking chair he'd bought after she'd commented how much she missed the one she used to have on her front porch, which had been destroyed in a wind storm. Lefty was on the couch with Kinley on his lap, Trigger and Gillian sitting with them. Lucky was hovering near Devyn while trying to pretend he wasn't, and the other guys were sitting in chairs they'd brought in from his small kitchen table.

They were talking about all the tropical storms that had been popping up in the Caribbean lately and how destructive they'd been, when Trigger cleared his throat and stood.

"I can't imagine a better place to do this than surrounded by the best friends we've ever had."

Brain felt Aspen go still next to him then whisper, "Oh my God."

He put down the pan he'd been scrubbing and quickly dried his hands, turning toward his friends.

Trigger was still talking. He'd turned to look down at Gillian, who was sitting on the couch, staring up at him with wide eyes.

"Gilly, every day I'm with you, I find out something new. You constantly keep me on my toes, and living a life without you in it would kill me. I admire your strength, I envy your ability to make friends, and I love waking up to you every morning and going to sleep with you in my arms. I want to spend the rest of my life learning what makes you tick and doing everything in my power to give you the best life possible. Will you marry me and make me the luckiest man in the world?"

Brain heard Aspen inhale deeply, and he pulled her back against him. He rested his chin on her shoulder and watched as one of the men he admired most in the world held his breath while he waited for Gillian's answer.

"You dork," she said lovingly and held up her left hand. "You already asked me, and I already said yes, remember? I'm already wearing your ring."

"I know, but we haven't actually gone through with the ceremony yet—and I'm tired of waiting to make you mine officially."

Gillian smiled. "I'll marry you whenever you want, Walker, but I already told you, I'm not planning it."

"Good. Because I've got the paperwork for you to sign, and next week we've got an appointment at the Justice of the Peace to get this shit done."

Gillian blinked in surprise. "You do?"

"Yup. What do you say?"

In response, Gillian leapt up from her spot on the couch and into Trigger's arms. "Yes!"

Everyone in the room clapped and broke into cheers.

Aspen turned her head and looked at Brain with a smile. "That was sweet."

"It was. You knew the second he started talking what he was doing, didn't you?" he asked.

She shrugged. "Well, yeah, it was pretty obvious. He didn't tell you guys that he was going to propose?"

Brain shook his head. "No. It took me a bit longer to

catch on since he'd technically proposed already, but I'm thrilled for them both."

"Me too. Women dream of this kind of proposal. Having the man they adore publicly declare his love and ask for her hand in marriage."

"You want that?" he asked.

"What?"

Brain gestured at Trigger and Gillian, still wrapped in each other's arms.

"Well, yeah." Aspen shrugged. "If you're talking about finding someone to love who wants to marry me, yes. Wait," she said, turning toward him fully. "Do *you*? I mean, someday, not right this second of course, but eventually?"

"Yes," Brain answered immediately. "I want someone I can rely on no matter what happens in our lives. I want to face challenges together and raise a family with her. I want someone who will love our kids no matter if they're super smart, or if they're handicapped."

"It's hard on you that you don't talk to your parents much, isn't it?" Aspen asked quietly.

Brain sighed. "Yeah. They wanted me to be the next Nobel Prize winner or something, and when my life took a different turn, it was as if they thought everything I'd done until joining the Army was thrown away."

Brain felt as if he and Aspen were the only ones in the room, which was a miracle considering the hoopla that was happening behind them.

"I'm sorry," Aspen said quietly.

"It's fine. Honestly? It's their loss."

"If the occasion ever arises, I'd still like to meet them... if that's okay."

"It's definitely okay. I don't hate them. I just don't go

out of my way to visit them, but for you, I'd make that effort. My parents and I are just very different people. I think they despaired of me ever finding a girl who wasn't like me."

"What do you mean?" Aspen asked with a tilt of her head.

"You know, someone who doesn't have her nose stuck in a book and wasn't constantly babbling about the periodic table or math formulas."

"There's nothing wrong with being smart," Aspen protested. "In fact, I bet your folks will be slightly disappointed I'm not a genius like you are."

"Want to bet, *dorogoy*?"

"Don't go spouting your Serbian sweet talk at me, trying to catch me off guard," she mock frowned at him.

"It was Russian," he said with a laugh. Then he got serious. "You keep me grounded in a way no one else has been able to. I'm not constantly wondering what other people are thinking about me when I'm too busy thinking about *you*. You accept me the way I am, and that means the world to me," he told her honestly.

"Because I like you just the way you are," she told him softly.

"If the time comes, and our relationship gets to that point, I'll give you a marriage proposal that you'll never forget," Brain vowed.

Aspen blushed and shook her head. "I don't need anything over the top, Kane. A simple 'will you marry me' would suffice...*if* things between us progress to that."

Brain nodded, but internally, he was already thinking of what he could do that would be both romantic and flamboyant at the same time. He should be freaking out that he was even thinking about how to ask Aspen to marry him, but instead he just felt...content.

"Come on, let's go congratulate your friends," she told him.

"*Our* friends," Brain corrected.

Aspen's smile couldn't have been bigger. "Our friends," she agreed.

But just as she turned to tow him out of the kitchen, making Brain flash back to when Kinley had done the same thing to Lefty, her phone rang.

Grimacing, Aspen sighed and shrugged. Brain didn't suggest she not answer it. He knew as well as she did that phone calls couldn't be ignored in their line of work.

"Hello?" she said as she put the phone to her ear.

Brain listened to her side of the conversation, his muscles tightening with every word.

"Yes, Sir. I understand, Sir. O-four hundred, yes, Sir, I'll be there. Thank you. You too. Bye."

By the time she hung up, Brain knew that not only had her plans for the evening changed, but she would also be leaving in the morning for the Middle East.

"That was the major," she told him.

"You're leaving in the morning," Brain finished for her.

Aspen nodded.

Without hesitation, Brain gathered her into his arms, and she went willingly.

"For the first time in my life, I don't want to go," she mumbled into his neck. "I've always been excited about being deployed. Happy to be *doing* something."

"I know," Brain soothed. And he did. He always felt the same way when he found out about a mission. But he had a feeling everything from this point on would feel differently.

He eased Aspen back and put his hands on her shoulders as he stared into her eyes. "This changes nothing between you and me," he said fiercely.

She nodded.

"I mean it. I don't care how long you're gone, nothing changes."

"It should only be around two months or so," she said quickly.

"Piece of cake," Brain told her, even though his stomach felt like it was in his throat. He didn't want to go two months without seeing her. For the first time, he understood what Gillian and Kinley might feel when they found out the team was going on a mission. Hell, he realized Trigger and Lefty probably felt the way he did right now, when they were called up. But he put on a positive face for Aspen.

"You'll write me, and I'll write you," he told her.

"Of course," she said, nodding quickly.

"All I ask," he continued in a gentler voice, "is that you watch your six. There's way too much I still need to learn about you."

Aspen nodded again. "And me about you."

"We'll write, and you can ask me whatever you want. I'll answer honestly," Brain told her. "Even if you think it's too personal, you ask. Okay?"

"Okay. Same goes for you."

"This isn't the end of us," Brain told her. "We just have to get used to it, unfortunately. You'll get deployed, and I will too. Life goes on, and we can either let our separations bring us closer together or push us apart."

"I don't get how I can be so emotional about this when we've only been dating for two weeks," she said with a small frown.

"Don't try to understand it," Brain advised. "I'm shocked myself, but I'm just going with it."

"Okay. Me too then. But don't forget who made the first move," she said cheekily, trying to lighten the moment.

Brain chuckled. "How could I? I wasn't all that keen on being used like that, but the second my lips touched yours, I was a goner. Don't let Derek give you shit," he said, just remembering that she'd be deployed with her asshole of an ex.

"I'll try not to."

'Good. I'm gonna miss talking to you," Brain admitted.

"Same here."

"Hey, this is a party!" Trigger yelled. "Break out some more margaritas for the women and beers for us. And okay, you can have your wine, Brain!"

He turned to his friends and shook his head. "Aspen has to go."

There were groans and complaints all around.

She shrugged. "Duty calls."

Those two words shut up the Deltas and they all got serious. One by one, they came into the kitchen and hugged her, wishing her well and telling her to stay safe. The other women realized that Aspen wasn't just leaving for the evening, but that she was being deployed, and they added their good lucks as well.

Brain walked Aspen to his door when all he wanted was to take her upstairs and lock her in his bedroom so she couldn't go anywhere. It was a shocking thought, considering what he did for a living. He held her hand all the way to her car, which was parked on the street with his teammates' vehicles.

He took her head in his hands and kissed her without asking permission first. He kissed her with all the frustration over the fact that he wouldn't get to see her for a while and the worry in his heart.

And Aspen kissed him back with the same level of emotion.

After a few moments, Brain pulled back and rested his forehead on hers.

"I'm serious, be safe out there, *dorogoy*. I won't be able to sleep well until I know you're home safe and sound."

"I will," she reassured him.

"Tell those Rangers if they don't have your back at all times, they'll find out *exactly* how vengeful I can be," Brain said a little too harshly.

But Aspen merely chuckled. "I love that you think nothing about threatening a platoon of Army Rangers."

"I'm a Delta, darling, I can kick their asses easily. And if I have to collect tarantulas and release them into their beds at night when they get back, I will."

Aspen laughed again and hugged him tight. Brain held on and inhaled deeply.

Gardenias. He'd never forget that smell as long as he lived.

Taking one last deep breath, he knew he had to let her go. She had shit she needed to do. He took a step back and shoved his hands into his pockets. "I'll call you at three-fifteen to make sure you're up," he told her.

Aspen smiled at him. "Thanks, I'd appreciate that. It

wouldn't be good if I overslept and missed formation. The sergeant major would kick my ass."

Brain couldn't make himself return her smile, and no further words would pass his suddenly closed-off throat.

He watched as Aspen opened her door and sat in the driver's seat. She started the engine and rolled down the window.

"I'll email as soon as I can," she told him.

Brain nodded.

"Thanks for a fun evening. Tell everyone I'm sorry I had to run, and congratulate Trigger and Gillian for me. I'm sorry I'll miss their courthouse ceremony."

Brain swallowed hard and nodded once again.

"Bye, Kane."

When he didn't answer, she put her car in gear and started to drive off.

"Aspen?" Brain blurted.

She stopped. "Yeah?"

"Kick some terrorist ass out there, okay?"

She smiled. "I will."

Then she was gone.

Brain watched the taillights of her car until she turned at the end of his street and disappeared from view.

"Fuck," he mumbled.

"Hurts, doesn't it?" Lefty suddenly said from behind him.

"Like hell," Brain agreed without turning around.

"When I found out Kinley had gone into WITSEC, and I had no idea where she was, if she was all right or safe, it about killed me. Brought me to my knees."

Brain nodded.

"But what kept me going was the fact that I knew how

strong Kinley was. That she felt to the bottom of her soul she was doing the right thing. I hated that I couldn't be by her side to keep her safe, but I had to trust that she could keep *herself* safe. That she was doing what she needed to do so she could return to me."

And just like that, Brain felt better.

He turned to his friend. "Aspen is fucking amazing. She's strong, has to be in order to be on a Ranger team. She's gonna be fine." And he truly believed those words. He hated not being with her. Hated that he couldn't keep her safe, but he couldn't be by her side every minute of every day. And he didn't need to be. She could take care of herself. And while she might not click with her Ranger team like she wanted to, he'd bet everything he had that if it came down to it, the men she worked with would come through for her.

He *had* to believe that, otherwise he wouldn't be able to let her go.

"She is," Lefty agreed. "Now, come back inside. We're planning a hell of a reception for Trigger and Gillian, because she refuses to plan anything. Winnie's talking about strippers and blow-up dolls and someone needs to talk her off the ledge."

Brain laughed; he couldn't help it. It was just like Winnie to want sexy strippers at a wedding reception. He walked back toward his house, but just before he went inside, he looked down the street where he'd last seen Aspen.

"Stay safe, darling," he whispered, before heading into the joyous fray in his living room.

CHAPTER SEVEN

From: Aspen

   To: Kane

   Subject: I'm here, finally!

   Kane,

Hi! We're finally here. Can't say where here is, as you know, but for as much sand as there is around us, I haven't had *one* chance to use my surfboard. ;) The flight was all right. I couldn't sleep, though. My seat was nothing like your couch. We're all set up in our accommodations and, like usual, I'm not in the same place as my team. I get it, I do, but it's frustrating. How can I get to know them and how can they get to know me if we're not together?

Anyway, I'm guessing we won't be here much, we're headed out to explore soon, but I wanted to send you a quick message to let you know I've arrived and everything is good. Talk to you later.

   -Aspen

. . .

From: Brain

To: Aspen

Subject: Re: I'm here, finally!

Aspen,

Thank you for writing. I've been waiting anxiously to hear from you. I'm glad the flight was uneventful and you made it there without any drama. I hadn't really thought about accommodations, but I can see how frustrating that would be. And you're right, a lot of the bonding happens before and after outings, when my team and I are hanging out informally. We talk about the day and everything that happened and what might be in store for us tomorrow. Keep your chin up.

Winnie and the other women all told me to tell you they're sending good thoughts your way. Gillian and Trigger are ready for their ceremony at the courthouse, and it was decided everyone's coming back to my house afterward for a small reception. Unfortunately, I know nothing about organizing a wedding reception, and Gillian still refuses to have anything to do with it—not that I can blame her, since she does that sort of thing every day because of her job. Got any suggestions for me?

I said it before and I'll say it again, be safe. Rogue waves can come out of nowhere and knock you on your ass. And I've heard there's a lot of nasty weather headed your way.

-Brain

From: Aspen

To: Kane

Subject: Weather

Kane,

Yeah, the weather's pretty nasty, and it's forecast to be shitty for the entire time we're here. But I'll be sure to wear my raincoat and carry my umbrella wherever I go. :)

As far as the party, I'm sorry to miss it. But I'm thinking the best thing you can do is serve a bunch of appetizers. They're easy for people to eat and pretty easy to make/buy. I think you should be able to buy a lot of things pre-made from the grocery store, but I would also ask everyone to bring something, that would save you a ton of time. Examples for what people could make are deviled eggs, caprese skewers, fruit kabobs, tortilla chips and salsa (or potato chips and dip), meatballs, cheese sticks, chicken wings, twice-baked potato skins, pigs in a blanket, or a charcuterie board (and now I'm hungry, darn it; the food here sucks).

Please congratulate Trigger and Gillian for me. Maybe I'll bring them back some sand as a present. Just kidding!

I know it's only been a few days...but I miss you.

-Aspen

From: Brain

To: Aspen

Subject: Re: Weather

I miss you too, *gráinne* (that's Irish, by the way. *grin*). Sometimes I wonder how we clicked so quickly, but then I tell myself not to worry about it so much. There are a lot of things in this world that I don't understand, and I'm enjoying feeling this way about someone.

How's the weather? My friends and I have been hearing some not-so-very-nice things about the storms over there, and it's making me nervous. Rumor has it we might be taking a vacation out there in the near future ourselves. I'll know more in a week or so.

Thank you for the suggestions. I called Kinley, and she was thrilled to help with the appetizers. She's calling Gillian's girlfriends, and they're going to help too. Winnie even offered to make a cake. It won't be a traditional wedding cake, but on short notice, it'll have to do.

I miss hearing your voice. I got so used to talking to you every evening that it seems weird to eat dinner and settle in front of the TV without being able to hear about your day.

Watch your six, *gráinne*.

-Brain

From: Aspen

To: Kane

Subject: Re: Re: Weather

Today sucked. There are some days I hate my job, and today was one of them. Remember when I came over to your house after that hard training session and was dehydrated? Yeah, things here are going like that training day. The guys I work with are being standoffish and I feel very alone, even when surrounded by people. I have to be an adult and suck it up. And God forbid I cry. I'll be called a pussy and told I can't hack it. Derek's an ass, and I'm ashamed I thought for one second that he was a good guy. He sucks as a leader, and the only positive thing about the day is that he's not my boss.

I'm sorry I don't have it in me to be upbeat and positive today. I miss you.

-Aspen

From: Brain
To: Aspen
Subject: Hang in there

I just got your email. I'm so sorry I'm not there to give you a huge hug. I wish I were. And I'm sorry Derek's being an ass. It makes me so mad that your team isn't supporting you like they should be. And you never have to be positive with me if that's not how you feel. I want you to be you, shitty emotions and all.

I miss you too. Confession: the quilt you used when you stayed the night still smells like you, and I've been sleeping under it since you left. It makes me feel closer to you.

-Brain

From: Aspen
To: Kane
Subject: Amazing Day!

Kane,

I had the most amazing day today! And I know, I know, my last email was pretty much a downer, but today was great. We were walking around seeing the sights like we've done every day we've been here, and we heard screaming coming from a house. A little boy was standing outside the door crying, and when he saw us, he frantically gestured for us to come closer. I stood back, letting the others do their thing, but the boy came right to me when he saw the red cross on my bag.

I went inside and found his mom was in active labor. She was screaming in pain, and she was all alone in the house. No one was helping her. I immediately got to work —and the guys with me helped out so much! They didn't seem irritated that they had to help a woman give birth. We worked as a team, and it felt *great*.

We ended up helping the woman birth a beautiful baby girl. I've only delivered one other baby, and really I just assisted that time. To see such an amazing gift of life is always so special. A miracle.

The mom was so grateful, she kept kissing my hand, and the little boy was adorable. I could've used your translation skills, but overall I don't think we did so bad.

Oh...how was the party? It was yesterday, right? Or is it tonight? I'm so bad at figuring out time zones.

-Aspen

From: Brain

To: Aspen

Subject: Re: Amazing Day!

I'm so glad you had a good day. That family was lucky you just happened to be there when they needed you. I'm proud of you!

The reception was good. The appetizers were a hit; thank you for the suggestion. The actual wedding at the courthouse was short, but very romantic (at least, I think you'd think so). Trigger surprised Gillian by arranging to have both her parents and his there. Wendy, Ann, and Clarissa, Gillian's longtime friends, attended, and of course, all of us did too. It was crowded in the room, but no one seemed to care.

Since you're a girl and probably want to know, Gillian was wearing a knee-length pink dress with a pair of pink Converse sneakers with sequins on them. She looked absolutely beautiful. Trigger decided to wear his dress blues, and I don't think the couple took their eyes off each other throughout the entire ceremony. I'm pretty sure Ann or someone videoed it, and I'll send you a copy as soon as I get it.

Winnie's cake was awesome too. A little lopsided, but no one cared. I wish you were here. Everyone asked about you and wanted to know if I'd heard from you. Whether you know it or not, you have a team back here at home. You're greatly missed.

-Brain

From: Aspen

To: Kane

Subject: Re: Re: Amazing Day!

I'm okay. I wanted to make sure I started with that so you wouldn't freak.

There was an incident today, but again, I'm okay. I wasn't sure what you might've heard or not heard about it. We were walking around like we've done all the other days we've been here when some not-so-nice guys decided they didn't like seeing us in their territory. Holman and Buckland, two of the guys in my group, were hurt, but not too bad. I hit my head on the side of a building when Hamilton tackled me to get me out of the way of one of the bad guys—but again, I'm fine.

You know, some days I feel like we're making a difference in ridding the world of evil, and other days it's as if the whole world is against us. I also feel like I'm on a roller coaster, one day happy and excited, and the next, feeling depressed and defeated. I know it's not healthy, and after days like today, I'm really questioning what the hell I'm doing with my life.

And there I go being all depressing again. Shit, I hate that.

So...what's going on there? Have Lucky and Devyn gotten their shit figured out yet? :) Have you talked to your parents? Tell me something normal, please.

-Aspen

From: Brain

To: Aspen

Subject: Normal

Aspen,

What's normal anyway? I totally understand what you're going through, and while that might not be very helpful, I hope it makes you feel not so alone.

I did hear about the incident, and I appreciate you emailing me so quickly after it happened, otherwise I would've been completely freaked out. And yes, men can get freaked out. I hate that you were hurt, but I'm glad Hamilton was watching out for you. That's how a team is supposed to work.

I don't know what's going on with Lucky and Devyn. Gossiping isn't really my thing, and we've been very busy. But no matter how busy we get, you're never far from my mind. It's been a whole month since I've seen you, and I seem to miss you more with each day that passes. I forgot how boring my life was until I met you. Now I come home from work every day and sit in my house by myself and watch TV until I fall asleep on the couch.

Back to the incident...

It scared me, sweetheart. I don't like thinking about you being in the middle of something like that, and the thought of you getting hurt makes me crazy since I can't be there to see for myself that you're all right. I trust you to do your job, it isn't that. I just...I worry. I need you to take care of yourself so you can come home and we can see where this thing between us goes. I haven't spent nearly enough time with you.

Be safe.

XOXO, Brain

From: Aspen

To: Kane

Subject: Thinking

Kane,

This trip is making me really think about what I want to do with my life. Again, I love what I do, love the medical field, but I think I could probably be just as effective, and happier, if I did it some other way. That doesn't mean I'm not going to work my butt off on this current job, but I've got some more thinking to do.

And you know what? I thought this trip would be good for me. To put some space between us because I was way too into you. I've never fallen for someone as fast as I have you. I thought the distance would be a good thing. But I realize that I feel the exact same way about you more than a month later as I did that evening when I said goodbye. I eagerly check my emails to see if you've written, and when you do, I read your email over and over, desperate to feel close to you. I guess the saying is correct, absence makes the heart grow fonder. At least on my part.

Of course, you could be reading this and cringing and thinking about the best way to ease off, to put some distance between us. More than we have right now. Lol.

On that note, I'm gonna sign off. We're going on a long walk tomorrow, and I already know Derek's gonna be an ass about it.

Miss you,

XOXO, Aspen

From: Brain

To: Aspen

Subject: Re: Thinking

I feel the same way about you, and I'm not cringing. Not in the least.

And...there might be less distance between us in the near future than either of us thought. The possibility of that trip my friends and I might be taking? It's looking like it's a reality.

See you *soon*.

Kane

From: Aspen

To: Kane

Subject: Trip

I haven't heard from you in a few days. I hope that means you've left for your vacation.

~Aspen

CHAPTER EIGHT

Aspen woke up after a shitty night's sleep. She was jittery and as excited as a six-year-old on Christmas morning.

Kane would be here today.

The missions she and the Ranger teams had been on over the last month hadn't gone as planned. They hadn't been able to find the man behind the most recent uprisings in the area, and the Army had called in a Delta Force unit to assist.

Derek was furious when he'd learned Kane was on the Delta team and would be arriving at the base soon. The last three days on patrol had been hell. Derek had pushed both his team *and* hers beyond what was safe in a bid to find the terrorist leader before the Deltas arrived. The two Ranger teams ran joint missions. And while Aspen generally felt there was more safety in numbers, especially when they patrolled the town outside the base's gates, just this once she wished her team and Derek's weren't working so closely together. It seemed to her that Derek was looking at the hunt for the terrorist as a competition, when it was nothing of the sort.

But Aspen hadn't said anything. Hadn't reported Derek to their commanding officer. He hadn't done anything illegal, had just walked a fine line between being reckless and determined. Instead, she suffered in silence alongside both platoons.

And finally, after all the emails over the last month in which she'd attempted to tell Kane what was going on without actually saying anything that would break security protocols, he was going to be there. She'd be able to see him, talk to him in person. Aspen knew nothing physical could happen between them, not while they were on deployment, but that was okay. It would be enough to simply see a familiar, friendly face.

Things between her and her own team had been better the last few days—danger tended to do that—but she still felt there was a wall between them that she simply couldn't breach. She'd asked to be able to bunk with them in their tent, but the Army had said not under any circumstance. Men and women had to have separate quarters, period.

Because Derek, Sergeant Vandine, and their commanding officers were meeting with the Delta team as soon as they arrived to go over intel, the Rangers had a rare morning off. Aspen knew they were all planning on going to the chow tent to eat a hot breakfast, then back to their tent to play cards. She hadn't been invited. A week ago, that probably would've devastated her. But nothing could faze her today because she was going to see Kane.

Feeling like a groupie or a desperate twelve-year-old waiting to see her favorite boy band, Aspen hung out near the landing pad where helicopters flying in from the nearby larger base arrived.

She'd had her hopes dashed twice already when the choppers that arrived weren't carrying the Deltas. But the third time was the charm, and she watched with a huge smile as seven familiar faces climbed out of the huge machine. She itched to throw herself into Kane's arms, but she controlled herself, barely.

The guys walked toward her, and Aspen was all ready to be professional and welcome them to the post with a handshake, but Trigger blew that out of the water when he dropped his rucksack and enveloped her in a huge hug.

Shocked and surprised, Aspen could only wrap her arms around him and hug back.

"Thank you for the wedding present," he told her when he finally let go.

"Wedding present?" Aspen asked.

"Yeah. From you and Brain. I've already taken Gillian shooting twice; that Glock you guys got her is a huge hit."

"Um...you're welcome," Aspen told him. She'd had no idea Kane had put both their names on a gift. It made her feel all tingly inside.

Then she was tugged into Lefty's embrace, as he told her how happy he was to see her and to find she was all right.

She went through the same thing with the other guys on the team as well, each one giving her a huge hug. Lucky was the second-to-last man in line, and he whispered in her ear as he held her to him, "It's so good to see you alive and well," Lucky said. "And in case you're wondering, we're not just hugging you because you're a friend...but also because we know Derek would do anything to make your life hell. He can't claim you're doing something inappropriate with Brain if we're *all* joining in."

They shared a grin when he pulled back, and Aspen wanted to cry. It made no sense how quickly these men had accepted her when her own team still held her at arm's length. But she wasn't going to think about it now. She was so thankful she'd get a chance to have Kane's arms around her, she could barely process anything else.

Then she was standing in front of Kane. His hazel eyes twinkled, and it was all Aspen could do not to throw herself at him. "Hi," she said shyly, thinking about everything she'd shared in her emails.

Without a word, Kane reached for her. It felt good to have hugs from his teammates, but having *his* arms around her, smelling his clean scent even after what had to be hours of traveling, had her melting into him.

"Fuck, this feels good," he whispered.

Knowing they couldn't do anything but share a quick hug, Aspen closed her eyes and did her best to memorize the moment. But of course the embrace ended way too soon. Kane was the first to pull back, but he didn't step away from her like the other guys did. He brought his hand up to her temple and brushed her hair away from her face, examining the bruise left when her head had hit a concrete wall the previous week.

"Does it still hurt?" he asked quietly.

Aspen shook her head. "I've got a dull headache, but it isn't too bad anymore."

He frowned, but said, "Good."

"We got Gillian a Glock for a wedding present?" she asked, wanting to lighten the mood, and to try to prevent herself from planting her lips on his.

He grinned. "Yup. It's dark purple, almost mauve. And it rocks, if I do say so myself." Then he sobered. "How bad has Derek been?"

Aspen shrugged. "He's frustrated we haven't been able to find Mullah Abbas Akhund. I think he wants the glory that might come from killing him."

"He's an idiot," Kane said with a shake of his head. "I mean, yeah, the man needs to die, but anyone who's more concerned about personal fame and glory in our line of work has no business being in charge of *anyone*."

"Agreed," Aspen said. "And rumors are that Abdul Shahzada is really the man to be worried about, anyway."

When Kane didn't say anything, Aspen bit her lip. "I'm telling you shit you already know, aren't I?"

"No, go on. I want to hear your thoughts on what's going on over here," Kane told her.

Looking around, Aspen saw that the rest of the team was listening intently to what she had to say as well.

"All right, well, Akhund is the face of the current uprising. He's the one who has the rallies and who the villagers taken into custody claim is in charge. But there have been a few who insist Akhund isn't really in control. They've mentioned Shahzada's name, but no one knows where he is or what alias he's using."

Kane nodded, letting Aspen know for sure she wasn't telling him or his team anything they didn't already know.

"We're gonna find Akhund," Doc said from her right.

"And he'll tell us everything we need to know about this Shahzada guy," Lucky added.

"We need to get going," Trigger said. "The post commander is waiting for us."

"Give me a second," Kane told his team, and they all nodded as they backed away.

Aspen looked at Kane and licked her lips nervously. She was so happy to see him, and it seemed as if he was glad to see her too, but when he didn't say anything for a long moment, simply stared down at her with a heavy look in his eyes...she had the crazy thought that maybe he was going to say he didn't think things would work out between them after all. Or maybe that they were moving too fast and needed to slow things down.

"Stop worrying," Kane said with amazing insight.

"I just...I'm so happy to see you."

"Me too. I've missed you so damn much, you just don't know."

"Actually, I think I *do* know," she replied with a small smile.

"Even though I can't touch or kiss you like I want to, simply standing here and seeing for myself that you're all right makes me feel better than I have in more than a month. I was really worried when I found out about you hitting your head."

It was a beautiful thing to say, and Aspen swallowed hard, doing her best to hold back her happy tears. "I'm okay. I promise."

She saw his gaze settle on the bruise on her head before once again meeting her own. "I'll be in meetings for a while, but do you want to eat lunch with me and the guys afterward?"

"Yes," Aspen told him without hesitation. She usually tried to eat with her Ranger team, but that was more about making sure she arrived at the chow tent at the same time, rather than the team actually asking her to join them.

"Good. We'll probably head out on patrol not too long after that, to get the lay of the land, but I want to spend every second I can with you in the meantime. Even if we're not doing anything but eating next to each other."

She didn't want to think about him or his friends heading outside the post to hunt down Mullah Abbas Akhund, as she knew firsthand how hostile the villagers were, but she had no control over what his superior officers had planned for the team, so she had to let it go. He was good at what he did, and he had a hell of a team of men at his back. "Same," she told him with as much feeling as she could muster.

"What are you going to do this morning?" he asked.

Aspen was well aware that he didn't have time for idle chit-chat, and yet here he was, doing just that. "My team is hanging out in their tent, so I'll probably just go back to my own. Maybe take a nap."

Kane frowned. "They didn't invite you to hang with them?"

Aspen shrugged.

"Assholes," he muttered.

"They really aren't," Aspen said. "Except for Derek, but thankfully he's not in my platoon. They just don't know how to treat me."

"They should treat you as a valuable part of their team," Kane groused.

"It's okay," she told him.

"Brain, we need to jet," Trigger called.

"I'll see you at the chow hall around lunch," she told him.

"Yes, you will," Kane said. "I missed you, *kochanie*."

Aspen tilted her head in question.

"Polish," he told her.

"God, I missed that," Aspen said.

Kane reached out and touched the back of his fingers to her cheek for a brief second, then leaned down and picked up his rucksack. "Later," he said quietly.

"Later," Aspen echoed, watching as the man she suddenly didn't think she could live without caught up with his friends and walked toward the post commander's tent on the small American base in the desert.

Brain could hardly concentrate on the meeting. He knew he should be taking notes and paying attention to what the post commander was saying, but all he could do was glare at Sergeant Derek Spence in anger. The man was conceited and cared nothing about the soldiers under his command. He was so concerned about "winning," i.e., getting to Akhund first, he couldn't see his own flaws.

And he had many.

It didn't help that the man obviously recognized him, and was throwing glares his way as well. The last thing he wanted was to get into a pissing match with the other soldier, but the way he treated not only Aspen, but everyone else, was going to get the jerk into trouble sooner or later. And unfortunately, anyone around him was going to pay for his mistakes.

When Derek and Sergeant Vandine finished telling the Deltas what they'd done over the last month to search for the Taliban leader, everyone began brainstorming their next steps.

There was concern about the mysterious Abdul Shahzada, but their target for this mission was Akhund. If they could kill him, it would take some time for the Taliban to regroup and appoint someone new to the area. If Shahzada was chosen, he'd have to show his face eventually, and the Army would be able to get more intel about him.

By the time the meeting came to an end, it was twelve-thirty and Brain wanted nothing more than to see Aspen again. He wondered how she'd spent her morning and hoped she'd been able to get a nap in like she'd planned.

He was walking out of the tent when Sergeant Spence caught up to him. He grabbed him by the arm and spun him around, catching Brain off guard.

"If you think you're going to come here and fuck Aspen, I'll turn you in so fast your head will spin," Derek growled.

Brain turned on the other man so quickly, he didn't have time to defend himself. He shoved him hard with a hand in the middle of his chest, and Derek bounced off the sturdy canvas of the tent behind him. "First, don't fucking *touch* me," Brain growled, sensing his team closing ranks behind him. He vaguely noticed there wasn't anyone there to back up dumb-ass Derek. "Second, if you think I'd do anything to hurt Aspen's career, you're an even bigger asshole than I thought—which is saying something, because I already thought you were a pretty big douchebag."

"Fuck you," Derek muttered.

"Unlike you, I can keep my personal feelings about

someone separate from my professional ones. You need to get over the fact that she dumped your ass and move on. Mesmer is a fucking great medic, and you're supposed to be working *with* her, not against her, and the rest of your team."

"You have no idea what you're talking about," Derek hissed. "I don't see you and *your* team lugging around extra female baggage. She holds us back, and we would've caught Akhund by now if we didn't have to constantly make concessions for her."

"What concessions?" Brain demanded.

"She slows us down," Derek told him, instead of offering concrete examples.

"Let me guess," Grover drawled, "you're upset you can't whip out your dick and piss wherever you want because there's a woman in your group."

Derek shrugged. "That's just one of a hundred ways we have to accommodate her. We should be worried about finding and killing a fucking terrorist. Instead, she's always on my case, wanting to coddle the teams. She whines about being dehydrated and about pushing everyone too hard. It's ridiculous that the Army allows chicks into the Rangers as it is, and to force us to drag one along with us as our medic is an insult!"

"You won't think it's an insult when shit hits the fan," Lefty sneered. "I bet you'll be the loudest one crying for her help over a fucking splinter in your little finger."

Derek's lip curled. "You guys think you're so fucking invincible. News flash—you aren't. You're no better than me. And you have to follow the same rules I do." He glared at Brain. "If I see you so much as touching Mesmer in a way inappropriate for a forward-deployed unit, I'll report you both. We'll see how invincible you are in front of a court-martial. Although," he mused with an evil glint in his eye, "on second thought, go ahead. Kiss the bitch the way you did in that bar. It'll give me a good reason to get her ass kicked off her team so we can get a *real* medic in her place."

Brain stepped forward to beat the punk-ass's face in, but Trigger and Oz each grabbed one of his arms, stopping him. He shrugged them off and leaned into the other man. Derek was taller than Brain, but that didn't intimidate him in the least. His hair was black as night and greasy from not being washed in who knows how many days. He stunk to high heaven, and the BDUs he wore were filthy.

"You're a sorry excuse for a soldier, let alone an Army Ranger. Look at you—you look like you just crawled out of a gutter. Modified grooming standards are one thing, but looking and smelling like you haven't showered in weeks is unacceptable. Be an example to your team, Spence, instead of an embarrassment. And if you *ever* give Mesmer or me shit again, you'll regret it."

"Don't threaten me," Derek growled.

"I'm not threatening you. I'm making you a promise," Brain told him in a low, even voice. Then he turned and stalked away from the other man before he did something that would hurt Aspen's career...like punch the sergeant.

Derek wasn't taking rejection well, which was ridiculous since he was a grown-ass man. Now Brain understood a bit more the ups and downs Aspen experienced from day to day. Working with someone like Derek would be enough to make anyone want to quit and find a new career.

"You handled that surprisingly well," Trigger observed as they headed for the chow tent.

"He's an ass," Brain said between clenched teeth.

"Yup."

Taking a big breath, Brain did his best to rein in his temper. The last thing he wanted to do was make Aspen anxious by showing up in a piss-poor mood and having to admit it was because of Derek. "We're headed out this afternoon, right?"

"Right," Trigger agreed. "You gonna have your head on straight by then?"

"Yes," Brain told him. And he would. Just seeing and being able to talk to Aspen would calm him down.

The team entered the chow tent, and Brain immediately searched for Aspen. He spotted her coming toward him with a smile on her face.

"Hi," she said, her eyes on his. "How'd it go?"

"As expected," Brain said. "We're headed out after we eat."

Her face dropped a bit, but she continued to smile for him. "Then we'd better get you something to eat so you can have some energy for walking around, huh?"

"You eaten yet?" Lucky asked.

She shook her head. "No. I was just reading a book on my phone while I waited for you."

Trigger, Oz, and Grover headed for the line, and Brain put his hand on the small of Aspen's back, urging her to fall in behind them. He made sure she was sandwiched between the seven of them, just in case Derek decided to come in and give her shit. Her Ranger team might not have her back, but he and his friends would.

They grabbed trays and went through the line. There

was a young woman standing behind a large tray of green beans with a name tag that said "Sierra." Her red hair was pulled into a bun at the back of her head and covered with a hairnet. She greeted Aspen with a huge smile.

"Hey!"

"Hi, Sierra," Aspen said, smiling back. "How's it going? Are you settling in all right?"

"I am. Thanks."

Aspen turned to Brain. "Sierra's new here. Just got in a week ago. She's working for the contractor supplying the food to the base."

Grover was behind Brain, and he leaned in. "What brought you all the way out here to the middle of nowhere?" he asked, a hint of interest in his voice.

Sierra shrugged. "I've always wanted to serve my country, but I can't shoot worth a darn, and I'm too short to be very effective at all the other Army stuff."

"Too short? You aren't that short," Grover argued.

Sierra took a step backward—off the box she'd apparently been standing on to serve the food. She lost several inches in height. "I'm five-two, and most people mistake me for a kid," she said, not sounding upset about that at all. She stepped back up on her box and smiled at them. "Everything about working out here has been fascinating so far, and I'm thrilled to finally be serving my country in some way, even if it's just by cooking and dishing up food to the soldiers who go out and risk their lives on a daily basis."

Brain liked the young woman immediately, even if she sounded a bit naïve.

"I don't know how long I'll be here," Aspen told her.

"But if you ever want to hang out, let me know. I could use some more friends around here."

"Deal," Sierra said with another huge smile.

"Most of the contractor tents are on the outskirts of the base. Tell me they didn't put you out there too," Grover said gruffly.

Brain looked at his friend in surprise.

"Um...yeah, of course that's where I live," Sierra replied.

"Hey, hurry it up!" a soldier called out from behind them, impatient with the delay in getting his food.

"See you later," Aspen told the other woman and moved down the line.

Brain followed close on her heels, and he heard Grover say, "Be careful, this isn't Mayberry."

"I know it's not," Sierra said in a harder tone that was totally at odds with her innocent appearance. "I might look like a child, but I'm *not* one. I'm perfectly able to take care of myself. I wouldn't have come all the way to Afghanistan if I was scared of being here."

"I'm just concerned," Grover told her. "You aren't a soldier, and things around here are heating up, fast. Just be careful...okay?"

Sierra and Grover stared at each other for a long moment before she said, "I will. And I'm sorry for jumping down your throat. It's nice to be worried about."

Grover nodded, then moved down the line with his tray.

Brain wanted to warn his friend about getting involved with anyone out here, since they'd soon be back in Texas, but he kept his mouth shut. Grover was probably just worried in a general way about the woman, like he would be about anyone he perceived to be in potential danger.

"There's a table over there," Oz said from in front of them, motioning toward an empty circular table with eight chairs. Everyone ambled over and sat. Brain moved his chair a little closer to Aspen's, resting his thigh against hers under the table.

She gave him a small smile, but otherwise didn't acknowledge his actions.

Brain should've been worried about how happy he was to see her. Should've been freaking out that his mood lightened immediately after hearing her voice. But he wasn't. Nothing intimate could happen between them while out here, but the weeks they'd been apart had seemed to bring them closer somehow.

"So, did you guys have a good meeting?" Aspen asked the group in general.

Doc nodded. "Yeah. It seems you and your team have been busy since you've been here."

Aspen grimaced. "For all the good it's done. Akhund isn't stupid, and he seems to always be a step ahead of us. It's annoying."

"You think someone's feeding him information?" Lefty asked quietly.

"I don't know," Aspen said, not dismissing his suspicion. "I'd like to say no, but it's possible. Seriously, every time we think we have a lead on his whereabouts, when we get there, it's as if he's a ghost. No one knows anything, no one's seen anything, and no one's heard anything. It's been an exercise in frustration."

Brain was only half listening to his friends, because the conversation going on at the table *next* to theirs had caught his attention. There were five Afghani men sitting together, speaking in their native Farsi. He wouldn't have thought twice about them...except what they were talking about disturbed him.

"I'll never get used to seeing females in uniform."

"It's disgusting."

"I agree. They should be at home cooking, cleaning, and raising children."

"That woman seems to get around. Look at her, sitting with the new men who arrived today."

One of the men snorted in disgust. *"As if it's not enough to flirt with the men she works with. Now she's moved on to the newcomers. Whore."*

That was enough. Brain was done. He didn't usually broadcast the fact that he could understand people when they were speaking a different language. He'd used his knowledge to his advantage on plenty of missions. But his need to protect Aspen, to stand up for her, overwhelmed his better judgement.

He pushed his seat back and stalked over to the other table. He heard his teammates moving, backing him up even if they had no idea what had set him off.

Putting his hands flat on the table, Brain leaned over and glared at the five men before addressing them in their own language.

"Sergeant Mesmer is a highly trained medic. She's an experienced Army soldier. If you can't handle working on this base, then you should seek employment elsewhere. The soldiers here are to be respected, regardless of their gender."

The men stared at him with wide eyes. It was obvious they were shocked an American not only understood their language, but could speak it.

"Of course," one of the men said in English, his accent thick but easily understandable. "We meant no disrespect."

Brain glared at him. *"Could'a fooled me. You need to apologize,"* he said, still speaking in Farsi.

"I'm sorry," the man said immediately.

"Not to me," Brain said, motioning to Aspen with his head. *"To the lady."*

All five men stood, bowed slightly at the waist and gave their apologies.

"Sorry."

"I apologize."

"Many sorries."

"No offense meant."

"So sorry."

Brain straightened. Then he said, *"In the future, you shouldn't assume no one understands what you're saying. If you're not on our side, you're our enemy. Remember that."* He nodded at the men, who hadn't sat back down, and turned toward his table.

All six of his teammates were standing behind him, looking pissed off, even if they didn't know what had just happened. They were somewhat used to this kind of behavior from him. The thing about understanding so many different languages was that he often overheard talk that was unpleasant. Many people disparaged Americans in general, felt free to gossip loudly about them in their presence, and generally had no problem saying exactly what they thought because they assumed there was no chance they'd be understood.

The second Brain turned his back on the Afghani men, he heard them picking up their trays and heading to the trash bins on their way out. He didn't even feel bad about making them cut their lunch short.

The team sat back down at the table, and when they did, Aspen asked, "What was that about?"

"They didn't think anyone understood what they were saying...and had some not-so-nice things to say about you," Brain told her.

Aspen frowned. "And?"

"And what?"

"That's it? That's all they were saying?"

Brain nodded.

She stared at him. "Kane, I don't know what they said, but honestly, it's probably nothing I haven't already heard from people on our own base. I've worked around men my entire career. I've had to claw and fight my way to where I am today. If I got all worked up and bent out of shape over people talking about me behind my back, I never would've made it. My skin's pretty thick."

"I. Don't. Care," Brain countered. "No one talks shit about you when I'm around."

She blushed, and Brain wanted to reach out and take her hand in his more than he could admit. But he'd just made a scene, and they were being watched. Derek had entered the tent after they'd all sat down, and if he made any inappropriate moves toward Aspen, the other man would definitely report it. Not that Brain was scared of him, but he'd never do anything that might reflect negatively on Aspen.

"Thanks," she whispered.

"So...want to tell us the gist of what was said?" Trigger asked after they all started eating again.

"No," Brain grumbled, still pissed off. "My bigger

concern is the fact that the Army's obviously employed some locals who aren't as supportive of the US as they might seem to be."

"You gonna say something?" Doc asked.

"Fuck yes," Brain told him. "It's hard enough to distinguish friend from foe over here. If we've invited the enemy to eat at our table and work with our soldiers, we're asking to be fucked over." He looked at Aspen. "I'm assuming they're employed as translators?"

Aspen shrugged. "I'm not really sure. I mean, they could simply be a part of the Afghani Army. From what I've seen, they rotate in and out, learning tactics from the units here."

Brain huffed out a breath. "Stay away from them," he told Aspen.

She immediately nodded. "Hadn't planned on inviting them to my tent for tea," she said with a small smile.

"I mean it."

Aspen frowned. "And I heard you. Despite meeting you guys when you got here this morning and eating lunch with you, I haven't had a lot of time to socialize. Today is one of the first breaks we've had in a long time. Usually we're out patrolling from sun up to sun down, and I fall into my cot at the end of the day, exhausted. I don't dilly-dally with the locals like you're insinuating."

Brain heard a muffled snicker from one of his team, but he didn't take his eyes from Aspen's. "Dilly-dally?" he said with a raised brow.

"Yeah. Hang out. Socialize. Chill. Whatever," she said with a huff.

"I'm sorry, I was out of line. I'm just worried about you," Brain told her.

She nodded. "Apology accepted. Was what they said so bad?"

"Not really. I just don't like hearing anyone talk smack about you. Especially shit that isn't true."

"Okay."

That was another of the one-thousand-and-one things Brain liked about Aspen. She didn't hold grudges.

He opened his mouth to ask her what was on her schedule for the rest of the day when Derek suddenly appeared by the table. "We're headed out in thirty, Mesmer. If you're not ready, we're leaving without you."

Brain clenched his teeth. What an asshole.

Aspen's platoon sergeant appeared behind Derek. "We've got a new lead on Akhund, and we'll be working with the Deltas to see if we can't corner him."

She nodded. "I'll be ready," she told the two men. Sergeant Vandine nodded back and immediately turned to head out of the chow tent. Derek glared at Aspen, and the rest of the men at the table for a beat, before following the other man.

"He's such a dick," Grover said under his breath.

"Yup," Aspen agreed easily, then she scooted back her chair and picked up her tray. "Looks like we're all about to be busy."

Everyone followed suit and picked up their trays and headed for the trash and tray depository.

Brain had worked with female soldiers before. He respected them as much as he did anyone else. But his protective instincts went into overdrive thinking about Aspen headed out into the villages to search for a murderous terrorist who wouldn't think twice about putting a bullet in her brain.

But he reminded himself that she'd been in the country for over a month and was damn good at her job. She wouldn't be attached to a Ranger unit if she wasn't.

After they'd deposited their trays and left the chow tent, Brain caught Aspen by the upper arm. The rest of his team headed off to the tent where their duffles and other equipment had been sent. "Be careful out there," he told her.

"I always am," she said immediately. "*You* be careful. You don't know the area yet and some of the villagers are pretty damn hostile."

"I can handle them," Brain told her.

Then Aspen smiled. "So...we'll be working together? I mean, sort of?"

He grinned. "Looks that way."

"You aren't going to be all cavemanish and protective while we're out there, are you?"

"Can't promise that," Brain said honestly. "But I'll do my best to rein it in."

"I'd appreciate it," Aspen said. Her eyes swirled with uncertainty though.

"What?" Brain asked.

"I just... Never mind, it's stupid."

"What, *mpenzi*? Tell me."

"What language was that?" she asked, stalling.

"Swahili."

"Seriously? Jeez, Kane, I think I doubted that you really knew so many languages, but I don't anymore. Swahili? Good Lord."

"What was that other thought?" Brain asked firmly.

She sighed before admitting, "I just don't want you to think less of me for any reason. I know you're the best of the best, and while I'm confident in my abilities, I'm probably not up to the standards that you and your team are used to. I want you to be proud of me. To make sure you don't regret standing up for me."

Not able to keep his hands to himself, Brain reached out and put his palms on her shoulders. He wanted to pull her into his embrace, but had to settle for this. "I don't expect you to be perfect, just as I hope you don't expect *me* to be. All we can do is keep our eyes out for the enemy and be prepared to act however we need to in order to stay alive to see the sun rise another day. Understand?"

She nodded.

"I'll always be proud of you," he told her softly. "From everything I've seen and heard, you're making the best of a shitty situation. Your team should always have your back, and for some reason, your guys can't seem to get their heads out of their asses. It's probably because the leaders —namely Derek—have them so confused they're retreating from you just to make things more comfortable for themselves."

"I don't blame them," Aspen said.

"Of course you don't. Because that's not the kind of person you are. But I do," Brain told her firmly. "Now, go get ready. We're gonna kick some terrorist ass and take down this Akhund guy. The sooner the better, so we can get back to Texas and move our relationship to the next level."

Her eyes widened at that. "You're assuming I want to," she said cheekily.

Brain smiled. "You're right, I am. But the need to taste your lips again, to strip you naked and feel you under me, can't be all one-sided."

She licked her lips and said shyly, "It's not."

"Good. Now...go before I fuck up and kiss the hell out of you right here and now."

"Kane?"

"Yeah?"

Aspen took a deep breath. "Thanks for sticking up for me today."

"Always," Brain told her.

She took a step away from him, and he dropped his hands. Then she turned and headed for her tent without looking back.

Knowing he needed to get his mind back in the game, and start thinking about the mission ahead of him, Brain stalked toward his own tent. He prayed they'd be able to find this Akhund guy and get the hell out of Afghanistan sooner rather than later.

* * *

Abdul Shahzada—known as Muhammad Qahhar to the officials on the American base—watched stoically from behind a tent as the cocky American soldier walked away.

Internally, he seethed.

He *hated* Americans. All of them. He was working on base as an interpreter, right under their very noses, to gain intel for the Taliban. And the fact that he'd just been lectured by one of the Americans didn't sit well with him. How dare the man listen in on a private conversation? How dare he lecture *him*, Abdul Shahzada? He wasn't a man anyone talked down to if they wanted to live—and yet that's exactly what the American had done.

Forced him to apologize to a *woman*.

That wouldn't go unpunished.

He'd learned more about base operations by just listening to other soldiers talking around him, assuming he wasn't listening, than they'd ever believe. For instance, he knew the Delta Force team had arrived to hunt down Mullah Abbas Akhund. But like the others, they were idiots. They didn't yet know for certain that Akhund wasn't the man they should be concerned about.

He was the public face of their group, but Abdul was, in reality, the man in charge in this region.

Abdul also knew he should inform Akhund that he needed to lie low, but honestly, he was sick of being in hiding. He wanted to publicly take his place as the head of their local faction. He wanted to prove to their leaders that he could take control—and keep it.

Akhund was on his own. If he got killed, so be it. It would be the will of Allah.

Abdul also wanted to make every single American who worked at the base pay. Pay for their interference in his country. Pay for their wicked ways.

His mind went to the female soldier. What if he ordered her to be taken? She was a whore, consorting with many groups of men on the base. She wore a uniform that should be reserved for real soldiers, and she acted too friendly with the local men. She was attempting to lure them away from Allah—and that wasn't acceptable. Taking her would also be a blow to the man who'd defended her. He'd probably go out of his mind, wondering where she was, what was happening to her.

It was a perfect scenario...except for a few things. Abdul had seen firsthand how crazy the American leaders got when one of their soldiers disappeared. They spared no expense or resource to find the person and bring them home. Not only that, but the whore was protected by not one, but two platoons of men. Three if he included the group that arrived today. She wouldn't be easy to obtain, no matter how much he wanted her.

Hearing something nearby, Abdul turned and saw an American food worker exiting the chow tent. She had hair the color of the devil, and she was so short it was unnatural.

As she walked away, oblivious to his presence, an idea bloomed in Abdul's gut.

What if it wasn't a soldier who was taken?

What if it was a lowly contractor?

He followed the small American at a distance, taking note of the fact she didn't interact with the soldiers she passed. It didn't look like anyone really even noticed her. She would make a good mark. If she disappeared, not many would notice or care.

He could take out his displeasure with the Americans on *her*.

It was doubtful the US government would put up much of an outcry if a contracted worker went AWOL. The Americans were stupid enough to believe she'd just left...and he'd be able to take as much time as he wanted with her.

She'd most certainly cry and beg him for mercy. But he wouldn't give it. Every drop of blood she spilled would make him stronger.

Taking revenge on the meddlesome, insufferable Americans was his main goal. Making the devil woman suffer, and teaching his followers how to interrogate and torture a real live person—much better than simply telling them how it was done—was a start. She would be a teaching opportunity for the movement.

Grinning to himself, Abdul continued to observe as she entered one of the tents on the outskirts of the base.

Perfect.

Knowing he wouldn't have long to wait before he was publicly in charge of the region, Abdul slipped back into the shadows. He could be patient. One day soon, the small devil woman would become a useful tool in his arsenal, and no one would even realize.

It was one more way to thumb his nose at the infidel Americans who dared try to tell him and his people how to live and what to believe.

His time was coming—and it was going to be glorious.

CHAPTER NINE

The hair on the back of Aspen's neck was sticking straight up and had been for the last fifteen minutes. Her platoon had been tasked with clearing three streets in a neighborhood on the west side of the city. Derek's platoon was clearing the area a few streets over. And she had no idea where Kane and his team were at the moment. She supposed they were doing the same...going house by house searching for Akhund.

The locals weren't exactly thrilled with their presence, which was nothing new, but today they seemed especially hostile. She wasn't sure why. But the men she was with were on edge, obviously feeling the anger and hostility in the air just as she was.

Derek had been pushing both Ranger teams especially hard all afternoon. He'd pulled rank on Sergeant Vandine twice, ordering him to stand down when he'd questioned his orders. Even though they were both platoon sergeants, Derek had been in his position longer than Vandine and unofficially outranked him. Between the growing discord between the platoon sergeants and the less-than-receptive welcome by the citizens as they searched for Akhund, Aspen was on high alert.

Apparently the Army had gotten notice that the Taliban leader had many supporters in this area of the city, and it was likely one or more of them were helping to hide him from the American authorities.

Taking position in the entrance of a small alley between two three-story buildings, Aspen held her rifle at the ready as sergeants Holman and Buckland flanked the doorway of yet another dwelling. Sergeants Hamilton and Vandine pounded on the door and announced who they were in Farsi. They ordered the occupants to open up and, when they didn't, warned that they would be entering.

Sweat dripped down the side of Aspen's face. Between the body armor and the Kevlar helmet she was wearing, along with the backpack full of medical gear she always carried, she was sweltering in the heat of the late afternoon. Her hands gripped the rifle tightly and her gaze swept the immediate area, looking for trouble. There were three other men from the Ranger team nearby, all watching the backs of the team members who were about to enter the house to search for Akhund.

But before the four men could get inside, all hell broke loose.

Eight men wearing black pants and shirts ran around the corner at the end of the street, yelling at the tops of their lungs and firing automatic weapons at the team at the same time.

Without hesitation, making sure none of her team were in her crosshairs, Aspen fired back.

The sound of gunfire was loud in the otherwise quiet

street. One of the men coming at them went down with a scream. Most of the platoon joined Aspen, the alley becoming a temporary haven for her team. Except for Vandine and Holman. They were pinned in the doorway of the house they'd been about to enter, no longer able to run for safety. Their best bet was to hunker down in the shallow space of the doorway until their team could clear the road.

The next minute and a half was chaotic and Aspen operated on autopilot. This wasn't training. The bullets flying through the air were real. The danger of dying was real.

Not letting herself think about that, Aspen lay on the ground, hugging the building as she peeked around the corner. The Taliban fighters shooting at them had taken up defensive positions and were trying to pick them off one by one as the platoon attempted to shoot from the alley.

Aspen didn't feel much of anything when the man she'd carefully aimed at, waiting for him to peek from behind a wall he was using for shelter, fell into the street with one of her bullets between his eyes.

She heard Vandine cry out when he was shot, and then her team yelling that Holman had also been hit.

"We can't wait anymore! Cover us!" Vandine yelled from his position in the doorway.

Without thought, Aspen helped lay down a barrage of gunfire to give their platoon sergeant time to get both himself and Holman to the alley, where the rest of the team was still hunkered down.

When they got within ten feet of the alley, Aspen whipped the rifle strap over her head, laid her weapon down, and rushed into the street to help the two men. When Vandine grabbed Holman, she'd assumed the younger man had the more serious injury, but the second she saw her platoon sergeant, she knew she'd been mistaken.

Vandine was white as a sheet and the entire front of his right pants leg was soaked with blood. Too much blood for the wound to be anything other than arterial. If she didn't do something fast, the man was going to bleed to death right in front of her.

Aspen was wearing a headset like the rest of the Rangers, and she immediately reported to the team—as well as Derek's team, who had to have heard the gunfire and were probably on their way to the location to assist. "We've got two down. We need backup to extract."

"Negative," came Derek's voice over the radio. "It's a distraction ploy. We've got Akhund pinned down over here. We need all able bodies to get to our location ASAP to make a perimeter. He's not going to get away from us again!"

Aspen blinked in shock. Maybe Derek hadn't heard her. She tried again. "I repeat, we've got two men down. Injuries are serious. We're pinned down and can't extract."

"And *I* repeat," Derek said nastily. "Our first priority is Akhund! Anyone who can walk needs to get their asses over to our position. *Now*. That's an order!"

Aspen looked at the five uninjured men of her platoon. For a second, they all stared at each other in clear disbelief.

"Did you copy?" Derek barked over the radio. "We need more boots on the ground over here. The second you all join us, they'll give up. Let the medic do her job and the rest of you get your asses over here. We'll be back to get her and the others in minutes after we find Akhund!"

Aspen heard Vandine groan and turned her attention to him. He'd slumped into the dirt in the alley and was barely conscious. Holman wasn't as bad off as their platoon sergeant, but it looked like his right hand had been shot off.

Between the time she'd looked down at the two injured men and back up, the remaining Rangers had disappeared.

She stared at where they'd been standing just moments before, in shock. She couldn't believe they'd left. *Fuck.*

Moving quickly, Aspen dragged Vandine farther back into the alley. She glanced nervously at the other end, where anyone could come up behind them, and swallowed hard. Shouts rose from the street, and she quickly ran back where she'd left Holman. She wished she had time to treat his hand, but they'd all be dead if he couldn't hold off the Taliban fighters.

She shoved her rifle at him. "Vandine's bleeding out. I have to put a tourniquet on him. Can you hold them off?" she asked.

Holman looked at her from where he was sitting on the ground and something intense passed between them. They both knew their chances of living through this were slim, especially now that they'd been left on their own. But neither was giving up. Holman was a Ranger, the toughest of the tough. He reached out with his good hand, his left one, and nodded.

Aspen put her hand on his shoulder for a brief second, then ran back to Vandine.

She couldn't believe Derek had abandoned his fellow soldiers. He hated her with a fervor that was completely irrational, but she knew he respected the others on the teams. Today, he'd put his desire to catch Akhund above everyone.

She threw herself on her knees next to Vandine and shrugged her medical bag off her back. Reaching into a pocket on her pants, Aspen pulled out the combat application tourniquet she always kept there. She grabbed the K-BAR knife out of the holster on her vest and sliced Vandine's pants from thigh to where it was tucked into his boot.

The blood was pulsing from a hole in his inner thigh. With every beat of his heart, blood pumped out. He literally had minutes to live if she didn't stop the bleeding.

Dropping the knife, Aspen wrapped the CAT around Vandine's upper thigh, put the end through the clip and, with one hand, quickly and efficiently turned the windlass rod to tighten the tourniquet. Thankful for the one-handed ease of the device, she looked toward the other end of the alley...

And swore when she saw two men peek their heads around the corner.

Without thought, she reached for Vandine's rifle. With one hand on the CAT, still tightening it, she awkwardly aimed toward the other end of the alley and fired two shots. Thankfully, the men she'd seen pulled back and didn't return fire.

"Fuck, fuck, fuck," she muttered. She might be able to get the tourniquet on Vandine's leg and stop the bleeding, but they were sitting ducks in the alley. Eventually the Taliban fighters would come for them.

"Take the rifle and you and Holman get the hell out of here," Vandine told her in a shaky voice.

"Fuck you," Aspen told him.

"That's an order," her platoon sergeant said.

Aspen ignored him and concentrated on locking the windlass into place. The CAT would hold until she could get her patient to an operating room. She had no idea if he'd lose his leg or not, but at least he wouldn't bleed to death in this fucking alley.

"Mesmer, did you hear me?" Vandine asked.

Aspen looked into her platoon sergeant's eyes. They hadn't always gotten along. She thought he wasn't assertive enough, especially when it came to Derek. He let the other man talk him into making decisions that she didn't think were especially good for the team. But she wasn't going to leave him here to die. No fucking way.

"I heard you," she told him, then turned to her medical bag, unzipping it and reaching for a vial of ketamine. The very powerful sedative and painkiller was more effective being administered by an IV, but they didn't have the time for that. Vandine had to be in an inordinate amount of pain, and she needed to take the edge off so they could get moving. Somehow, the three of them had to get out of that alley and to safety before they became "guests" of the Taliban.

She picked up her K-BAR and slit through Vandine's shirt, exposing his arm and vein.

"You should've gone with them," Vandine told her in a weak voice.

Aspen took a deep breath and concentrated on drawing just the right amount of ketamine into a syringe. Then she turned back to her platoon sergeant. She stretched his arm out and, as she was inserting the needle into his vein, said, "I recited the Ranger creed just like you

155

did, Sergeant. And part of that was, 'I will never leave a fallen comrade to fall into the hands of the enemy.'" She looked into his eyes as she pushed the sedative into his vein. "I might not be a real Ranger in your eyes, or the eyes of the rest of our team, but I take my oaths seriously."

For a second, she thought he'd lost too much blood to really understand what she was saying. Then he nodded once. "Sit rep?" he asked, his voice way too weak.

"Holman is at that end of the alley," she said, motioning behind her with her head. "Holding off the unfriendlies. We're gonna have to go out the other side."

Vandine tilted his head to look behind him at the other end of the alley. And as he did, Aspen saw the two men from earlier once again peer around the corner. She lifted the rifle and blasted off a few shots. Heading in the direction of those men wasn't ideal, but facing off against two was better than trying to fend off the six or more men who'd been shooting at them from the other side.

Knowing they were in deep shit, she kept the weapon trained on the end of the alley. The ketamine needed three minutes to take effect, then they would have to move.

She'd done her job, stabilized her patient and made him as comfortable as the situation would allow. If the team was there, they could've easily helped her carry Vandine and get them all out of there, but at the moment they were on their own.

At the sound of shouts and more gunfire at the end of the alley where she'd left Holman, Vandine said, "Go. I might be hurt, but I can still get off some shots if those two assholes show their faces."

Aspen nodded and hurried toward Holman.

"What's going on?" she asked.

Holman didn't look good. He was still sitting on the ground, but his upper body was weaving back and forth. Shit.

"Don't know. There were a bunch of guys who looked as if they were about to make their way down the street toward us, but then they turned around and ran back the way they came. Sergeant Spence might've been right, and they all followed the others when they left."

More shouts sounded from what seemed like the next street over, and Aspen thought this might very well be their one shot to get the fuck out of there.

"Time to go," she told Holman. "Wait here."

She ran back to her pack and shoved in the few materials she'd taken out to help Vandine. Taking precious seconds to grab a roll of gauze, a second vial of ketamine, and a new syringe, and putting them aside, she slung the pack over her shoulders again. Then she went back to Holman. "Give me your arm."

He didn't ask any questions, just held out his left arm. His mangled right hand was cradled against his stomach. Glancing at it, Aspen saw that he was missing at least three fingers, and the other two seemed to be hanging on by only tendons and muscles. He was going to lose it for sure. One of the Taliban fighters had definitely landed a lucky shot.

Feeling as if she were trying to run through syrup, Aspen went through the motions to inject her teammate with a dose of the painkiller. She didn't need to tell him what the side effects of the drug would be, they were all well aware of what could happen. They'd learned all about it in the many classes they'd had on battlefield medicine.

She also took fifteen seconds to wrap his mangled

hand. He couldn't exactly run around with his fingers dangling the way they were. Her wrap wouldn't help him much, but it wouldn't hurt either.

"I'll be right back with Vandine, and then we can get the hell out of here," she told Holman when she was done. He nodded.

Hoping like hell Holman wasn't going to suffer hallucinations, as some people did after being given ketamine, Aspen ran back to her platoon sergeant. By the time she got to him, he was unconscious. She figured that was probably a blessing. She was also very glad the men who'd been shooting at them from the other end of the alley had seemed to vanish into thin air. She didn't know what was going on, but took two precious seconds to appreciate whatever had caught their attention. It gave them a small reprieve, and maybe, just maybe, they'd all get out of this clusterfuck alive.

Taking a deep breath, Aspen turned Vandine on his side and positioned him so she could pick him up. This was the hardest thing she'd had to accomplish in training. Picking up a two-hundred-pound man when he was dead weight was almost impossible.

Just as she leaned over, she heard gunfire erupt from the other end of the alley, and it gave her the adrenaline dump she needed.

She hefted her platoon sergeant over her shoulder in a fireman carry, knocking her radio off kilter in the process. The earbuds were ripped out of her ears; she'd lost her ability to communicate with both her team and the other Rangers.

Knowing if she put Vandine down now, she might never be able to pick him up again, she staggered back to where she'd left Holman. He'd managed to stand, even if it looked like the wall was the only thing holding him up.

"Time to go," she said.

"Where to?" Holman asked.

Surprised that the man was deferring to her when he'd never given her the time of day before, Aspen peered out from around the alley. She didn't see anyone. The civilians were probably hiding in their homes, and the men who'd shown up out of nowhere seemed to have disappeared as well.

She motioned to their right with her head. "That way. Away from where the men were shooting at us. We'll circle back around toward the base once we're out of this neighborhood."

Holman nodded and stepped away from the wall. His strides were unsteady and he walked as if he'd been out drinking for hours, but he held the rifle firmly with his good hand.

Staggering under Vandine's weight, Aspen followed. The three of them made their way out of the alley without getting shot, which she figured was a good sign. They walked to the end of the street, and she leaned against the side of a house while Holman peered around a corner.

When he signaled that the coast was clear, they turned south.

They'd gone just over a block when the hair on the back of Aspen's neck rose once more. Swearing, she said, "Hold up, Holman."

The other man stopped immediately, and they both scanned the area.

Aspen wasn't sure what had caught her attention at

first—and then she heard it. Men speaking in low tones, as if they were trying to sneak up on someone.

That *someone* being Aspen and her two wounded charges.

"Fuck," she swore. "Tangos coming up behind us," she told Holman. They had nowhere to go. There weren't any alleyways in the immediate vicinity and they were sitting ducks on the open road. "Go, go, go!" she told him, and they both took off at a run.

If they could make it to the end of the next block and around the corner, they might have a shot at evading capture.

Shots rang out, and Aspen winced as she felt something hot and extremely painful lodge itself into her calf. But she didn't stop running. They turned the corner—

And for a split second, Aspen's life flashed before her eyes.

Holman bounced off the chest of a soldier standing there and almost went down. But the man grabbed hold of him and prevented them both from falling.

One second, Aspen was ready to fight to the death, and the next, she felt a sense of relief so great, she almost passed out.

They'd literally run right into Kane and his team.

The seven Delta Force operatives were dressed entirely in black, looked extremely pissed off and dangerous—and she'd never been so glad to see anyone in all her life.

Without a word, Trigger, Lefty, and Oz slid around her and began firing back at the men who'd been trailing them. Grover grabbed ahold of Holman's arm and helped keep him upright, just as Kane took her elbow in his grip.

"The others will hold them off," Lucky said as he and

Doc turned and led the way in the opposite direction from where the firefight was happening.

"We can't leave your team," Aspen said a little frantically as she tried to walk and look behind her at the Deltas who were taking care of the tangos.

"We aren't," Kane told her calmly. "They'll join up with us the next block over."

"Swear?" Aspen couldn't help but ask.

"Yes," Kane said.

Breathing out a sigh of relief, Aspen believed him. Kane had one hand on her, helping her walk without falling, and held a pistol in the other, ready to take out anyone who might surprise them.

He hadn't offered to take Vandine. Hadn't taken over.

She respected Kane and his team more in that moment than she could even put into words.

They didn't go far, only two more blocks, but Aspen knew if they had to walk any farther, she wouldn't have been able to. Vandine was getting heavier with every step, and she was aware of the fact that Kane was using more and more strength to help her.

The most beautiful sight of her life was the large Army truck parked in the middle of the street after they turned one last corner.

The Deltas operated like a well-oiled machine. It was both impressive and depressing. The latter because it was what she'd always wanted in a team of her own, but had never had.

"Let me take him," Kane told her.

She'd barely nodded when Vandine's weight was lifted from her shoulders. The relief was immediate, and she reached up to take Lucky's hand. He'd already jumped into the back of the truck and was waiting to help her up. She put her right leg on the bumper and winced as pain sliced through her.

Ignoring it, and with Lucky's help, she hauled herself into the back of the truck.

Scooting back to give the others room, she watched as Kane, Doc, and Grover easily lifted Vandine as well. They lay him down on his back, and Aspen quickly moved to check the tourniquet, to make sure it hadn't loosened in their mad dash for safety.

Satisfied that the CAT was still doing its job, Aspen turned to Holman once he was helped into the truck. They hadn't started moving yet, and she hoped it was because they were waiting for the other three Deltas.

Before she could open her mouth to speak to Holman, Kane put his hand on her arm. "You're bleeding," he said.

"I know," Aspen told him, shrugging off her medic bag once more. She knew she'd been shot but she wouldn't stop right now. Holman's hand needed attention. Her wound obviously wasn't serious, as she wasn't lightheaded. She'd deal with it after she took care of her team.

As if sensing her determination, Kane didn't say another word about it. When she opened her pack though, he did say, "What can I do to help?"

Thankful for an extra set of hands, Aspen said, "Give me a second." Then she turned to Holman. The sergeant was sitting up, his mangled hand still cradled to his stomach.

"I need to take care of that," she told him gently.

"I know," he said, but didn't otherwise move.

"You need more ketamine?" she asked.

She watched as Holman took a deep breath. His gaze

went from her, to Kane, to the other Deltas in the truck.

She had a feeling Holman wanted to say he didn't need any more painkillers.

Grover was the one to make the decision for him. "He needs it," he said.

Holman grunted and looked at the other man.

"There's no need to try to be macho, man," Grover told him. "Take the fucking painkillers. It doesn't make you less of a soldier."

Holman looked back at Aspen and nodded. It was just a dip of a chin, but it was enough. She quickly got a dose ready and he held out his good arm, allowing her to administer the drug. The second she was done, he gripped his rifle once more.

"You want to lie down?" she asked.

Holman shook his head. "I can't protect you if I do."

Aspen swallowed hard. She had no idea if the ketamine was making him act protective toward her or what, but she wasn't going to demean his good intentions.

"Okay." She turned to Kane. "Can you hold his arm for me?"

"How?"

"Get next to him and grip his elbow and his forearm. This is gonna hurt. He won't remember it because of the ketamine, but he's going to yell."

"I won't," Holman said in a whisper. "Yelling will bring the enemy."

Without another word, Kane moved into position. He held Holman's arm exactly how Aspen instructed. She unwound the bloody gauze she'd put on earlier and took a second to really look at her teammate's hand. It was gruesome, barely recognizable as a hand. She knew at a glance that there was no way the surgeons were going to be able to save it.

Moving as quickly as possible, she wrapped a new bandage around the wound tightly. She needed to stop the bleeding and do whatever she could to prevent any more infection from setting in.

Holman squirmed in Kane's grasp, but not one sound left his lips.

Just as she was tying off the bandage, she heard the other three Deltas return.

"Let's roll," Trigger said, jumping into the back of the truck.

He was obviously talking to the other two men, who had gotten into the front, because the second the words left his lips, the engine started and they were on their way.

"Don't you need to stay and find Akhund?" Aspen asked.

It was Grover who answered. "We act as a team. We'll get you three to base and safety, then we'll head back out. That asshole Spence is giving away the Rangers' every move, with as much fucking noise as they're making. After his fuckup of a search today, we're going to make sure he's off the hunt. We can find Akhund a hell of a lot quicker without Spence's so-called *help*."

Aspen should've been offended. After all, she'd been looking for Akhund for the last month and a half too, but all she could think about was the fact that all seven Deltas were going back to base with her, Holman, and Vandine. They didn't have to, but they were sticking together. Like a team.

If she had any doubts about how a team was supposed to operate, she didn't anymore.

But she knew for a fact that even if she requested reassignment, she'd always be the odd man out. The Army might have opened up the Rangers and combat specialties to women, but for now, the price for acceptance was just too high. Derek proved that by leaving her alone today.

"Thank you for your help," she told Kane as she eased Holman's hand back into his lap. His eyes were glassy and his breathing was way too fast, but she wasn't surprised. Not after what they'd just survived.

She turned back to Vandine, who was lying on the floor behind her, and checked his vitals. He was still unconscious, but he was breathing and his heart was still pumping what blood he had in his body, which was a plus. His blood pressure was way too low, and she considered putting in an IV, but decided they were close enough to the base that it could wait.

"Can I look at your leg now?" Kane asked from beside her. He was so close, it startled the hell out of Aspen, and she jerked away in reaction.

"Easy, *polyagapiménos*. You're safe."

She couldn't help but laugh. "Poly-a-what-tos?"

But Kane's lips didn't even twitch. "Greek. *Polyagapiménos*. You're still bleeding."

Aspen craned her neck to look at her calf. Her pants were covered in blood, but she honestly barely even felt any pain. She flexed her foot and winced. Yeah, okay, that hurt. But she didn't think it was anything more than a graze. She wasn't bleeding out and, while it was painful, she was more concerned about the others at the moment.

She shook her head. "I can't right now. I need to make sure Vandine doesn't crash and get him into the OR. Holman's not out of the woods either. It can wait."

She couldn't interpret the look in Kane's eyes, but she flushed from the intensity of it. "What?" she whispered.

"I've never seen anything more impressive in my life," Kane told her.

Aspen couldn't take her eyes from his.

"We saw you and Holman running down the street and knew you'd turn toward our direction. We couldn't shoot back at the men chasing you down because we didn't want to hit you."

Aspen nodded. She understood and appreciated that.

"Damn, woman!" Lefty exclaimed. "Watching you run while carrying a man way taller and heavier than you was pretty damn impressive."

"And did you notice she had her rifle at the ready too?" Doc asked.

"Not only that, but she still had her pack on as well," Grover added.

"And she kept going even after she'd been shot," Lucky said.

"Like I said...impressive," Kane finished. He hadn't taken his eyes from hers while his teammates praised her.

Aspen shrugged, but deep inside their praise soothed her soul after what she'd just been through. "I wasn't about to leave him behind. I made an oath."

"An oath the rest of your team obviously doesn't give a shit about," Lefty grumbled.

Aspen forced herself to look away from Kane then. "They were given a direct order," she defended.

"I don't give a shit if God himself ordered them to abandon their team, they shouldn't have done it," Kane growled.

Aspen's gaze went back to him.

"Seriously. Your team is your lifeline. They knew they were leaving you three to your deaths, and they did it anyway. That's *fucked*," Kane said in disgust.

"But—"

"He's right," Vandine said in a whisper.

Aspen's head whipped around. "Sergeant!" she exclaimed, surprised he was conscious.

"It's my fault," the man said. "I've been deferring to Spence for weeks. I should've stood up to him way before now. I didn't take leadership of my team, and as a result, they were confused about their mission and where their loyalties lie." His hand came up and he blindly reached for Aspen.

She grabbed hold of it, putting her fingers on his pulse point to try to monitor his heart rate as the truck drove way too quickly through the town and back toward the base.

"The way he's been treating you isn't right. We're Rangers, not fucking seventh graders. You really carried me?" he asked.

Aspen's head was spinning with his topic change, but she nodded anyway. "You always partnered me with the biggest man on the teams just to see if I'd fail."

"And you never did," Vandine said with what sounded like pride. "You're good people," he said softly. "And I'm not just saying that because you saved my life."

Aspen nodded again, not sure what to say in reply.

"Am I gonna lose my leg?" he asked, his eyes boring into hers.

Aspen wanted to lie. Wanted to tell him that he'd be fine. That he'd be up and walking in no time, but she wasn't one hundred percent sure, and the last thing she'd do was blow smoke up his ass. "I'm not sure. But I've done everything in my power to help the surgeons out when we get there. I *am* sure if it's at all possible, you'll wake up with all four limbs."

He nodded. Then his eyes focused on Holman for a moment before returning to her. "His hand?"

Aspen pressed her lips together and shook her head slightly.

"Akhund?" Vandine asked.

It was Trigger who answered him. "In the wind. Spence and the others went after him, and I'm sure he's long gone by now. But we're gonna get him," he said with confidence.

Vandine nodded. "Once we're out of the way, you mean," he said with a small chuckle.

"Damn straight," Grover said. "As long as he's free, no one's safe."

The truck slowed, and Aspen tensed.

"Easy," Kane said, putting his hand on her arm. "We're at the gate."

She nodded. For a second she had visions of them being ambushed. They'd really be sitting ducks in the back of the truck.

Within a minute they were moving again, and Aspen could see the familiar sights of the base passing behind them as they raced toward the hospital. She knew Holman and Vandine would be checked out and stabilized as much as possible there before being flown out to Kuwait, and then on to Germany.

The truck came to a stop in front of the tent being used as the clinic/hospital, and Aspen readied to help her patients inside. She looked back down at Vandine and saw that he'd fallen unconscious once more. It was probably better, considering his condition and the treatment that was ahead.

When she looked up again, she saw a crowd of doctors and nurses were waiting at the truck. There were three gurneys as well.

"Three?"

"You've been shot," Kane said by way of explanation.

She frowned. "I'm fine. I'm not going in on a gurney. I need to debrief the teams on my patients."

It was Kane's turn to frown. "Aspen—"

"No," she said firmly. Then gentler, she continued, "It hurts, but it's not life threatening. I'll get it looked out after I make sure my team is taken care of." Then she scooted forward on her knees, keeping her hand on Vandine's chest as he was moved to the back of the truck. She observed as he was transferred to the gurney and whisked inside.

Then she turned her attention to Holman. "I can walk," he protested as the nurses and doctors were attempting to put him on a gurney.

"Of course you can walk," Aspen reassured him. "But we need to let the doctors earn their keep, right?"

He rolled his eyes and shook his head at her, but he sat on the gurney.

Breathing a sigh of relief, Aspen turned to grab her pack, and saw that Kane already had it over one shoulder. "I got it," he told her.

Thankful for his help, Aspen started to climb out of the truck but hesitated. Her leg had really started throbbing, now that the adrenaline that had been coursing through her veins had dissipated somewhat.

A nurse pushed the third gurney closer, but Trigger and

Grover intercepted him. "She's got this," Trigger told the man under his breath.

Kane hopped out of the back of the truck and held out his hand. "Lean on me," he ordered.

In any other situation, she might've complained about him ordering her around, but she was too grateful for his help at the moment. She took his hand—and it felt as if a jolt of electricity arced between them.

Surprised, she glanced up at him...and saw a look of possessiveness so strong in his gaze, it made her stumble. But Kane didn't let her fall.

His other hand went to her waist and he all but lifted her out of the truck. He gave her a moment to catch her balance then dropped her hand, but his arm didn't fall from around her waist. He walked at her side as they made their way into the tent. Aspen knew she was limping, and hated that show of weakness, but somehow the man next to her made her feel way stronger than she was.

If she'd been by herself, she knew she'd be worried about what everyone was thinking, how they'd gotten separated from the team, where the rest of the Rangers were, what exactly had happened. But with Kane and his team at her back, she felt almost invincible.

It took about twenty minutes to debrief both teams of doctors about Vandine and Holman's injuries. She explained what she'd done in the field and how much ketamine both had received. She gave her professional opinion about how bad she believed their injuries were and then, just like that, her job as a medic was done.

Kane and Oz led her into an open exam room while Trigger went to find someone to finally look at her own injury. Lefty put her pack on the floor and got to work straightening the contents after she'd rummaged through them in the alley.

Grover asked if she was hungry, and even though she said she wasn't, he said he'd go find Sierra and see if she could prepare something for her. Doc offered to go to Aspen's tent and bring her something to change into, because it was obvious her pants were a lost cause.

Tears sprang to her eyes.

"What's wrong?" Kane asked urgently.

Aspen just shook her head. "I just...why are you all still here?"

Kane took her head in his hands after she sat on the side of the examining table. "This is what a team does, *chérie*."

"I'm not on your team," she whispered.

"The hell you're not," Kane retorted. She swore his head started to lower, but just then, a doctor entered the room and he had to take a step back.

"I heard you were shot," the doctor said curtly. "Let's see the damage."

Aspen turned onto her stomach and let the doctor and nurse cut her pants leg so they could see her calf. She lay still as they cleaned and sutured the wound. It hurt, but somehow having Kane in the room, leaning against a wall with his arms crossed, watching over her, made it not quite as painful as it might've been.

When she was all bandaged up, she put on the uniform pants Doc had brought her. It was painful to put her boot back on, but since he'd also brought her a pair of flip-flops, she was good to go.

While she was being cared for, she learned that the base docs were moving both Vandine and Holman to

Germany as soon as possible—and surprisingly, they were shipping her out with them.

When she'd heard the news, she opened her mouth to question it, but pressed her lips together when Kane shook his head at her. Aspen had no idea why she was being medically evacuated when she wasn't all that injured, but Kane cleared it up when they had a minute alone.

"Vandine insisted on it," he told her. "Said you were his teammate and injured as well. I think the base general was more than willing to send you home early after hearing from Holman about what happened out there today. He's not happy with Spence, or about how the other men on your team left you guys behind. I think he realizes that putting some distance between you and the others right now is probably best."

"So I'm being punished for Derek's actions. Great," Aspen muttered. Then sighed and looked up at Kane. "What happens when we all get back to Texas?"

"I don't know, but I'm sure you'll figure it out," Kane told her.

"You guys are staying, right?"

"Yeah. As soon as you leave, we'll head back out for recon. We're gonna get Akhund."

"Of course you are," Aspen said with conviction. "The top brass should've saved us all the time and heartache by sending you guys in the first place."

Kane smiled, and once again, Aspen thought he might kiss her, but they were interrupted by a nurse who came into the room to clean it for the next patient.

The next thing Aspen knew, she was standing next to a huge medic evac helicopter, ready for the long journey to Kuwait, then Germany, then back to Texas. Doc had gone back to her tent and packed her things, and Aspen tried not to be embarrassed that he'd seen her underwear.

Trigger, Lefty, Oz, Lucky, Doc, and Grover were all standing behind Kane in their black pants and shirts as the helicopter was fired up. They'd already given her hugs and wished her well before saying they'd see her soon.

Then it was time to say goodbye to Kane.

"I'd say I'll write, but there's a chance we might beat you home," Kane quipped.

"Be safe," Aspen said, not quite able to joke. Not when she'd experienced the danger in the village firsthand. There had been several times over the last few hours when she'd thought that was it. That she'd be shot and the only way she'd go back home was in a body bag.

"I will," Kane told her.

They stood silent there for several tense seconds. Aspen wanted to let him know how much she cared about him, but couldn't find the words.

Then he muttered, "Fuck it," and reached for her.

One hand went behind her neck and the other grabbed her around the waist. He pulled her into him, Aspen gasping in surprise. Her hands landed on his chest...and then his lips were on hers.

The kiss was even more intense and breathtaking than the one they'd shared in the bar so many months ago.

Aspen's eyes closed, and she dug her fingers into his chest as he tilted his head to take her deeper. She'd never truly understood the allure of kissing until now. It felt nice, but she'd never gotten super turned on when she'd made out with past boyfriends.

But the second Kane's lips landed on hers, it was as if her body had been plugged into a socket. Every hair on her

173

body stood up and she shivered in response. Aspen knew she should pull away. That they shouldn't be kissing in front of what seemed like half the base. But she couldn't take her lips from his if her life depended on it.

Way too soon, Kane was the one who lifted his head first. She watched as he licked his lips, and his fingers tightened momentarily on her neck.

"If you get shot, I'm gonna be pissed," she whispered.

Kane chuckled. "Noted. Take care of that leg. Don't let it get infected," he told her.

"I won't." She knew she had to go. Had to get on the helicopter, but she literally couldn't pull herself out of Kane's hold. She felt safe there. As if nothing could hurt her while in his arms. Not Derek. Not the Taliban fighters. Nothing.

With a big breath, she took a step back.

His arms dropped, and she immediately felt bereft. She both hated and loved the feeling. Hated it because she'd always been independent. Loved it because having such deep feelings about a man was a new and exciting thing. And it was obvious that she wasn't the only one affected.

Kane gave her a chin lift and backed away to join his team. All seven watched as she climbed into the helicopter and it took off. Aspen kept her eyes on the Delta team as long as she could, until they were too small to see anymore.

Only then did she close her eyes and rest her forehead on the small window next to her seat. She and Kane had only been in Afghanistan together for a few hours, but somehow, Aspen knew today had changed her life forever.

CHAPTER TEN

A week and a half.

That's how long it took to find Akhund, kill him, report on their investigation to the head honchos at the base in Afghanistan, and get back to Texas.

Brain was more than ready to see Aspen again.

He'd only managed to communicate via email twice since she'd left the base, since much of his time had been spent hunting down Akhund. But he'd learned that Aspen's leg was mostly healed, and she hadn't seen or talked to Derek or the rest of her team yet.

She'd been in Germany a few days before flying home. Her parents had flown down from Minnesota after they'd heard she'd been shot, and had just left the day before.

Brain also knew Aspen would be returning to work soon, and that she wasn't looking forward to it. Even though they'd only shared emails, he could read the uncertainty in her words.

"You going to see Aspen?" Oz asked.

Brain nodded. They were at the airport at Fort Hood,

and for the first time, he understood Trigger and Lefty's urgency to see their women after a mission.

"She know you're back?"

"I'm gonna text her right before I leave here to head to her apartment," Brain said.

"You sure that's a good idea?"

Brain frowned. "What do you mean?"

"Just that she might want more of a head's up that you're coming over. Chicks like to dress up and look their best when they see their boyfriends."

Brain pressed his lips together for a second. Then said, "We aren't really boyfriend/girlfriend yet."

Oz raised his eyebrows. "Really? That goodbye kiss said differently. And...all the more reason for you to give her a proper head's up."

Brain hadn't thought about anything besides seeing her, but he thought Oz might just have a point. He pulled out his phone without a word.

Brain: Any chance you'll be free in about an hour and a half, and I can stop in?

Three dots immediately appeared as she typed a response.

Aspen: You're back?!?!?!?!
    Brain: Lol. I am.
    Aspen: YAY! Are you hungry? Can I cook something?
    Brain: I'm good, thanks though. I'm looking forward to seeing you.

Aspen: Same!

Brain: How's the leg?

Aspen: Good. The scar's pretty gnarly, but that's the least of my worries.

Brain: A scar just means you're tougher than whatever tried to hurt you.

Aspen: I like that. Are you all right?

Brain: What do you mean?

Aspen: You weren't shot, stabbed, tortured, or beaten or anything?

Brain: No.

Aspen: Good. I'm looking forward to seeing you.

Brain: Me too. Gotta go. See you soon.

Aspen: Soon.

Brain put his phone back in his pocket and knew he had a moronic grin on his face, but he couldn't help it. "Good call," he told Oz.

"For the record, I like her," Oz said. "I know you don't need my permission to date anyone, but Aspen's pretty okay for a Ranger."

Brain rolled his eyes at his friend then punched him in the shoulder.

"Hey, you guys comin' or what?" Trigger yelled from across the tarmac. "We've got a lot of shit to put away and we still have to debrief. I want to get home to Gillian sometime tonight."

"We're comin'!" Brain shouted back. But his mind was still on Aspen. He couldn't wait to see for himself that her leg really was healing properly. He wanted to explore the crazy chemistry he felt when he was around her and when they kissed. He simply wanted to hear her voice. He had a feeling he was a goner, but he didn't even care.

Two hours later, after an intense debrief where the team didn't hold back about everything that had happened in Afghanistan—with both the Ranger teams, and with their own successful search for Akhund—Brain was standing in front of Aspen's apartment door. He'd showered and changed into a pair of jeans and a plain black T-shirt.

Two-point-three seconds after he knocked on her door, it opened, and Aspen stood there. And suddenly, the week and a half since he'd seen her seemed more like years.

"Hi!" she said eagerly.

Without a word, Brain took a step toward her. She backed up, and he shut the door behind him. Then he kept walking.

Aspen had a grin on her face, but she kept backing away from him.

Neither said anything, but Brain felt as if he were a male lion stalking his mate. Aspen bumped into a small table and veered around it, still smiling. Eventually, she backed herself into a wall near her kitchen.

Brain caged her in by putting his hands on the wall next to her shoulders and leaning forward. He nuzzled the side of her neck, and she tilted her head, giving him room. Her hands gripped his waist, and nothing had felt better.

"Gardenias," he whispered as he inhaled deeply.

"My lotion," she told him as she tightened her grip on his T-shirt.

Brain pulled back just enough to look into her eyes. "Hey," he said quietly.

"Hey," she echoed.

There was so much Brain wanted to say, but he couldn't do anything but stare into her beautiful brown eyes. Her lashes were long; he hadn't noticed that before. She wasn't wearing any makeup, but she didn't need to. Her skin was flawless, and the longer he simply stared at her, the more color bloomed in her cheeks.

"Kane?"

"Yeah?"

"Um...are we going to stand here all night staring at each other or what?"

"Maybe."

She grinned. "Well...all right then."

Brain couldn't help but smile back. He wanted to kiss her. Wanted to touch her...all over. Wanted to claim her, mark her, make her his. But he also didn't want to freak her out. So he settled for saying, "We haven't really talked about it, but I want to go out with you. And I want to be exclusive. I don't want you seeing anyone else while we're together." He waited, almost holding his breath to see what she'd say.

"Okay."

He let out his breath in a whoosh. "That's it? Okay?"

She shrugged. "Yes. And the exclusive thing goes both ways, right?"

"Fuck yeah," Brain said. "Women aren't exactly beating down my door," he said honestly, then immediately regretted it.

But Aspen didn't seem fazed. "Their loss," she told him. "I'm thinking we need to seal this deal with a kiss," she went on.

Brain was more than all right with that. He was having a hard time thinking about anything other than feeling her lips on his again. Without a word, he leaned in and kissed her.

Aspen moaned, and one of her hands slipped under his T-shirt to touch his bare skin as she kissed him back.

Goose bumps immediately broke out on Brain's arms, and he honest-to-God growled before tilting his head and practically devouring her. But Aspen gave as good as she got, not backing down from his aggressive kiss.

How long they stood against the wall kissing, Brain had no idea, but when he felt her hands slip under his waistband in search of...more, he pulled back.

They were both panting, and he saw that Aspen's pupils were dilated. She was so gorgeous—and for some reason, she liked *him*.

For a brief second, Brain panicked. If she knew how much of a nerd he was, she probably wouldn't be so interested. But he pushed down the self-deprecating thoughts. He wasn't a child, and Aspen wasn't one of the cruel kids he'd grown up with, making fun of him for being smart and not allowing him into their circles because he was so young.

"That was...fun," she said with a smile.

Brain just shook his head at her and stepped back. He kept hold of her hand and towed her into her living room. He motioned for her to sit, and when she did, he pushed her coffee table back and kneeled in front of her.

"What are you...my leg is fine, Kane," Aspen told him.

But Brain ignored her as he pushed up the leg of her loose cotton pants to see for himself. He twisted his neck and examined the still-healing gunshot wound. There was no bandage, and he could see the stitches clearly. The bullet had grazed her, taking a large chunk of skin with it.

The skin was pink and still a bit swollen, but, as she'd said, was healing well.

"I'm assuming you've been cleared for light PT?" he asked.

Aspen nodded. "No running or weights yet, but I can do a lot of the other stuff."

Brain ran his thumb next to the scar, remembering how she'd carried her first sergeant while she ran. He'd be the first to admit that at one time, he probably would've been skeptical about women as combat medics attached to elite teams like the Rangers. But in the span of a few minutes, Aspen would have single-handedly changed *anyone's* mind. He cupped her calf in his hand, making sure not to touch her still-healing wound, and looked up at her. "How're the others?"

"Vandine's still in Germany. He'll be flown to Dallas as soon as the doctors think he's ready. The bullet nicked his femoral artery. Doctors were able to repair it, but they won't want to move him until they're sure it won't tear."

"He would've bled out in minutes if you hadn't been there," Brain said. It wasn't a question.

Aspen merely nodded. She'd done what she'd been trained to do. She was grateful both men were alive, but she'd just been doing her job.

"And Sergeant Holman?"

"The doctors removed his hand in Germany. They couldn't save it," she told him.

"But he's back in Texas, right?" Brain asked.

Aspen's eyes narrowed. "If you already know how they're doing, why'd you ask?" she asked, slightly irritated.

"Because I wanted to find out what you know," Brain said with a smile, not turned off in the least by her snark.

"And bring you up to speed if you didn't know everything I did."

She felt better about that.

"What's your schedule tomorrow?" Brain asked her.

"I have PT in the morning. Then a meeting with the major."

"What about?"

Aspen shrugged. "I'm assuming it's about my returning to regular duty."

Brain wasn't so sure, especially after everything the Deltas had had to say about what happened that day when she'd been hurt in Afghanistan, but he let that go for now. "What about the afternoon?"

"I'm still on half days. Why?"

"I thought you might like to drive down to Austin to see Holman."

"Really?" she asked.

"Yeah."

"Why?"

"Why what?" Brain asked.

"Why would you want to go see him? Don't think I don't know you aren't my team's biggest fan," Aspen said.

"I'm not. But you told me in an email that you were worried about him. And as his medic, I know you're probably dying to see for yourself that he's okay. I can put aside my differences if it means giving you what you want."

Aspen looked down at him for so long, Brain began to worry he'd said something wrong.

"Thank you," she said after a long moment. "I'd love to see how he's doing. But don't you have to work tomorrow?"

"Nope. We always get a few days off after a mission."

Her eyes lit up. "Really?"

"Really. Why does that amuse you so much?"

"I was just thinking about how much Trigger and Lefty must love that...not to mention their girlfriends."

Brain laughed. He finally stood and held out a hand to Aspen. "They do love it. It's obnoxious, if you want to know the truth."

"You wouldn't think that if you were the one getting some," Aspen told him with a laugh.

"True," Brain said, gripping her hand and pulling her upright.

But he didn't stop there. He yanked her right into his body, wrapping an arm around her waist until they were plastered together from hips to chest. He knew she could probably feel his erection against her, but she didn't pull away. She simply wrapped her arms around his shoulders and smiled.

"I'd love to spend the next few days with you...after you get home from work, of course. I feel as if in some ways, I know you really well, but in others, I don't know you at all. I'd like to remedy that."

"I'd love to," Aspen agreed.

"Good." Brain moved his hands to her waist and couldn't help but slip his thumbs under her shirt to caress the bare skin there.

"Things in Afghanistan went well?" she asked.

Brain opened his mouth to instantly say he couldn't talk about his mission, but then realized that Aspen knew exactly where he'd been, and why. There would be times in the future when he couldn't discuss his assignments with her, but he felt more relieved than he knew how to put into words that he could talk about Akhund.

"We got him," he told her.

"Good," she said firmly. "It didn't take too long, if you're already back home."

"Took longer than any of us wanted, but because of Spence's amateur actions, Akhund went to ground. It took a bit of sleuthing to figure out what rock he was hiding under."

"By sleuthing, I'm assuming you mean using your super language powers to eavesdrop," Aspen said with a smile.

Brain wanted nothing more than to lift her shirt over her head, throw her down on the couch and show her without words how much he loved her teasing, but instead, he sat on the couch and pulled her down with him. He settled into the corner of the surprisingly comfortable sofa, and she immediately curled up next to him. Brain put his arm around her shoulders and sighed in contentment when her own arm wrapped around his stomach, her knees resting on his thigh.

He'd never been a cuddler, but he decided right then and there he could definitely be one with her.

"Something like that," he admitted. "Anyway, he'd barricaded himself in a house and had surrounded himself with as many women and children as he could find. Bastard knew we wouldn't kill innocent civilians if we could help it."

"What about the men who were shooting at us?" Aspen asked.

"They weren't an issue," Brain told her, not going into detail about how they'd hunted down those men and made sure they couldn't hurt anyone else ever again.

"Right. How'd you get to Akhund?"

"With a loud speaker."

Aspen raised an eyebrow in question.

Brain shrugged. "I used it to tell the people in the house, in Farsi, that if they surrendered, they wouldn't be hurt. That they could take their children and go."

"And just like that, they came out?" Aspen asked in disbelief.

"Not exactly. It took two days, but eventually, little by little, they came out. Akhund wasn't happy. I heard him screaming at the people in the house, threatening them, but for some reason, he didn't strike back at his people when the first woman left. That gave the others the courage to exit the house themselves. Then it was just a matter of going in and ordering Akhund to surrender."

"He didn't though, did he?"

Brain shook his head. "No."

"What about Shahzada?"

"In the wind," Brain said. He turned to look at her. "And what I'm about to say goes no further than this apartment."

"Of course. I'm aware I don't have the same level of security clearance as you do, but I know enough to keep my mouth shut," Aspen told him seriously.

"Before Akhund died, he bragged that we'd never find Shahzada. That he was smarter than everyone. That the villagers were loyal to him, and any attempt at finding and killing him would fail."

"Did he give you any clues as to where he is or *who* he is?"

"No," Brain said in frustration. "We're pretty sure he's still in the area, but that's all we know. There are reports that he's got an extensive network of followers, and his MO is to take prisoners of war to gain information."

Aspen sucked in a breath. "Shit, seriously? Are there any POWs right now that are still in captivity in the area?"

"It's hard to tell. There have been people who've gone AWOL, but most have been accounted for," Brain said.

"I'm glad I'm not there anymore," Aspen muttered.

"You and me both," Brain agreed.

Aspen took a deep breath. "Well, I'm relieved Akhund is no longer an issue. He terrorized the villagers."

"He did. And hopefully our negotiations with them, and the fact we didn't have to kill any innocents, went a long way toward helping the US/Afghani relations in that region."

"I hope so," Aspen said with a nod of her head.

They were both quiet for a moment. Then Aspen asked, "Are you sure you aren't hungry? I can find something for us to eat if you want."

"I'm sure. But if *you* are, don't let me stop you."

"I'm good," Aspen reassured him. "I just…I don't want you to be bored."

Brain looked down at her and smiled. "I don't care what we do together, *skat*, just being with you is amazing."

She frowned. "*Skat?* Please tell me that's darling in some other language and you didn't just call me excrement."

Brain chuckled. "It's Danish."

"I think I prefer *chérie* or something," she told him with a pout.

"Noted."

Brain had never been much of a talker. He preferred to read a book or listen to music. But for the next few hours, he and Aspen talked nonstop. Sometimes they discussed serious topics like global warming, affects of war on children, or the coronavirus. But other times they talked about nothing important, like their preferences in fast food.

It was getting late, and Brain knew he should leave since Aspen had to get up for PT in the morning, but he couldn't tear himself away. He liked hanging out with her. Liked that she seemed perfectly comfortable around him. It almost felt too good to be true.

And that thought abruptly brought another woman to mind.

He hated thinking about anyone other than Aspen when they were together. He tried to push away thoughts of that other bitch, but since his mind had chosen *now* to remember what she'd done, he couldn't stop it.

His body must've tensed under hers, because Aspen lifted her head and asked, "What're you thinking about so hard?" She'd lain down at one point in the evening, her head resting on his thigh. Brain was running his hand through her hair over and over, loving the sight of the strands covering his lap.

He sighed and didn't even consider lying. To Aspen, he was an open book. He wanted her to know everything about him, even if that meant sharing some of his insecurities. "Remember when I told you I hadn't been with a woman in two years?"

She lifted her head and furrowed her brow. "Of course I do."

"You have to understand...I was always the youngest person by far in my classes growing up. In high school. In college. Women didn't really see me as anyone other than someone they could get notes from, or who could do their homework. So when I joined the Army and was suddenly surrounded by men and women my own age, it was pretty overwhelming for me. I wasn't treated like the 'smart guy' at first. In fact, most people didn't even know about my degrees or anything about my intellectual abilities."

"That's good," Aspen said softly.

"Yeah. I dated a bit, but it was awkward for me. I didn't really know what to say or do, and I don't even want to get into how long it took for me to get comfortable with my sexuality. Anyway, I met this woman, Deidre, a few years back. The team and I had gone to a bar to chill out after a particularly gnarly mission and saw some other guys from the post we knew. We were having a few beers when a group of women came in. They were also soldiers, and they made a beeline for us. We all started talking, and somehow it came up that I was good at languages. Everyone seemed duly impressed...but Deidre was especially interested."

"Please tell me this isn't going where I think it's going," Aspen said, sitting up and curling her arm around his chest once more.

Brain shrugged. "I got her number and before I knew it, we were talking every day and she was hanging out at my place. I enjoyed talking with her, and she admitted that she was trying to learn Farsi and was having a hard time. So I gladly helped her. She was very dedicated to studying, and I admired that. I liked her a lot. She was pretty, tall, had long blonde hair, and it was flattering that she'd picked me out of all the other guys who were at the bar that night."

"I think I don't like Deidre very much," Aspen said heatedly.

Brain felt a little weird that he was enjoying the fact

that Aspen was getting worked up on his behalf. He needed to finish this story and make his point. "Right, well she was never very affectionate, but I chalked that up to her strict religious upbringing, which she'd told me about. We kissed a little, and fooled around, but it wasn't until after she'd taken her Farsi language test for the Army—and passed—that we slept together.

"We'd both gotten a little drunk, and one thing led to another. We ended up in bed, and I thought everything was great between us. But the next morning, she woke up...and she definitely wasn't happy. I just thought it was because she was hungover, but she quickly enlightened me. Told me that she didn't think things were going to work out between us, and she appreciated my help with Farsi, but now that she'd passed her test, she was breaking up with me."

"What a bitch!" Aspen seethed.

"I can look back now and see the signs. They were all there. Not wanting to hang out in public. Never wanting to do anything with me but study. Being reluctant to do more than kiss. Hell, she had to get *drunk* in order to fuck me. The thing of it was...I'd truly thought we'd connected. But the bottom line was that she was using me for my smarts. It really *was* too good to be true, but I was the dummy who'd thought we were on our way to something serious."

"And what? You think that's what I'm doing too? Using you for some unknown reason? Is that why you're thinking about her?"

"No, not really. But sometimes I can't help but remember that sometimes when something seems too good to be true, there's a reason."

Aspen shocked the shit out of Brain when she threw a leg over his lap. She straddled him and took his face in her hands and met his gaze as she said, "I don't care that you know French, or German, or Farsi, or any other language. I mean, it's amazing and wonderful, and I admit to feeling a bit inadequate as a result, but that's not why I'm going out with you. You want to know why?"

Brain stared at her. "Yes," he said simply.

"Because when I'm with you, it's as if we're the only two people in the world. Being with you makes me happy. I feel a connection to you that I've never felt with anyone else in my life. If anything, *I'm* the one who should be worried about you deciding I'm not worth *your* time. This isn't too good to be true. At least, I don't think so."

"Me either," Brain said.

"Good. So put the bitch Deidre out of your mind. She's not worth thinking about for one more second." Then she scooted closer, and Brain felt his dick twitch. If they were naked, they'd be as intimate as two people could be. He could shift just a bit and he'd be inside her.

"Kiss me," Aspen whispered.

She didn't have to ask twice. Brain gripped the back of her neck and held her tight as he brought his lips to hers.

At first their kiss was sweet. They nipped and teased each other playfully. But Brain needed more. Always more.

They kissed for several long minutes. Until Brain knew he needed to go before he exploded in his pants. Aspen was rocking against him, caressing his cock with her unconscious movements. He wanted her. More than anything else, *ever*. More than his first Master's degree. More than a spot on the Deltas.

But he didn't want to rush things. Wanted her to know

he respected her and, if he was being honest, he kind of liked the buildup of anticipation. He hadn't felt this alive in a very long time. Tonight didn't feel like the right time to make a move on her. She had to get up early, and he was tired as well.

He pulled back and watched with lust as she licked her lips, puffy and slick from his kisses.

"You'll really take me to Austin tomorrow to see Holman?" she asked.

"Yes."

"Thank you."

Brain nodded once. "I'll pick you up around one-thirty. Text me if something changes and you don't want to go anymore."

"I'm not going to change my mind," Aspen told him gently. "And wouldn't it be easier if I came to your house?"

"No. Because then you'd have to drive back here when we get home, and I don't know what time that'll be. I'd prefer for you not to be driving around after dark," Brain told her.

Aspen smiled. "I've been driving at night for a long time," she told him. "And I'm practically a Ranger. I'll be fine."

"Humor me," Brain told her, not changing his mind. He wasn't usually paranoid, especially about driving around Killeen at night, but everything was different now. He couldn't stand the thought of Aspen getting hurt. Not when he could prevent it.

"Okay. Fine."

Brain nodded, then he leaned forward, kissed her once more—because he couldn't keep his mouth off her—and stood, with Aspen still in his arms.

She screeched, then laughed as she clung to him.

Smiling, he let go of her legs and wrapped his arms around her waist. They stood intertwined together in front of her couch. Since they were about the same height, he could look straight into her eyes. "I had a good time tonight."

"Me too. I'm glad you got home safely," she told him.

"Get off that leg," he ordered.

"I can walk you to your car."

"No. It's late. If you walked me to my car, then I'd have to walk you back up here to your apartment."

She grinned. "Fine. Are you ever going to see me as competent when it comes to safety?"

"It's not about competence. It's about me wanting to be the one keeping you safe. I know you're on a Ranger team. I know you're a combat medic. You've had a lot of the same training I have. But, as your boyfriend—and when we aren't in the middle of a firefight in Afghanistan —I simply can't see you as anything but a vulnerable woman. *My* woman."

Brain internally winced. He'd mucked that up royally. He wouldn't blame her if she dumped his ass right then and there.

But she simply smiled wider. "I'd be stupid to take offense to that," she told him. "As long as you do realize that I'm not helpless. I'll never be the kind of girlfriend who lets her man take over her life. I've been on my own for a long time, and I don't need anyone to take care of me."

"Noted. I'll do my best to rein in my caveman tendencies," Brain said, relieved she wasn't pissed.

"So I can walk you to your car?" she teased.

"No," Brain said with a shake of his head.

Aspen laughed. "I was kidding." She leaned in, kissed him, then took his hand and towed him toward her door. Brain followed docilely, sneaking a peek at her ass as she walked.

She stopped and turned. "Were you checking out my butt?"

"Yeah," Brain admitted immediately. "It's pretty damn nice."

She grinned. "Turnabout's fair play. You can't complain in the future when I check *you* out."

"Deal." Then he ran his thumb over her cheekbone. "Thanks for letting me come by."

"Anytime. And I mean that," she told him.

Brain backed through the open door, knowing if he kissed her one more time, he might not be able to stop. "I'll see you tomorrow."

"Drive safe."

"I will."

"Text me when you get home?"

Brain tilted his head. "I'm sure I won't have any issues getting home."

"Humor me."

"Fine. See you tomorrow."

"Bye, Kane."

"Bye."

Brain forced himself to turn and walk down the hall and away from Aspen. It was almost scary how much he cared about her. He was going to do everything in his power not to fuck this up...even if he had no idea how.

CHAPTER ELEVEN

Aspen was waiting when Kane knocked on her door the next afternoon. The morning had been...stressful. She'd gone to PT with her team, but everyone was subdued and didn't really talk to her much. They'd never been chatty-Kathys with her, but this morning they were even more reticent. They'd gotten a new platoon sergeant, and Aspen liked him well enough. At least he didn't talk down to her like some Rangers did. And Holman's replacement was also there for his first workout with his new team.

Then later that morning, she'd met with the major. Aspen had thought he wanted to discuss her return to full-time duties, but instead, he'd asked a million questions about the op in Afghanistan. He wanted to know every-thing about how Vandine and Derek had handled various situations, including a second-by-second accounting of when everything had gone to shit that last day.

Aspen had been uncomfortable saying anything derogatory about anyone, even if they'd fucked up. But in the end, it was obvious the major already knew most of what had occurred. So she'd done her best to recount what happened with as little emotion as possible. She just told him the facts.

When she was done, the major sat back in his chair with his fingers steepled under his chin and stared at her.

Aspen refused to fidget. She hadn't done anything wrong.

"Do you like your job, Sergeant Mesmer?"

"Yes, Sir."

"Do you *love* your job?"

At that, she paused. She loved being a medic. Craved the adrenaline rush she got when she had to make life-or-death decisions. She especially loved being able to make a difference in someone's life...like with Vandine and Holman. But she definitely didn't love all the other shit that came with the job. Being looked down on because of her gender, being shot at, being treated like a second-class citizen.

"That's what I thought," the major said before she had a chance to respond to his second question. He leaned forward and rested his elbows on his desk. "You're a damn good medic, Mesmer. I've taken a look at your service record, and it's impeccable. You're coming up on eight years in, right?"

"Yes, Sir."

"You'll need to decide on whether or not you'll be reenlisting soon."

"Yes, Sir," Aspen said again.

"I don't want to lose you. I don't want the Army to lose you. But you're not happy."

Aspen blinked, surprised the man would come right out and say it.

"I could sit here and promise you all sorts of things to try to get you to stay. I could tell you that Sergeant Spence will be reassigned, that I could move you to a new Ranger unit. Give you your choice of duty station, reenlistment bonuses...but I don't think any of those things will make you happy."

He was right. She'd never been the kind of woman to need a huge salary, or to live in a gigantic house. She wanted to *belong*. And the bottom line was that she wasn't sure she'd ever really belong in the Army. Especially in the special forces teams.

She frowned at the man in front of her.

"I'm confusing you, and I'm sorry. I want what's best for all my soldiers, and if that's getting out and finding what they need to be happy outside the Army, so be it. I don't know what your plans are. I don't know anything about your social life or your family. But after hearing how well you conducted yourself in that shit-show in Afghanistan, despite all the factors against you, I feel as if I need to impart some advice.

"Before you reenlist, think about what you want. What you *really* want. And if that isn't another four years doing what you're doing now...walk away."

Aspen had been shocked at the major's words. But she couldn't deny that having a superior officer come right out and say what she'd been thinking, and validating it, felt like a weight had been lifted off her shoulders.

Despite that, she'd left the meeting without any decisions being made, and fairly stressed out about what might happen if she did decide to get out of the Army. But knowing that she'd be seeing Kane that afternoon made it easier to push everything to the back of her mind

—all the heavy decisions she'd have to make in the near future, and the strain of her reunion with her Ranger team.

When Kane finally knocked on her door, Aspen practically skipped to answer it.

"Hey. I thought you'd never get—"

Her words were cut off by Kane's lips. He wrapped an arm around her waist, pulled her into him, and kissed her... hard. And Aspen couldn't help but smile at his enthusiasm.

When he pulled back, she tried again. "Hi."

"Hi," he echoed. "Ready to go?" He took a step back but kept hold of her hand.

She loved that kissing was no longer a huge step in their relationship. It already seemed natural. "Yeah. Let me just grab my purse."

He squeezed her hand once before dropping it, and even that made Aspen feel all giddy inside. She ran back into the small apartment and grabbed her purse, which she'd left on the counter in the kitchen. She was back in front of Kane in seconds. "Ready," she told him.

She locked the door behind them, and once she'd dropped her keys in her purse, Kane took hold of her hand again. It had been a long time since Aspen had held hands with someone, and she couldn't remember it ever making her feel as happy as it did right now.

When they were settled in his Challenger and headed toward Austin, he asked about her day. "How'd your morning go? Your leg holding out all right?"

"My leg's fine," she told him, not admitting that all the activity from the day had it throbbing a bit. She'd taken an over-the-counter painkiller before he'd picked her up, and she knew it would help. "And my morning was weird." She proceeded to tell him about the strain between her and the Ranger team, and about her meeting with the major.

"What do you think?" she asked him when she finished.

"About what?"

"About me getting out of the Army? I have no idea what I'd even do."

Kane glanced over at her. "Be an EMT. Or get your paramedic license. You told me once that it was a paramedic who made you want to join the Army, after you'd seen them in action when you were on that ride-along with the police department. You already have your national license for EMT. You could get your state certification and find a job with an ambulance company."

Aspen blinked. Kane sounded so sure. So positive she'd find a job easily, and that she'd pass the tests to get her licensure. The more she thought about it, the more excited she got. For some reason, she'd never even thought about working on an ambulance. She'd been so worked up about the thought of leaving the military, she'd had a hard time thinking about anything else.

"And I'm sorry your team can't get their heads out of their asses. For what it's worth, most are probably embarrassed as hell at their actions. They never should've left you, Holman, and Vandine."

"They were ordered to by someone who had a higher rank," Aspen defended.

"I've said it before and I'll say it again. I don't care if the Chairman of the Joint Chiefs of Staff, the highest-ranking officer in the Army, ordered me to leave anyone on my team behind. I wouldn't do it."

Aspen reached out and put her hand on Kane's thigh.

He immediately wrapped his hand around hers.

Several miles passed in silence before Aspen said, "I don't blame them."

"You should," Kane said, with no ire in his tone. "A team is sacred. Everyone has their strengths and weaknesses, and you work with each other to accomplish your missions. My team needs me to translate. To listen and report and to talk our way out of situations when they arise. I don't know what I'd do without them, and I'd like to think they feel the same way about me."

"They do," Aspen told him immediately. She hadn't hung out with Kane's friends all that much, but even the little time she'd known them had shown her what she was missing out on.

"I can't sit here and tell you what to do with the rest of your life. But I do know that I want to keep seeing you. I want to be involved with whatever it is you choose to do. If you stay in the Army, I'll do whatever I can to make things between us work. It won't be easy, as either of us could be moved tomorrow, but I'm not the kind of man who'll insist on you giving up your career to follow me in mine."

Aspen stared at him. "Are you saying you'd get out of the Army if I didn't want to?"

Kane shrugged. "I don't know. I mean, we just started dating and things might not work out between us. But I do know I've never felt the connection to another woman that I do with you, and I'll only be in the military for another ten or so years...I'd like to think I'll be with the woman I marry for way longer than that. Put in perspective, it's a no-brainer."

Aspen felt like crying. She knew Kane wasn't proposing

marriage, but for him to sit there and basically tell her that he'd put her above his own career, a job he loved, was startling and humbling. "I don't know what I'm going to do."

"And that's fine. You have time to think about it. All I'm sayin' is that I'll support your decision. I honestly think you'll find the team atmosphere you've been looking for in the medical field. It might take a while to find someone you click with in the ambulance service, but you'd be an amazing addition to any company, and your patients would be lucky as hell."

"You need to stop talking," Aspen told him, doing her best to blink back tears.

He looked over at her in alarm. "Why?"

"Nothing. I just can't handle you being so damn sweet."

Kane's face smoothed out when he realized nothing was wrong. "Sorry, no can do. That shit just seems to pop out when I'm around you."

She felt him squeeze her hand, and she closed her eyes and rested her head on the back of the seat.

As if knowing how tired she was, Kane didn't say anything else. He turned up the music a bit, and between that and the smooth ride, Aspen was soon dozing off.

She woke up when Kane squeezed her hand. "We're here, *kallis*."

Aspen raised a brow in the now-familiar silent question.

"Estonian," he told her.

Smiling, Aspen nodded and climbed out of the car. As soon as he came around to her side, Kane took her hand again. He was always reaching for her. Holding on to her. Touching her. She'd never dated anyone who was so touchy, and she had to admit she loved it.

They went into the VA hospital where Holman was being treated and found out which room he was in from the lady at the reception desk. They took the elevator up in silence, and it gave Aspen time to stress about what she was going to say to her teammate.

"Stop worrying," Kane ordered.

Aspen shook her head. "How'd you know that's what I was doing?"

"You have a worry line right here," he said, running a finger between her eyes.

"Great, *now* I'm worrying about wrinkles," Aspen muttered, but she smiled when Kane merely laughed.

When they got to Holman's door, she knocked, and when he bade them to enter, Aspen pushed the door open.

She stopped in her tracks upon seeing the number of people in the room.

A pretty woman maybe a few years older than Aspen was sitting in a chair next to Holman's bed. A young teenage girl was leaning against a wall, fiddling with a cell phone, and a boy—probably around six or seven—sat cross-legged at the end of the bed.

"I'm sorry to interrupt," Aspen said quickly.

"Mesmer!" Holman exclaimed. "Come in!"

She stepped into the room, the feel of Kane's hand on her back giving her more confidence than she might've had if she'd arrived by herself.

"What a surprise! This is my wife, Lynn, my daughter, Laurie, and my son, Max."

Aspen greeted each person with a smile and a nod.

"And this is Sergeant Mesmer. Aspen. She's the one who saved my life."

With those last seven words, everyone in the room stared at Aspen.

She did her best to shrug off his statement. "I'm not sure I'd say that. All I did was wrap some gauze around your hand."

"Max, hands over your ears," Holman ordered, and Aspen smiled at how the little boy immediately did as his father ordered.

The second his son couldn't hear him, Holman said, "Bullshit. I'm not an idiot, Mesmer. You were as calm as a cucumber. You gave me your rifle, dealt with Vandine, all while keeping the enemy from entering that alley. Then you threw the sergeant over your shoulder like he weighed nothing more than a sack of potatoes and got us all the hell out of there."

"Daddy, can I listen again now?" Max asked a little too loudly.

Holman smiled at his son and nodded. Then he turned his attention back to Aspen. He held out his good hand and gestured with his fingers for her to come closer.

Surprised, Aspen shuffled forward and took her teammate's hand. He'd never touched her before, not like this. They'd had to touch each other in training, but this was way different.

"They shouldn't have left us," he said quietly, and Aspen knew he was referring to their teammates. "But what sucks the most is knowing that if it had been Buckland, or Hamilton, or anyone else who'd been injured instead of me...I would've done exactly what they did. I didn't realize, Mesmer."

"Realize what?" she asked quietly.

"How vital you were to our team. That you were actually the most valuable person there.”

Aspen felt her throat close up and she was literally speechless.

“I've done a lot of thinking while I've been laid up,” Holman went on. “None of us were happy when you were assigned to our team. We thought you'd slow us down. That we wouldn't be able to do our job as effectively. We were so pissed about what you didn't have between your legs that we didn't consider what you had between your *ears* was so much more important. I know I'm a day late and a hell of a lot of dollars short, but I'm asking for your forgiveness.”

“Done,” Aspen said immediately.

Holman nodded at her in relief.

“How're you really doing?” she asked.

He shrugged. “I'm okay. Losing my hand is gonna take some getting used to though.”

Aspen winced.

“Nothing could've been done, Mesmer. I knew from the moment I looked down and saw there wasn't much left, I'd lose it. You couldn't have saved it, so don't even go there.”

Aspen nodded.

“Thanks to you, I'm here,” Holman said. He glanced over at his wife, and the look of love that passed between them was so intense, Aspen was almost embarrassed to be witnessing it. “I get to see my beautiful Lynn's face every day, hear my daughter sass me, and listen to my son tell me all about the frogs and snakes he's found out in the yard.”

Aspen glanced at Holman's family again, and it occurred to her that she hadn't even known they existed until right this second. She had no idea if the others on the team were married or if they had kids. They'd never talked about them. But then again, she hadn't asked. She'd been so concerned with trying to fit in as part of the team that she hadn't attempted to connect with her teammates on a personal level. She realized some of the distance between them was her own fault. Not all of it, not by any stretch, but she'd made plenty of mistakes too.

Holman's gaze moved from her to Kane, still standing in the doorway. "I know you, right?"

Aspen dropped Holman's hand to gesture to Kane. "This is Sergeant Temple. He helped us get to the truck, remember?"

Holman gave Kane a chin lift. "I do. Thank you."

Kane shrugged. "We didn't do much. I'm sure if we hadn't shown up, Mesmer would've hot-wired a truck, thrown both you and Vandine inside, and run over anyone who dared get between her and the hospital."

Holman chuckled. "I have no doubt, but thank you all the same."

Kane nodded.

"So...what's next?" Aspen asked Holman.

"I'll be medically retired, then spend the rest of my life playing the role of a pirate with a hook hand." He said it in jest, but she could hear the pain behind his words.

"Why did the one-handed man cross the street?" Max asked.

Aspen looked at the little boy in surprise, but Holman smiled huge and said, "I don't know, son, why?"

"To get to the second-hand shop."

Everyone laughed, but Laurie rolled her eyes. "That's rude," she told her brother.

"You laughed," he shot back.

"Whatever."

When Aspen glanced back at Holman, she saw he was looking at his kids with love in his eyes. He met her gaze and said quietly, "I don't know what I'm going to do. All I've known is the Army. Joined right out of high school after Lynn and I got married. But I'll figure it out. I'm alive, and I have a family who loves me. Everything else is secondary."

Aspen nodded. Holman had a good attitude. She wasn't surprised to see moments of doubt and uncertainty in his eyes, but he had everything to live for...and he knew it.

She spent another thirty or so minutes in the room talking with Holman and his family, but when she saw his eyes drooping, she knew it was time to go. She turned to Lynn. "If you need anything, anything at all, please don't hesitate to get in touch with me."

"Thanks," the other woman said.

Aspen scribbled her number on a whiteboard in the room. "I mean it. Holman's part of my team, and that means you are too. Whatever you guys need, just let me know."

"I appreciate it. We're good for now," Lynn assured her.

Aspen wasn't surprised by her answer. It wasn't as if they knew each other, which made her a little sad. She smiled at the other woman and gave Holman a chin lift. "See ya, stumpy."

For a second, she was appalled at the words she'd blurted without thought, but when Holman burst out laughing, she relaxed.

"See ya, Mesmer."

She left the hospital room and felt the familiar weight

of Kane's fingers on the small of her back. When they got into the empty elevator, she turned and rested her forehead against his shoulder. Kane didn't say anything, just lifted his hand and massaged the back of her neck.

When they got back to his car, he took her into his arms before she could get inside.

How long they stood there, hugging each other in the parking garage, Aspen had no idea. But by the time she pulled back, she felt a lot better.

Kane studied her for a long moment, then nodded. "Hungry?" he asked.

"Starving."

"Mexican?"

Aspen's eyes lit up. "Uh...duh."

Kane smiled. "How 'bout Torchy's Tacos?"

"Oh, yeah," Aspen said. She'd eaten at the popular Austin restaurant a few times and had never left unsatisfied.

What had started out as a very weird and unsettling day was turning out to be pretty darn wonderful...and she had Kane to thank for it.

* * *

Hours later, Aspen once more stood in her doorway saying goodbye to Kane. They'd eaten some amazing tacos then driven back to Killeen, where he'd brought her to his house. They'd talked, made out, made out some more, then he'd reluctantly told her that he needed to get her home since they both had to be up the next morning. Even though Kane still had another day off, he was meeting his team for PT bright and early.

Aspen had wanted to protest, but she knew he was right, they both needed to get some sleep. "When will I see you again?" she asked as they stood in her doorway.

Kane frowned. "I'm not sure. The team and I are headed down to San Antonio after PT to help some firefighter acquaintances with a fundraiser thing."

He blushed when he said it, which piqued Aspen's curiosity. "What fundraiser thing?"

Kane shrugged. "They're raising money for firefighters and other public service members who suffer from PTSD. It's a carnival-type thing, where kids get to try to dunk firefighters and other volunteers into a dunk tank, throw pies in our faces, things like that. There'll be three-legged races and even a petting zoo. Several organizations with emotional support animals will be there too."

Aspen felt her heart melt. "You're a good man, Kane Temple."

"I'm glad you think so," he said. "But to answer your question, I don't know when we'll see each other again. I'll be sure to text though. Okay?"

"More than okay," she told him with a smile.

"Go get off that leg," Kane ordered. "You've been on it most of the day."

That wasn't exactly true, as she'd been in the car for a lot of the time, and when they'd gotten to his house, they'd been on his couch, making out or talking, but she nodded anyway. It was nice to be fussed over.

"Drive safe tomorrow."

"I will. Come here," Kane said, even as he was pulling her into him.

Ten minutes later, and feeling out of breath from his kisses, Aspen finally shut the door, making sure to lock it up tight. She ran to the window and waited until Kane had pulled out of the parking lot before heading to her bedroom.

As she lay in bed, in the dark, staring at the ceiling, Aspen thought back to what both the major and Holman had said earlier in the day. She wasn't happy with the Army anymore. When she'd joined, she'd been gung ho and excited about making a difference. Paving the way for other women to be in special forces. But now she was just tired. She wasn't sure she'd paved anything, and it was time to do something she enjoyed. Time to find the team she'd been searching for.

She wasn't going to find the same kind of camaraderie Kane had with his team, not while still in the Army. But maybe she could find it elsewhere.

And a little voice inside her head whispered that she could slip into the team Kane and his friends had already made. He'd talked about Gillian and Kinley, how important they were to Trigger and Lefty, and, in turn, the rest of the guys as well. She wanted that. Wanted girlfriends she could trust. Wanted a job she loved, working with people she enjoyed spending time with.

But more than all that, she wanted Kane. Wanted him in her bed, or to stay with him at his house. She wanted to cook with him then not have to go back to her lonely apartment because it was getting too late. Kane made her happy, and it had been way too long since she'd felt that way.

She didn't know what would happen in the future with her team, the Army, and some unknown career, but she hoped she'd have Kane by her side through it all.

CHAPTER TWELVE

One month, one week, and four days. That's how long it'd been since Brain had gotten back from Afghanistan, and since he and Aspen had been exclusive. They'd talked every day, had seen each other as much as their schedules allowed, and still Brain wanted more.

They hadn't had sex yet, but he wasn't too worried about that. Their relationship was moving along at a comfortable pace. He was happy to make out and simply hold her. They hadn't spent the night together, not all night, but they'd fallen asleep on each other's couches a time or two. Waking up with her in his arms always felt so right.

Today, they were spending the day relaxing with his team. Everyone was coming over to his house. Trigger and Lefty were bringing Gillian and Kinley, of course, and Grover was bringing his sister, Devyn.

He'd talked about his friends so often, Aspen pretty much knew everything about them. She knew their funnier quirks, and all about the troubles Gillian and

Kinley had been through. He knew Aspen and his friends had gotten along at the previous get-together at his house, and he hoped they continued to click.

A knock on the door brought him out of his musings and he answered it with a smile. Aspen was standing there with her arms completely full. Brain quickly reached for the casserole dish she was holding, and she smiled gratefully.

"You should've let me help you," he admonished her lightly.

"But then I would've had to make two trips to and from my car," she said with a laugh.

Brain simply shook his head. He'd already learned his girl would do *anything* to avoid making two trips to her car, even at his house, where it wasn't a big deal to walk the ten extra steps it took to get to his driveway and back. He supposed it came from the fact her own parking lot was so far from her door. Regardless, it always amused him. Aspen would load herself down with twenty grocery bags just so she wouldn't have to make two trips.

She came into his house and, as soon as the door closed behind her, Brain leaned into her. Both their hands were full, but that didn't mean the kiss they shared was any less hot.

"I feel as if I haven't seen you in forever," she said after they'd broken the kiss.

Brain led the way into his kitchen and turned the oven on low. He opened the door and placed the casserole inside to keep it warm until the others arrived. He turned back to see Aspen unloading one of the bags she'd brought.

"I told you I had all the food covered," he told her.

"I know, but I was at the store, and I thought it couldn't hurt to have more food than we might need. Your friends are *big*. I'm assuming they eat a lot, and I figured having a few vegetables wouldn't go unappreciated."

Brain reached out and pulled her into him. She let out a small, surprised screech, but smiled when they were plastered together chest to chest.

"Hey," he said quietly. He took some time to admire the view. She had on a black tank top and a pair of jean shorts, the latter of which showed off her long, muscular legs. She wore a pair of flip-flops, and he loved seeing she'd painted her toenails pink. She'd left her hair down, and the curly locks tumbled over her shoulders, making him want to see it spread out on his pillow.

In short, Aspen looked casual and comfortable, and Brain still had a hard time believing she was with *him*.

Aspen smiled. "Hey."

"It feels like I haven't seen you in forever either. How was work yesterday?" They'd texted a bit the night before, but it was mostly about today and when she should come over.

Aspen sighed. "It was all right."

Brain hadn't been in many long-term relationships, but even he knew that meant things weren't going well. "What happened?" he asked.

"Derek's just being a jerk," she mumbled, not meeting his eyes.

Brain put a finger under her chin until she was looking at him. "What happened?" he repeated.

He was alarmed when Aspen's eyes filled with tears. Every muscle in his body tensed.

"It's stupid," Aspen said, unconsciously petting his

chest as if she knew how on edge he was at seeing her upset. "As you know, everyone's kinda been doing their own thing during the day, and we've only been together at PT. Well, in the last week, we've all been training again, and Derek's been trying to command both teams, just like he did before. My new sergeant isn't happy with the way Derek's trying to order him and his platoon around, especially since they're the same rank, so he's pushing back.

"Yesterday, Derek made some smartass remark about females not being strong enough to cut it in the Rangers. He wasn't specifically talking about me, it was more of a blanket statement, but it was obvious he was *including* me in his disparagement. My team's been a little more receptive and friendly toward me in the last few weeks, probably because of all the equal-opportunity classes we've been taking, and maybe after what happened with Vandine and Holman. Anyway, my new platoon sergeant told him he didn't know what the hell he was talking about, and they kinda got into an argument. It was awkward and uncomfortable for all of us. I just...I hate being the reason no one is getting along."

"You aren't to blame," Brain told her. "Derek is. And you're fighting decades of discrimination. I'm glad to hear your new sergeant isn't putting up with Derek's shit though."

"Yeah, I was surprised. At first I didn't think he was the kind of guy who'd even tolerate a woman on his team, but he's actually encouraged me quite a bit in training," Aspen said.

Brain knew how badly Aspen wanted to be on a team like his own. A supportive one, comprised of people who would do absolutely anything for one another. He couldn't make the Rangers accept her, but he could give her the team she craved when she was off duty. He'd gladly share his own team with her.

"You made any decisions about your upcoming reenlistment?" he asked. They'd talked at length about the pros and cons of getting out of the Army, and what her options might be if she left, but as far as he knew, she hadn't made a final decision.

"No," she told him. "But I'm leaning toward getting out. I looked into it, and I'm qualified nationally as a paramedic because I passed the exam, but I have to get my Texas state licensure. I haven't actually looked at what jobs might be open, but I'm pretty sure I'll be able to find one. If not here, in Austin for sure."

"What's holding you back?" Brain asked.

"I just...I feel as if I'd be letting down all the other women who are still trying to claw their way into combat specialties."

Brain shook his head. "Fuck that. You can't think that way. Aspen, you've already broken so many barriers, it's not even funny. You're attached to a Ranger team. Hell, you *are* a Ranger, for all intents and purposes. Even if you get out now, no one can take that away from you. And as your new platoon sergeant has shown, not everyone thinks the way Derek does. Even *he* was all right with you being there until his ego took a hit when you didn't want to go out with him anymore. He's made it personal, which is bullshit."

"Thanks," Aspen said quietly. "The last few months have just been really stressful. One day I'm determined to stick things out, and the next I'm ready to throw in the towel."

"Well, today you don't have to make a decision. You can enjoy spending time with our friends."

She smiled. "I'm not sure I can call them my friends yet, since I've only hung out with everyone that one time, before I was deployed."

"They're your friends," Brain told her firmly. "Don't ever doubt that. If you need anything, you can call any one of them, and they'll bend over backward to help you, no questions asked."

"That's because of you," she said. "Not me."

"Maybe right now, yes. But after you get to know them better? Nope," Brain said.

"You know, that first time might've been a fluke," she said. "They may not like me once they really get to know me."

"Whatever. You're likable," he told her. "And you put up with *me*. So there's that."

"Because you're sooooo hard to put up with," she quipped as she rolled her eyes.

Brain laughed with her, then dug his fingers into her sides, tickling her.

Aspen screeched and tried to wiggle away from him, but Brain held on.

They were both laughing when they heard someone clear their throat from not too far away.

Brain looked up and saw Trigger and Gillian standing nearby. He straightened and wrapped an arm around Aspen, turning her to face their guests.

"Oh, hey," he said, still smiling.

Gillian returned his greeting, then said, "I like her *more* than I did before. Anyone who can make you laugh like you just did is okay in my book."

Aspen looked up at him. "You don't laugh much?"

Gillian answered before Brain got a chance. "Lord, no. I mean, he's not all broody like Doc is, but close."

Aspen stared at Brain for a moment before she turned back to Gillian. "Let me help you with that." She reached for the bottle of wine the other woman was carrying, and Gillian gladly handed it over.

Trigger gave Brain a chin lift. "Sorry if we interrupted anything. I should've known better than to just walk in."

"No problem. You know my house is your house," Brain told him.

"Yeah, but now that you've got Aspen, I wouldn't want to get my ass kicked for walking in and seeing something I shouldn't."

Brain chuckled and nodded. "Okay, good point."

"Whatever," Aspen muttered. "As if we'd get naked five minutes before people were supposed to arrive."

Gillian shook her head. "Never say never around these guys," she countered.

Everyone laughed.

There was a knock on the door but before Brain could answer it, Oz, Lucky, and Doc wandered in.

"Heard we're having a party," Oz called out cheerfully.

Grover and Devyn arrived next, and Lefty and Kinley weren't too far behind.

The four women quickly huddled together in the kitchen, getting reacquainted. Brain hesitated to leave Aspen, but Trigger pulled him away. "She'll be fine," he told him.

"Of course she will. I just wanted to make sure they had everything they needed," he bluffed.

Trigger smiled knowingly, but didn't comment.

Luckily, it was a nice day outside, so the seven men hung out on Brain's deck, shooting the shit. Normally, Brain loved hanging with his team when they weren't at work. Just relaxing and enjoying each other's company. But today, he couldn't keep his gaze from straying inside, where Aspen was still hanging out with the other women. She looked like she was having a good time, but the last thing he wanted to do was abandon her if she was uncomfortable.

"You had time to translate the latest bullshit message from Shahzada?" Lefty asked.

Pulling his attention away from Aspen was harder than he thought it would be, but Brain did his best to concentrate on the conversation at hand.

Shahzada hadn't wasted any time, ordering one of his followers to read a manifesto on a local radio station about the evils of the Western World, and how they were going to be the downfall of their way of life and religion. He'd also threatened any and all Americans working in the area and warned that no one was safe.

Brain nodded at Lefty, telling him and the others everything he'd been able to decipher from the message, which led into a deep political discussion about the United States' presence in the Middle East.

* * *

Aspen glanced out onto the patio and saw Kane and the rest of the guys engaged in a somewhat intense-looking conversation.

"They're probably talking about work," Gillian said with a small shake of her head. "Walker always swears that they're going to keep things light and not talk shop when they get together, but they always do. They can't help it."

Kinley laughed. "I've noticed that. Although, to be fair, when we join them, they'll stop."

"Of course, they can't let us mere mortals know what they're talking about," Devyn added. "Although, I suppose if you went out there, Aspen, they'd probably keep on talking shop, since you're one of them and all."

Aspen blinked in surprise. "No, I'm not."

"Sure you are," Devyn returned.

"I'm a combat medic," Aspen said.

"Right, who's on a Ranger team. And Rangers are special forces. So are my brother and his friends. Therefore, you're one of them," Devyn reasoned.

Aspen couldn't help but laugh. "Okay, but officially, on paper, I'm a combat medic, not a Ranger. And Kane and the others have way higher clearance than I do, so whatever they're talking about is probably need-to-know only, and the only thing I need to know is how long my team's going to be gone and how many medical supplies I need to pack."

Gillian leaned against the counter and, after taking a sip of the glass of wine in her hand, asked, "So...how is it being the only woman on your team? Walker told me that, by the way. I'm not just being stereotypical and assuming."

"It's...hard," Aspen said. That wasn't really the right word, but it would do for now.

"I bet. Are the guys all as good-looking as our team is?" Kinley asked.

Aspen chuckled. "Our team?"

Kinley smiled. "Well, yeah. I might be with Gage, but they're all kinda ours."

That was true, Aspen realized. The men had all greeted the women with huge hugs and genuine affection. They weren't just tolerating them because three of them were going out with their friends.

When she realized the others were staring at her, she remembered Kinley had asked her a question. "Oh, well, if I'm being honest, I'd have to say no, they aren't as good-looking as them." She gestured to the men out on the patio. "They're all in shape though, six-pack abs and all that stuff."

"There's more to a guy than looks," Devyn chided them.

"Oh, really?" Gillian teased. "So the lustful looks I've seen passing between you and Lucky don't have anything to do with his looks?"

Devyn blushed and took a large gulp of her wine before she shrugged. "Hey, I'm not saying he's isn't nice to look at, but I'm not going there. I've said it before and I'll say it again. Guys are trouble."

"Are you into girls then?" Aspen asked.

"No. I've just learned the hard way that most men are manipulative little fucks. They'll use you until there's nothing left, then they'll still try to make you out to be the bad guy. I've had enough of it. Give me a nice, shy man with no siblings and no other family and I might give him a chance. In five years. No, ten."

Aspen wanted to laugh, but there was so much bitterness in Devyn's words, she couldn't. She didn't really know her all that well yet, but she couldn't help saying, "Hey, if you ever want to talk...I've been told I'm a pretty good listener."

"Same here," Kinley said.

"Me three," Gillian added. "I think we've all had our share of asshole exes, and we're happy to share whatever burden you're carrying."

"I never said it was an ex," Devyn mumbled, then shook her head. "But thanks, guys. I'm just a little resentful right now, I'm sure it'll pass. And in the meantime, you're right, there's nothing wrong with looking at a little eye candy. Although you'll have to forgive me if I say that lumping my brother in with that gives me the willies."

They all laughed.

"But Grover's hot," Gillian said.

Devyn rolled her eyes.

Aspen enjoyed the gentle ribbing the women gave each other. It had been a very long time since she'd been included in any kind of teasing among female friends. And while she hated that Devyn seemed to be going through a hard time, she liked how she was doing her best not to wallow in whatever was going on.

"So, Aspen...you and Brain, huh?" Kinley asked.

Aspen hid a smile in her wine glass. She'd wondered when the topic would come around to her and Kane. "Appears so," she said.

"I'm happy for you both," Kinley said. "Brain seems... different from the rest of the guys."

"How so?" Aspen asked, genuinely curious as to what his friends thought of him.

"I don't know...less in-your-face alpha," Kinley suggested.

Aspen couldn't help it. She laughed.

"I guess that's not true?" Gillian asked with a grin.

"I can see how you'd get that impression," Aspen said. "Kane's not the kind of guy to strut around barking at people or ordering them about. And I'm not sure what your definition of 'alpha' is, but make no mistake, he can be as bossy as the next guy."

Kinley raised an eyebrow. "Really? Because to me, he seems like he's perfectly content to chill in the background. Don't get me wrong, that's not a bad thing, but it just surprises me that you think he's bossy."

"The other day, he noticed that one of my tires was a little low on air. I told him I'd take care of it on my way home. He shook his head and held out his hand for my keys. I protested, telling him I was tired and would deal with it later. He said he was taking care of it right that second, and I was going into his house to sit down and relax," Aspen said, smiling at the recollection.

"That sounds like something Walker would do," Gillian commented.

"Right. Another time, I was cooking dinner at my apartment and forgot to get milk. I needed it for the sauce I was making, so he immediately got up and headed for my door. I tried to convince him that I'd figure something out, but before I could finish a sentence, he'd walked back, kissed the hell out of me, then left without another word.

"*Then* there was the time he got out of a meeting early, and he knew my team and I would be working out on the obstacle course. He came to watch, and when Derek started berating me for something that was out of line, Kane yelled, 'Yo!' and stood on the side of the course with his arms crossed. That was literally all he said, and Derek backed off, ignoring me for the rest of the afternoon. So again, I don't know what you guys consider alpha, but to me, Kane's pretty damn intense sometimes."

"Wow," Gillian said. "I had no idea either. He just doesn't strike me as the type. He's...*Brain*, you know?"

"No, I don't know," Aspen said a little harsher than she'd intended. When Gillian's eyes widened in surprise, she did her best to temper her tone. "I know he's smart, there's no denying that. But a guy can be both smart and tough as hell. I think he's been stereotyped most of his life, and I know how he feels, because people take one look at *me*, a woman, and can't believe I can cut it in the Rangers. But it's all bullshit. Kane is more than just the brains of the team, even if everyone keeps trying to force him into that role."

The other women were silent as they digested Aspen's words. Then Devyn said, "I don't know my brother's friends all that well, but I know by experience that sometimes the quietest men are the ones you have to watch out for."

Once more, Aspen wanted to ask Devyn if she was all right. Find out what was bothering her, because it was more than obvious something was going on. But she didn't get the chance before Gillian spoke up once more.

"I didn't mean to offend you," she said.

"No," Aspen countered. "I didn't mean to offend *you*. I just...Kane's an alpha when it counts...when it's something he feels strongly about. And I'm not insinuating that he feels strongly about *me*, but he can be just as dominant as anyone, no matter how smart he is or how many languages he knows. I think, to be in special forces, it kind of comes with the territory."

"Thanks for letting me off the hook. And...I don't think there's any doubt that Brain feels strongly about you," Gillian said with a small smile. "Walker isn't one to gossip, but he's mentioned more than once that Brain seems happier than he's been in years."

Aspen liked that. A lot.

"I'm sorry I missed your wedding," she told Gillian. "I heard it was awesome. And I'm jealous about the pink sparkly Converse sneakers that I heard you wore."

Gillian beamed. "Thanks. They're pretty awesome. And thank you for telling Brain about the appetizer thing for our reception party. That turned out really well."

"You're welcome," Aspen said with a smile.

Just then, the door leading onto the patio opened and all seven men filed into the house.

"Hope you guys are hungry!" Oz said, holding a platter of hamburgers. "The meat's ready."

"I'd say," Devyn muttered under her breath.

It was all Aspen could do not to burst out laughing. She turned to grab the casserole out of the oven instead.

Within minutes, the chatter in the small house had fallen to a minimum as everyone began to eat. Between the side dishes the others had brought and the hamburgers, which were cooked to perfection, the meal was one of the best Aspen had eaten in a long time.

Some of the guys ate standing up, giving the women the seats at the table. There was good-humored teasing and lots of compliments over the food, and Aspen loved every second of it.

An hour and a half later, everyone had settled into Kane's living room and were telling stories and joking with each other. They'd given her a recap of Gillian and Trigger's wedding, and how hilarious Winnie had been at the reception.

Aspen was sitting on the floor in front of Kane, who

was on the couch. She had her arms draped over his legs, which were stretched out on either side of her.

Gillian was sitting next to Trigger on the other end of the couch, and Devyn sat between Kane and Trigger.

Kinley was on Lefty's lap in the easy chair, and the other guys were spread around the room. Some standing, some sitting. But everyone seemed comfortable and relaxed, which made Aspen smile in contentment. This wasn't her house, wasn't her party, but somehow it still felt as if it was. Maybe because she'd spent a lot of time here over the last month and a half.

Oz was in the middle of telling a funny story about a time when they hadn't understood the local culture of an unnamed country, and how they'd gotten into trouble as a result, when Grover's phone rang.

He was standing on the other side of the room, leaning against the wall. He smiled when he looked at the readout and didn't bother to leave the room to answer the call.

"Hi, Mom, how are you? I'm good. No, you're not interrupting anything. I'm just hanging out at Brain's house with the team. Oh, and Devyn's here too... She hasn't?" Grover frowned over at his sister.

Aspen looked up at Devyn to find the other woman was shaking her head at her brother.

"Do you want to talk to her?" Grover asked, and when his mother apparently answered in the affirmative, he brought the phone over to where Devyn was sitting and held it out. "Mom wants to talk to you."

"No," Devyn whispered. "I don't want to talk to her."

Grover blinked in surprise. "Why not?"

"Because."

"That's not an answer," Grover told his sister. "Just talk to her. She says you haven't called since you moved here."

"I know, and maybe there's a reason for that, Fred," Devyn countered tersely.

Brother and sister stared at each other for a long moment before Grover brought the phone back up to his ear. He didn't go back to his spot against the wall. Instead, he stood in front of the couch and stared at Devyn while he spoke to his mom. "She can't talk right now, Mom, she's helping in the kitchen. What's going on between you two?"

There was silence in the room while Grover listened to whatever his mom was saying.

"Okay," Grover said after a moment. "I'll talk to her."

At that, Devyn was clearly done. She stood from the couch abruptly and turned toward Brain. "Thanks for letting me join in tonight. I'm gonna head out."

Grover was still on the phone, and Aspen heard him trying to end the call so he could talk to his sister. But Devyn wasn't waiting. She was up and by the door before anyone could move.

"Devyn, wait!" Grover called out after he'd hung up.

Devyn turned to face him. "What?"

"We need to talk."

"No, we don't," she fired back.

Grover walked toward her, the pair standing in front of Kane's door, but because the house wasn't all that big, everyone could hear what they were saying.

"Yes, we do," Grover countered. "Why have you been ignoring Mom? She's worried about you."

Devyn snorted. "It doesn't matter."

"What do you mean? Of course it matters," Grover said urgently.

"I love you, Fred," Devyn said. "But you can't fix this."

"Tell me what 'this' is, and I'll try," Grover insisted.

"Mom was disappointed that I left Missouri," Devyn said after a long moment. "And she wasn't shy about telling me how big of a mistake I was making."

"Maybe she's trying to fix things between you now," Grover said.

"She wants to try to 'talk some sense' into me. Convince me that I was wrong. That I shouldn't have left Missouri and everything was a big misunderstanding. But it *wasn't*."

Brother and sister stared at each other for a moment, then Grover reached out and pulled Devyn into his arms. He hugged her tightly and said something into her ear. She nodded and pulled back. Then, without another word, she opened the door and headed out.

Lucky leapt up from his spot on the floor and hurried after her. "Thanks for the food, Brain," he called as he went. "I'll make sure she gets home all right," he told Grover when he passed him at the door.

Grover nodded, and just like that, Lucky was gone.

"Sorry about killing the mood," Grover said when he came back into the living room.

"Don't worry about it," Brain assured him.

"It's just...our mom's always been overprotective of Devyn because she was so sick when she was little. I just can't imagine what the hell's going on or what caused the rift between them."

"She'll talk to you when she's ready," Gillian told him.

"But if you push, she'll just clam up even more. She seems pretty stubborn."

Grover snorted. "You have no idea."

The conversation switched to something less serious, and it wasn't long before the previous mood was restored.

"You ever hear from that chick from Afghanistan, Grover?" Oz asked.

"What chick?" Aspen asked, her curiosity piqued.

"The short one," Doc said. "The one from the chow tent."

"Sierra?" Aspen asked.

"Yeah, her," Grover said. "And no. I sent her an email but never heard back. Guess she wasn't really interested."

Aspen was surprised. She didn't know Sierra all that well, as she'd arrived not too long before Aspen had left the country. But she'd always been extremely friendly, if not a little naïve. She couldn't imagine her giving Grover her contact information and then blowing him off. "You think she's all right?"

"Why wouldn't she be?" Grover asked. "She works in food service. It's not as if she's out there patrolling the village or anything."

Aspen frowned. Grover was obviously still in a mood over what had happened with his sister and mom, and bringing up Sierra wasn't making him feel any better. So she did her best to change the subject. "Are you guys going to the organizational day this weekend?"

An organizational day was an event planned by the Army intended to get soldiers and their families together in a social setting. There were usually games, obstacle courses, face painting, and other activities for the children to enjoy.

"Yeah, we'd all planned to head over around eleven and meet up there. I know Ghost and his team will also be there," Trigger said.

"Ghost?" Aspen asked.

"He's the leader of a former Delta team," Kane told her, leaning forward and resting his arms over her shoulders. Because she was below him on the floor, it was as if he was hugging her from above and behind at the same time. Aspen loved feeling surrounded by him. "He and his team are retired from missions now, but they're still heavily involved in training and in planning missions."

"One of those guys is Annie's father, right?" Gillian asked.

"Yup," Lefty answered.

"Who's Annie?" Aspen asked.

"Sorry, yeah, Annie's thirteen now, I think, and she's amazing. I went to an obstacle course competition she was in, and she was killing it, but when one of the kids in her heat was struggling, she went back to help him rather than go on to win herself."

"Awesome," Aspen said.

"It was," Gillian agreed.

"Anyway, the answer is yes, we'll all be there. Are you going with your team?" Doc asked.

Aspen stiffened, and Kane squeezed her shoulders. "No," she told him. "I mean, we haven't talked about it. I don't...we don't hang out when we aren't at work like you guys do."

"Their loss," Kane said quietly from behind her.

"Well, you can come and chill with us," Kinley told her with a smile.

"Thanks. I'd like that."

227

"On that note, it's getting late, and we should probably get out of your hair," Lefty said.

Aspen couldn't help but chuckle. It wasn't that late, and it was obvious that Lefty just wanted to get Kinley home so he could have his wicked way with her. The two had been eyeballing each other all night, and if the way Kinley had been squirming in Lefty's lap was any indication, she was more than all right with calling it a night.

Everyone else agreed, and soon it was just Aspen and Kane in his house. She turned to him at the door after they'd said goodbye to everyone. "Was it something I said?" she quipped.

Kane chuckled and tugged her into his side, leading her back to the living room. He pulled her down on the couch and lay back, taking her with him.

Aspen stretched out beside him happily. There were things she could be doing. Taking out the trash, cleaning the counters, doing dishes, but she was perfectly happy where she was at the moment.

"Don't take it personally. That's kinda how these things always end. When one person calls it quits, everyone else usually follows close behind. I'll see them at work soon enough."

"True," Aspen mused.

"So...what'd you think?"

"Of your friends?" she asked, propping herself up to look at him.

"Yeah."

"They're just as great as they were when we hung out the first time. It's as if months haven't passed since then."

"Grover and Devyn's spat notwithstanding," Kane said on a sigh.

"Honestly? That made me feel even closer to everyone," Aspen told him. "I mean, I'm not happy something's up with them, but the fact that they didn't hesitate to have it out in front of all you guys...it just means they trust you. That they feel comfortable around you. It was nice, in a weird way. Does that make any sense?"

"It does," Kane reassured her.

Aspen put her head back on his chest. "I'm happy for you, Kane."

"For what?"

"That you have friends who are like family."

"They'll be family for you too, if you let them," he told her quietly.

"I know. And it kinda scares me."

"It shouldn't," Kane said. "They're good people. Anything you need, they'll be there for you."

Aspen let that sink in. It felt nice. And she freaking loved knowing that Kane had such loyal friends at his back. It made the missions she knew he'd be sent on in the future not seem so scary. Trigger, Lefty, Oz, Lucky, Doc, and Grover would do whatever it took to make sure Kane came home, just as he'd do for them. She couldn't say the same about her own team, which sucked.

As the day got closer to when she was going to have to make a decision about her reenlistment, Aspen already knew she was leaning more and more heavily toward getting out. She was sad about that, as she'd been so excited the day she'd learned she was attached to a Ranger team. But as hard as she'd tried, she hadn't been able to fit in, not the way she wanted.

And for the first time, she wondered if her presence on

the team was hindering the other men from connecting the way they should.

That thought was painful, but she couldn't deny it might be true.

"What are you thinking about so hard?" Kane asked.

"Nothing much," Aspen said. How could she admit out loud that she felt as if she'd failed? Once upon a time, she'd wanted to make a difference. Wanted to pave the way for her fellow women soldiers to be able to join whatever unit they wanted.

"I'm proud of you," Kane whispered. "You've worked your ass off to be where you are today, and even if your team can't appreciate it, I've seen for myself how much of an asset you are to the Army, and to the Rangers."

And just like that, Aspen felt better. "Thanks," she told him quietly.

"I know we haven't gone there yet, except for that one night, which I'm not sure counts since it was accidental, but...do you want to stay tonight?"

Aspen's heart rate spiked.

"Not for sex. Just to sleep. Neither of us has to go to work in the morning, and I thought it might be nice to fall asleep with you in my arms and wake up to your beautiful face in the morning."

Aspen couldn't think of anything better. She lifted up to look at him again. "It depends...what are you gonna make me for breakfast?"

He smiled. "Whatever you want, *hubibi*."

"I can't even begin to guess what language that was," she said with a laugh.

"Arabic."

"Right. And I was teasing. I'm not much of a breakfast person. As long as you have coffee, I'm good."

"I've got coffee," he told her, smiling. "And I can go out and get some fresh doughnuts or kolaches if you want."

"Oooh, I want," Aspen told him.

"Deal."

She lay her head back on his chest and sighed in contentment. She loved making out with Kane. Loved how he always put his hand on the back of her neck and held her still as he took what he wanted. But she also loved *this*. The feel of his hand on her back, gently stroking. The sound of his heart beating in his chest under her ear.

For the first time, she admitted to herself that she was addicted to Kane Temple. Not a day went by when she didn't think about him. The fact that they could also be in the same room together, each doing their own thing, was just icing on the cake. She didn't have to entertain him; he didn't have to entertain her. They were comfortable with each other, and that was something she'd never had with anyone else in her life.

Kane could be *the one*.

She could see them fifty years from now, lying just like this, simply soaking in each other's company. And she liked that thought...a hell of a lot.

CHAPTER THIRTEEN

The park was packed.

Aspen hadn't been to an organizational day in a very long time. Since she didn't have kids, and none of the teams she'd been on had attended together, she'd just never gone.

But walking around with Kane and their friends was a blast. She especially loved holding Kane's hand. Since this was a social event and they were in civilian clothes, public displays of affection weren't frowned upon. Kane had grabbed ahold of her hand as soon as they'd gotten out of his car and hadn't let go once.

They'd met up with his team and had wandered around the park, getting the lay of the land. Kane said hello to what seemed like almost everyone. Sometimes he stopped to chat for a minute or two; other times he gave a simple chin lift in greeting.

"You know a lot of people," she observed after he'd greeted what seemed like the hundredth person.

He shrugged. "Been stationed here a while, and the

team and I try to stay busy when we're in town, volunteering and helping out."

"How come we never met before that night at the bar?" Aspen asked.

Kane looked at her. "Don't take this the wrong way, okay?"

Aspen couldn't help but tense.

"Breathe, *dar*. And before you ask, that was Kurdish."

Aspen let out a breath. "Right. I asked. Hit me."

"Never," he muttered. Then said in a more normal tone, "I'm guessing your team doesn't do a lot of volunteering on the base?"

He stated it as a question, but it was obvious he already knew the answer. Aspen shook her head.

"Right. So before we met, your days consisted of going to work, then going home and decompressing."

Aspen thought about it, then nodded.

"You didn't have much of a chance to run across me or my team," Kane said. "And don't think I'm judging you. I'm not. You needed the time away from post for your own sanity. I get it. With the way you've been treated, I can't blame you for wanting to go home and not hang around anyone from work."

"I still feel stupid for dating Derek," Aspen muttered.

"Don't. Guys like him are good at only letting women see what he wants them to. He only showed who he really was after you rejected him," Kane said easily.

"It doesn't bother you to talk about my past boyfriends?" Aspen asked, genuinely curious as to his answer.

Kane stopped and put his free hand on the side of her

neck, his thumb rubbing along the underside of her jaw. It felt good. Really good.

"No," Kane said simply. "I'm not saying I want you to go into a blow-by-blow, no pun intended, of your history, but you're thirty-one years old and gorgeous. I know you've had plenty of boyfriends."

"Not *that* many," she told him.

But Kane just grinned. "I like having an older and wiser girlfriend."

"I'm only a year older than you, Kane, let's not get crazy."

His smile widened. "You're a cougar. *Grrrrrr*."

Aspen burst out laughing and playfully shoved his shoulder. "Shut up."

Kane caught her around the waist and pulled her into him. He leaned in and kissed her, a hard and fast meeting of their lips that was over way too soon.

And in that moment, Aspen realized that she was done waiting for him to make the first move. She hadn't pushed to go further than they had as far as their physical relationship went. But feeling his hard body against hers in the middle of a family friendly carnival made a bolt of lust shoot through her. She wanted him. Bad.

"What was that thought?" he asked.

Licking her lips, Aspen leaned into him and wrapped her arms around his shoulders. She nuzzled his ear for a moment, then whispered, "I loved sleeping with you last night."

She heard a contended rumble deep in his throat as he agreed.

Feeling daring, Aspen nipped his earlobe, loving the

shiver that ran through Kane. "Can I stay with you again tonight?" she asked.

"You're welcome anytime," he said quietly. His hands had moved to her waist, and she felt one slip under her T-shirt. How she wanted that hand to do more than just gently caress her lower back. She wanted to feel his hands all over her.

"I want you," she admitted softly in his ear.

Every muscle in Kane's body stiffened. She felt his cock harden against her...and smiled.

He pulled back, but kept her plastered to his front, studying her for a long moment. "You sure?" he finally asked.

"Yes," Aspen told him simply.

Then the most beautiful smile formed on his lips.

She could stare at his smile all day, but they were interrupted by shouting from nearby. They both turned to see a group of boys on the obstacle course equipment that had been set up on one side of the park. They were facing a girl, who was standing in front of them with her hands on her hips.

"Shit, that's Annie," Kane said, looking around. "I don't see Fletch or Emily. Come on," he said, pulling away and heading for the kids.

Aspen wasn't sure who Fletch and Emily were, but she recognized the name Annie. She was the little girl who Gillian had watched compete in an obstacle course race a while ago. She was the daughter of one of the Deltas on another team. Looking around as they headed for the confrontation, Aspen didn't see the guys from Kane's team either. They must've been lost in each other for longer than she'd thought, and his team had gotten ahead of them as they continued to wander the park.

"You're a girl," one of the boys sneered. "You can't play with us."

"Why not?" Annie demanded, sounding irritated.

"Because," another boy said. "You're slower and weaker."

"I am not!" Annie protested.

"Are so!"

"My dad says girls should stay in their lane and do things like ballet and cheerleading and leave the dangerous stuff to guys."

Aspen frowned at that. She hated knowing there were still men who thought that shit. Was even more irritated that they were teaching their sons to be discriminatory as well.

"That's stupid," Annie said, but her tone lacked the self-confidence it had a moment ago.

"Why don't you go over to the arts and crafts tent where you can make something you can use in the kitchen?" one of the boys taunted.

Before Aspen and Kane could reach them, Annie rushed forward, kicked the boy who'd just spoken in the shin, then stalked toward the obstacle course, ignoring the other boys, who were now yelling at her.

"I've got Annie, if you take care of the boys," Aspen told Kane.

He nodded, and she saw a muscle in his jaw ticking.

Squeezing Kane's hand before she dropped it, Aspen jogged over to where Annie was on her belly crawling under a set of ropes strung across the ground.

"Hey," she said as she approached.

Annie looked up, but didn't say anything.

"I'm Aspen. You're Annie, right?"

"How do you know my name? I'm not supposed to talk to strangers," she said sulkily.

"My boyfriend is friends with your dad," Aspen told her. She wasn't sure exactly how well Kane knew Fletch, but she figured that didn't matter at the moment.

Annie merely shrugged.

"I heard what those boys said to you. I hope you aren't taking their words to heart."

The little girl pulled herself out from under the ropes, but didn't stand. She stayed on her belly and looked up at Aspen. "What's it to you?"

The teenage attitude wasn't exactly unexpected, and Aspen gave the girl a pass since she was obviously upset. "I hate when boys say stuff that's so blatantly untrue. It's true that *some* girls are weaker than boys, but a blanket statement like that is just stupid."

She saw that Annie seemed a little more interested in listening to what she had to say, so Aspen kept going.

"I mean, look at me. I'm not as tall as some men are, but I'm also not exactly short. I might not be able to do as many pullups as the men on my team, but I can do way more sit-ups than them."

"What kind of team are you on?" Annie asked, sitting up and crossing her legs.

Aspen sat on the ground next to her and said, "A Ranger team."

At the look on the little girl's face, Aspen smirked. She had her attention now.

"You're a *Ranger*?" she asked, the awe easy to hear in her tone.

"Well, not technically. I'm a combat medic attached to a Ranger unit. So that means that wherever they go, I go. Whatever they do, I do. I have to be in just as good shape as they are in order to keep up with them. It wouldn't do for me to fall behind, especially if a firefight broke out and someone got hurt. I need to be there to help patch them up."

"Do you have to kill people?"

Aspen winced at the question, but did her best to answer honestly. "My main job is making sure the guys on my team are healthy. But yes, sometimes I have to engage in combat alongside my team. I protect them, just as they protect me. But my primary job is to be a doctor for them, not to kill people."

"I want to do that," Annie whispered.

Aspen felt more proud at that moment than she could remember being in a very long time. If she could inspire a girl like Annie, then it felt as if she was doing something right. "It's not an easy job," she warned.

"I know. But you get to do all the cool stuff without having to shoot people all the time. That's what I want to do. I know girls aren't allowed in the Deltas, like what my dad is, but he told me that there are women in the Rangers now. I read about the Rangers online, and while I know I can make it through the training, because I'm tough, I don't really want to have to shoot people. But maybe I can be a combat medic like you and still do what the Rangers do."

Aspen smiled. "I have a feeling you can do anything you set your mind to. But...one thing you're going to have to do is control your temper. You can't go around kicking people if you're going to be a combat medic."

Annie frowned. "Mikey's a poophole."

Aspen wanted to laugh, but managed to control herself. The girl had obviously been warned about swearing and was doing her best to not disobey her parents, but still get her point across. "Be that as it may, there will be lots of poopholes you'll have to deal with if you want to be a combat medic attached to a Ranger team. A lot of people still don't think women can physically do the job. And they'll tell you that over and over, to try to get you to quit. You'll have to work twice as hard as a man to get the job too. It's not fair, but if you want it bad enough, if you can show the officers in charge that you're the best person for the job and that you can do it without losing your temper, then you'll get it."

Annie studied her. "Being a girl is hard," she said after a minute.

Aspen laughed. "It can be, especially when you want to do something that in the past has mostly been done by boys. But that doesn't mean you shouldn't go after what you want. It might be harder, but when you accomplish it, you'll feel twice as good as the boy because you worked hard for it."

Annie nodded.

"I heard you're pretty darn good at the obstacle course."

"I am," Annie said without a shred of bashfulness.

"Want to run through it with me?" Aspen asked.

"Sure."

Aspen stood with Annie and they went to the beginning of the course. Kane had finished talking with the boys and was standing off to the side having a conversation with his team. Gillian and Kinley were there too, and they both waved when they saw Aspen looking in their direction. Aspen waved back, then returned her attention to Annie.

"You go first," Annie said, and once again Aspen had to hide her smile. It was obvious the girl didn't quite believe that Aspen could manage the obstacle course; it was going to be fun to show her otherwise.

Glad that she'd decided to wear a pair of jean shorts and a loose T-shirt today, Aspen nodded at Annie and started going through the course. It wasn't all that hard, since it was set up for the kids to run through, but it wasn't a walk in the park either.

She scrambled under the ropes, ran toward the wall and climbed up and over it without hesitation. Then she climbed up a pole and rang the bell at the top before sliding back down. She leaped over three logs and jumped up and grabbed a horizontal pole. Flinging one leg up and over it, she shimmied hand over hand across it, upside down, before using her leg muscles to pull her on top of the pole. She sat atop it and reached for the bell hanging above her head.

Hearing applause, Aspen looked down and saw Annie jumping up and down and clapping her hands enthusiastically. She'd drawn an audience, and everyone who'd been watching her was clapping as well. Flushing, Aspen flipped herself over and hung from the pole by her hands for a second before dropping to the ground.

"You're good!" Annie said, her eyes dancing. "Will you teach me how to do that leg thing on the pole? My arms are usually really tired by the time I get to that point and it's hard for me to pull myself up to get to the bell."

Loving that Annie was asking for assistance, Aspen

said, "Of course. I'm happy to help. Just remember, you might be strong, but you need to save your strength whenever possible. Work smarter, not harder. And that means using your leg muscles wherever you can."

Annie nodded.

"Come on, let's start at the beginning. You show me what you can do, and I'll give you pointers along the way, all right?"

"Awesome! My own Ranger combat medic coach. Totes cool!"

Turning to head for the beginning of the course, Aspen stopped in her tracks when she almost ran into Derek.

"What the hell, Mesmer?" he bit out.

Aspen had no idea what Derek was all pissed off about now, but she quickly took a step to the side, putting herself between Annie and her ex. He didn't give her a chance to say anything.

"It wasn't bad enough that we had to deal with you on the teams, but now I get word that you're considering not re-upping? Figures you'd quit. You should've stepped aside a long time ago and given us the chance to train a *real* medic. Someone who wouldn't divide the team like you did."

Aspen saw red. "How dare you!" she hissed. "How *dare* you belittle everything I've done for the Rangers. I'm as much a Ranger as you, probably more. I paid attention in training and would *never* leave a teammate behind. Unlike you, who not only left three teammates behind, but two who were *injured*. They would've died if that Delta team hadn't come upon us."

"A real Ranger would've been able to handle it," Derek shot back.

"I did handle it," Aspen told him. "While you were busy having a dick-measuring contest with the Deltas. Too worried you'd come up short if you didn't find Akhund before they did. We'd been there a month and a half and hadn't managed to catch him, and they did what we couldn't in less than a *week*. Leaving me, Holman, and Vandine behind made *you* look like an ass, not me."

Derek glared at her, and Aspen raised her chin. She could see the anger in his eyes. This whole situation was crazy; she hadn't done *anything* to make him so mad at her. But then again, her simply existing seemed to anger him.

"Stand down, Spence," a deep voice said from behind her.

Aspen didn't have to turn around to know it was Kane.

"Stay out of this, *Brain*," Derek snarled.

"I'm already in it," Kane returned, stepping up beside Aspen. She appreciated more than she could say that he didn't step in front of her, pushing her behind him. That would've pissed her off just as much as Derek's words did.

"Look around you, man," Kane said. "You're standing in the middle of a park surrounded by your peers. Walk it off."

Derek took a deep breath and his hands curled into fists, but he did take a step backward. "She's no peer of mine," he ground out. "This isn't over, Mesmer. You can't come into my team and fuck everything up, then just walk away."

"I'm not on *your* team—and I'm not walking away," Aspen told him. "I've done everything possible to be accepted. I've done the same training, crawled through the same shit you guys have. I've studied my ass off and gotten my paramedic license through the state of Texas, just to prove I know what I'm doing when it comes to your safety. I even saved the lives of two Rangers! Yet time and time again, just when I think I'm making progress with *my* team, you do something to sabotage it. I'm done with your bullshit, Derek. You're lucky I haven't reported you for making us work in unsafe conditions—and the hundred other little things you've done."

Derek glared at her, his gaze flicking behind her briefly, then he abruptly turned and stalked away.

Aspen breathed out a frustrated sigh. She should've been glad he hadn't attacked her, but all she could feel was pissed off that things between them had deteriorated so badly.

"I have *no* idea what I ever saw in him," she muttered between clenched teeth.

"That was kinda hot," someone said from behind her.

Aspen spun around to see Trigger, Lefty, Oz, Doc, Lucky, and Grover standing there. She wasn't surprised to see them—but she was shocked to see the seven men behind *them*.

"*Chérie*, let me introduce another Delta team that we're friends with. This is Ghost, Fletch, Coach, Hollywood, Beatle, Blade, and Truck."

"What an idiot," the man named Hollywood said with an eye roll.

"Dad! Did you see that? That was so cool!" Annie said enthusiastically.

Fletch's muscles visibly relaxed at hearing his daughter's words. "Yeah, squirt. I saw."

"He gonna be a problem?" Truck asked.

Aspen stared up at him. He was almost a foot taller than her, and all muscle. But she wasn't scared of him.

How could she be when he was more than obviously on her side? She sighed. "Yeah. But I can handle it," she told Truck and the others.

"Maybe I should talk to his commanding officer," Ghost suggested.

Aspen shook her head. "Just drop it."

"He threatened you," Doc said. "He can't get away with that."

"Here's the thing," Aspen told the dozen men around her. "This kind of thing happens all the time simply because I'm a woman. I can handle men like Derek, they're mostly bluster. He's threatened by me simply because I'm a chick. I've been dealing with this for the entire eight years I've been in the Army. *Eight years.*"

"It's not right," Lefty said.

"You're right, it's not," Aspen agreed. "But that doesn't mean it doesn't happen. If you want to help, take a look at how you interact with the women *you* work with. Do you talk down to them? Do you assume they can't handle something just because of their gender? Discrimination is both a state of mind and a conscious decision. Just because you don't think you aren't being discriminatory, doesn't mean your actions aren't."

Everyone stared at her in silence, and Aspen felt uncomfortable for the first time. She didn't often get up on her soap box about this kind of thing, she was used to sweeping it under the rug and just dealing with it.

"You mean like when Dad opens the door for Mom?" Annie asked.

Smiling, Aspen turned to the little girl. "There's being polite, and then there's belittling. There's a difference." When Annie's brow furrowed, Aspen tried to think of an example. "So your dad holding open a door, or carrying the grocery bags, or wanting your mom to let him know when she gets home while he's at work and can't be there to meet her...that's polite. It's a part of loving someone and wanting them to be safe.

"But assuming a girl wants to wear pink instead of blue, or when a teacher spends extra time with the boys on math and science, and encourages the girls to draw or write, *that's* discrimination. A man getting promoted over a woman, when the woman is more qualified, is discrimination. A dad only telling his little girl she's pretty when she's wearing a dress or skirt, and not when she has on a pair of pants...that *could* be discrimination."

"I wanted to sign up for shop at school, so I could learn how to fix a car engine, and my teacher, Mr. Smithy, told me it wasn't appropriate and I should take home ec instead," Annie said.

Aspen nodded. "That's discrimination. If you want to learn how to repair cars, go for it. If you want to go into construction, do it. But on the flip side, you shouldn't assume all boys want to do that kind of stuff either. Some would probably be more than happy learning how to sew, dance, and how to cook, and don't want to play football and other sports. Discrimination goes both ways."

Annie nodded. "That guy was a poophole. Can you show me how to be better on the obstacle course now?"

Aspen heard chuckles all around her. She'd almost forgotten that she had an audience. Before she could get embarrassed, she felt Kane's hand on her waist.

"Thanks for having our backs," Kane told his friends.

"You're welcome at my table anytime," Fletch told her. "And for what it's worth, we all think you're a hell of a medic. And if the Deltas used them, and if we were still doing missions, we'd personally request you be attached to our team."

Aspen blinked in surprise. "Thanks."

The seven men nodded and turned to head back to their families, who were standing nearby, watching. Fletch stopped to tell Annie that she had fifteen minutes before they'd be heading home. She wrinkled her nose, but nodded before he headed for a woman standing next to a little boy.

"No way," Oz said grumpily. "They aren't allowed to steal you away. *Our* team would request you."

Aspen couldn't help it, she laughed. "Thanks, guys. I appreciate it." She looked over at Annie, who was obviously more than impatient to get some obstacle course time in.

"Give me fifteen minutes?" she asked Kane.

"You can have as much time as you want, *dušo*."

She raised an eyebrow.

Kane leaned in, kissed her lips, then whispered, "Bosnian."

"Are you ever just going to call me darling in English?" she couldn't help but ask.

Kane shifted so his lips were by her ear and said quietly, "When I'm so far inside you that neither of us can tell where we start and where we end...I'll call you darling." Then he pulled away with a grin and stepped back.

"That was mean," Aspen said, shifting where she stood, feeling how damp she'd gotten between her thighs.

"So was turning me on by looking like you were ready to pound Spence into the ground," Kane retorted. Then he gave her a chin lift and turned to walk back to where he'd been standing with his team before Derek had appeared out of nowhere.

"Kane?" Aspen called.

He turned. "Yeah?"

"Thanks for standing next to me and not in front of me."

He nodded, and Aspen could see the respect shining in his eyes even with the distance between them.

"Ready?" Annie asked.

Aspen nodded and turned to face her. "Sorry you had to see and hear all that," she told the little girl as they began walking toward the start of the course.

Annie shrugged. "I understand more about what you were saying earlier now. That guy didn't like that you were on his team."

"Nope," Aspen agreed.

"Even though you did all the same work he did to be there," Annie continued.

"Correct," Aspen said.

"Are you really quitting?" Annie asked.

"I don't see it as quitting," Aspen said. "Am I getting out of the Army? Yeah, I think I am. I've worked my butt off to give women and girls like you the chance to make a difference. I hope that by helping to pave the way, it'll make things easier on *you* when you grow up. But I'm tired. I want a team like your dad has. Like my friends have. I want to know I can one hundred percent count on someone to have my back."

"Like they did today," Annie said confidently.

"Yup. They didn't care that I was a woman. They had my back anyway."

"My boyfriend's that way," Annie said proudly.

"You have a boyfriend?" Aspen asked in surprise.

"Yeah. His name is Frankie and he lives in California. But when we get older, we're gonna get married. I know I can count on him to have my back no matter what, just as I'll have his. He's deaf and gets picked on a lot, but he doesn't care because he knows the other kids are the poopholes, not him."

Aspen couldn't help but smile every time she heard the word poophole. It wasn't exactly nice, but the little girl wasn't swearing, so she couldn't reprimand her. "It's good to have a boyfriend like that."

Annie nodded. "So when you get out, what are you going to do?"

"I'm going to use my paramedic license and help people around here. I'd like to get hired on an ambulance and go to people when they need help."

"Ooooh, like when people call 9-1-1?"

"Exactly."

"Cool. We had to do that when our house blew up. Come on! I want you to show me how to be faster and better at the pole thing!"

Aspen shook her head. When her *house blew up*? She'd ask Kane later about that. For now, she wanted to forget about Derek, discrimination, and just enjoy Annie's enthusiasm.

CHAPTER FOURTEEN

Brain vacillated between being pissed off on Aspen's behalf, and impressed as hell at how she'd treated the entire nasty incident with Spence. He couldn't believe Derek had the nerve to confront Aspen at the organizational day. Of course, the ass probably thought she was alone, and he could say whatever he wanted and not have any repercussions.

But Derek clearly hadn't planned on Aspen being willing to take him on right then and there. Nor did he suspect she'd have so much backup. As soon as Brain saw what was happening, he'd headed for Aspen. He knew his team would have his back, and he wasn't surprised Ghost's team was there too. Fletch had probably been watching Annie, and when he saw something going down around her, everyone mobilized.

While Brain was still pissed about the entire incident, Aspen seemed to let it slide. She'd talked about Annie all the way back to his house and was as happy as she could be to mentor the teenager.

"She's amazing," Aspen said happily. "She caught on immediately and realized how much faster she could shimmy across that pole if she hooked her knee around it and used her leg muscles to take some of the weight off her arms. That gave her enough strength to be able to pull herself up at the end and ring the bell. I loved seeing her smile."

And Brain loved seeing *Aspen* smile. He squeezed her hand resting on his leg. "You did good."

"I did, didn't I?" she asked.

"Are you okay about what happened with Spence?" he couldn't help but ask.

Aspen sighed. "Yeah. It was bound to happen sooner or later. He's a dick, and he obviously thought he had the upper hand."

"He's going to cause problems at work," Brain said. "Well, *more* problems."

"He'll try," Aspen agreed.

Brain liked that she wasn't trying to blow off his concerns.

"But after today, he made my decision on whether to get out or not easy. I'll tell the major tomorrow that I'm done."

"You okay with that?" Brain asked. He couldn't imagine leaving the Army, but then again, he had a hell of a close-knit family he'd be leaving if he did.

"Yeah. I am. I'm actually excited about what's ahead for me. I've got about two more months, and I'm sure the major will take me off the team to make room for my replacement. It's probably best for everyone involved anyway."

"It sucks. I'm sorry," Brain said.

Aspen shrugged. "You know what? I'm okay with it. Even if they replace me with a man, I still feel as if I helped smooth the way for someone like Annie in the future. Maybe she won't have as hard a time as I did, simply because she isn't one of the first women to be on the teams. At least I hope so."

"I know so. I'm proud of you."

"Thanks. I'm proud of myself," Aspen told him.

"I talked to my commander about the hurricane that's brewing out in the gulf," Brain told her.

Aspen blinked at his change in topic. "Yeah?"

"Yeah. They say it's supposed to keep on gaining strength, and it's heading straight for Houston."

"Fuck," Aspen breathed. "They've been hammered with storms in the last few years."

"They have. And if this one continues on the same trajectory, they're probably going to ask for volunteers to head to Houston to assist where necessary."

"Are you going?" she asked.

Brain shrugged. "We'll decide as a team if we are or not. It'll depend on if something more important crops up elsewhere."

Aspen huffed out a small laugh. "You know, in the past when things like a storm or tornado or something happened, my team was asked if we wanted to volunteer, but it was an individual thing. Like, the last time, Hamilton couldn't go because one of his kids had a thing at school he felt he needed to be at, and Buckland just didn't want to go. It was never an all-or-nothing thing on whether we'd go or not. Knowing that you and the others decide to be all in, or all out, just hammers home the fact that I'm making the right decision." She squeezed his hand

and turned a little in her seat. "If you guys say yes, I'm going too," she told him.

Brain smiled. "Okay."

"Just like that?" she asked skeptically.

"Just like that," he agreed. "You've more than proven to me and the rest of the guys that you can hold your own. You'll be a huge asset, and we'd be happy to have you at our side."

Aspen smiled. She tugged her hand out of his grasp and flattened it on his thigh. "I think I need to thank you for rushing over to my aid today, even if I didn't really need it."

"Yeah?" Brain asked.

"Uh-huh."

Her fingers brushed against his inner thigh, and Brain caught her hand in his once more. "You want me to wreck?"

Aspen shook her head. "Nope. I'm hoping you'll drive faster. I want you, Kane."

He glanced over at her and saw she was staring right at him. Open. Honest.

Without a word, he pressed his foot to the gas and his Challenger shot forward.

Aspen laughed and beamed at him.

Brain had wished to have Aspen under him more times than he could count, but he'd never wanted to push her too fast. He'd known months ago that he wanted more from her, but had been content to move at her speed. To get to know her. To make out and hold her, but not go further.

He would've waited as long as it took for her to want

him with the same intensity, but thank God he didn't have to wait anymore.

"You sure?" he asked, not wanting any misunderstandings between them.

"Yes," she said simply.

Needing to distract himself from the feel of her hand on his thigh, Brain said, "I've got condoms. I'm clean, but I don't want you to worry about anything besides enjoying yourself this first time."

"I'm on the pill," she told him. "I had an ovarian cyst when I was a teenager. The docs put me on the pill so they wouldn't keep forming."

Brain's adrenaline spiked. But he tamped down his excitement. "Still, this first time, until I can prove to you that I'm clean, I'll stay gloved to protect you."

"Okay. But, Kane? I trust you. I wouldn't be agreeing to sleep with you if I didn't. And for the record, I don't jump into bed with just anyone. It's been three years for me."

Brain split his concentration between her and the road. "Three years?"

"Yup. But that doesn't mean I didn't take care of myself in those three years," she said breezily.

She was killing him. Talking about touching herself was enough to make his cock jump in his jeans.

Aspen obviously felt it because she chuckled. "You like that thought?"

"Fuck yeah," Brain breathed. "I'll be lucky if I don't shoot off like a teenager the second I get inside you, just from imagining what you look like touching yourself and getting yourself off."

"If you do, you can make *me* feel good until you're ready again," she told him easily.

"Oh, that's a given," Brain told her. "I'm not coming until you do. At least once."

"At least?" she asked with a quirk of her brow.

"At least," he confirmed.

"I think you're driving too slow," Aspen told him breathlessly.

Brain smiled and nudged his speed up another mile an hour. The last thing he wanted was to be stopped by a cop. That would delay his getting inside Aspen, and at the moment, that was all he could think about.

Aspen knew she was coming on strong, but she couldn't help it. She was more than ready to make love with Kane. When they'd officially started dating, after they'd gotten back from Afghanistan, she wasn't so sure about the intense feelings she had for him. She'd felt as if they were moving too fast, that she was falling for him too quickly. But the more time she spent with him, the safer she felt... both her body and her heart.

Kane was one of the good guys. She knew that down to her very bones. And lying in his arms last night made everything crystal clear.

She loved him. Loved being in his arms. Loved falling asleep with him and waking up in the morning with his arms still around her.

He could be moody and grumpy, but he never took out his moods on her. He was a good friend, a good teammate, a hell of a soldier, and she wanted to connect with him on a more intimate level.

Sleeping with him could break them apart. Giving in to the sexual tension might make them realize that was all they had...but she didn't think so. She wanted to think that being intimate would only bring them closer. Time would tell.

She wanted to forget about Derek, and getting out of the Army, and all the other stressors she'd experienced lately, and just enjoy being with Kane.

He pulled into his driveway and into his one-car garage and was out and walking around to her side before she'd even undone her seat belt.

Grinning at his eagerness, she let him help her out of the car and, without a word, he wrapped his arm around her waist and led her into the house. The second the door shut behind them, his lips were on hers, and he backed her against the wall.

For the first time in her life, Aspen truly let herself go. She didn't worry about seeming too eager, or not eager enough. She didn't think about what she should do with her hands, or if she was moving too fast or too slow.

She just did what felt right.

As Kane devoured her mouth, her hands slipped under his shirt and up his chest. She dug her fingers into his pecs and flicked his nipples. Kane growled and lifted his head, but Aspen didn't want him to stop. Didn't want him to slow down. She wanted him, now.

She pushed his shirt up, and he got the hint, ripping it off. Aspen ducked her head and took one of his nipples in her mouth, nipping at it, then sucking—hard.

He grunted, and before she was ready to let go of him,

he picked her up. She wrapped her legs around his waist and laughed as he started for the stairs.

She wasn't worried in the least that he might drop her. She felt completely safe in his arms. Hooking her own around his shoulders, she held on as he carried her into his bedroom. His sheets were still thrown back from when they'd gotten out of bed that morning.

Without warning, Kane dropped her onto the mattress.

Aspen chuckled once again. But the second she saw the look of lust in his eyes, her humor fled.

"Off," he said in a guttural tone, motioning to her shirt with his chin.

Aspen wanted to tease him. Should probably make him work harder to get her naked, but they'd both waited long enough. Grabbing her shirt, she peeled it over her head, then reached for the clasp of her bra.

Kane had taken off his socks and boots and, while she watched, he unbuckled and unzipped his jeans, pushing them, along with his underwear, down and off. Aspen lay back on the bed and undid her shorts. She toed off her shoes and lifted her hips. Kane's hands were there immediately to help pull her shorts and panties down, until she was completely naked.

Aspen didn't feel self-conscious about being naked in front of Kane. Raising her arms above her head, she stretched, arching her back and spreading her legs apart slightly. The look in Kane's eyes, not to mention how hard his cock was, made her feel beautiful.

Kane stood stock still next to the bed, staring at her as if trying to memorize the display before him. Aspen could feel her nipples go tight and hard on her chest, and while she definitely wanted to get on with the festivities, she knew she'd remember this moment for the rest of her life.

"Fuck," Kane breathed. "I don't know where to start."

Aspen smiled and held out a hand. "How about a kiss?" she asked.

He took her hand and the next thing Aspen knew, Kane had settled on top of her. Not next to her, literally *on* her. She felt a smear of precome against her thigh as he got settled, and she spread her legs apart, giving him more room.

Because they were about the same height, she could feel his throbbing cock against her mound, and his chest hair felt ticklish against her extremely sensitive nipples. He propped himself up on his elbows and speared both hands into her hair, holding her head still.

He stared down at her for a long moment. It didn't feel awkward in the least. His gaze bored into her own, and she swore she could see into his soul. Corny, but true.

"I want to go slow. Memorize every inch of your beautiful body. Learn what turns you on and what makes you moan. I want to lick your pussy and taste you. I want to see you explode in my arms, then immediately make you come again, even if you think you're too sensitive."

With every word out of his mouth, Aspen felt herself getting wetter. He hadn't even touched her and she was more than ready for him.

"But I'm on the verge of coming just looking at you," he continued. "Feeling your tits against my chest, seeing your pupils dilated with lust, feeling your hips push up into me just from my words...I can't think about anything beyond getting inside you."

"We have plenty of time to explore...later," Aspen told him. "I want you. Inside me. Now."

Without another word, Kane leaned over and opened a drawer next to his bed. He grabbed a condom and expertly opened it with his teeth. He leaned up on a hip and covered himself with one hand, then returned to the same position he'd been in a moment ago.

"Slick," Aspen teased.

Kane actually blushed. "I practiced. I knew when I got you in my bed, I'd have no coordination. So I bought a box, and every night before I jacked off, I'd practice putting on a condom with one hand. Then once it was on, I'd rip the damn thing off and fantasize about you being in here with me."

He was adorable. Practicing putting on a condom was his nerdiest moment yet, but she couldn't fault him because all she could think about was getting him inside her—and that practice meant he was ready in seconds. Shifting until one hand was between them, she tapped his thigh. "Lift up," she whispered.

He did, and Aspen wrapped her hand around his cock. He wasn't huge, but he wasn't small either. He was the perfect size for her.

She couldn't help squeezing him, and Kane moaned.

Then, not wanting to prolong their foreplay, Aspen notched the head of his dick between her soaking-wet folds.

"As I said, it's been a while," she told him. "Go slow."

Kane nodded, and she felt him slip into her a little. She grabbed his waist but didn't take her eyes from his. Slowly, ever so slowly, he pushed all the way inside her.

There was a small pinch of pain, but then she finally

felt his pubic hair brush against her own. He was in. She squeezed her muscles, and he groaned.

"Fuck, darling, you're so damn tight. Am I hurting you?"

"No," she reassured him. "You're perfect."

They stayed like that for a long moment. Long enough for Aspen to ask, "Kane?"

"Give me another few seconds," Kane said between clenched teeth. "If I move, I'm gonna blow, and I want to enjoy this for as long as possible."

Aspen smiled. Feeling ridiculously pleased that he was having a hard time controlling himself. She knew many women would get upset if their man couldn't hold off, but to her, it was the ultimate compliment.

Then Kane took a deep breath, one she felt against her belly, and he lifted up, looking down between them.

"God, that's so hot," he said, more to himself than her.

Aspen looked down and had to agree. She could see her nipples sticking straight up, the pooch of her small belly that she'd never been able to lose, but more importantly, she saw the way their body hair meshed together. She always kept herself trimmed, and he obviously did too.

Then Kane moved his hips back, and she saw his cock appear from inside her, the condom shiny with her excitement.

"Watch," he ordered, but Aspen wasn't about to look away. He pushed back inside her, and somehow the sight of him entering her body made what they were doing all the more intimate.

"That's right, take me," he said softly. He pulled back and pushed in again. Then again. Aspen couldn't take her eyes away from the erotic sight of him slowly fucking her.

"You feel so amazing," he told her. "Hot, wet, and tight. You're like a fucking glove, squeezing me."

Discovering Kane was a dirty talker was surprising. For someone who called himself a nerd, he certainly wasn't acting like one now.

Then he startled her by thrusting so hard, the smack of their flesh hitting together was loud in the quiet room.

They both groaned.

"Sorry," he said immediately.

"Don't be! Do it again," Aspen ordered.

Kane grinned and ever so slowly pulled out of her, until only the tip of his cock was inside, then he slammed in once again. Aspen threw her head back on his pillow and moaned.

"You like that," he said.

It wasn't a question, but Aspen nodded again. "Slow is nice, but fast is fucking amazing," she told him.

"Can you come from this?" he asked as he thrust hard into her again.

Aspen shook her head. "No, but it feels really good."

"Touch yourself," Kane ordered.

Blinking in surprise, Aspen looked up at him.

"I want to feel you come around me, and I'm not going to last very long, especially not if I'm fucking you hard and fast. You feel too good. But I'll be damned if you don't come our first time."

"It's okay, Kane."

"It's not. Touch yourself, darling, show me how you like it. Slow and steady, or fast and hard?"

Feeling a little self-conscious, Aspen moved her hand back down between them. Kane came up on his hands, keeping them connected and looked down as she began to strum her clit.

She'd masturbated more frequently than she was comfortable admitting, even to Kane, but nothing felt better than having him stuffed inside her while she stroked herself.

"I can feel your muscles contracting around me," Kane said as she moved her fingers faster. "That's it, God, this is amazing. Keep going."

Aspen tuned him out as her orgasm got closer and closer. She tried to buck up, but couldn't move because Kane was on top of her. Then she tried to slam her legs together, but again, Kane's body prevented her from moving. The orgasm rising inside her was so huge, it was somewhat frightening, so she stopped touching herself.

But Kane wasn't having that. He shifted until he could get one of his own hands between them and took up where she left off.

His fingers were calloused and felt rougher against her sensitive bud than her own touch. Her folds were soaking wet, and his fingers slid easily against her clit, taking her higher and higher. Aspen grabbed hold of his biceps and dug her fingernails into his skin, trying to delay her orgasm. She knew she was going to shatter into a million pieces and he was the only thing holding her together.

His touch almost hurt, but in a good way. One second she was hanging on to the precipice and the next, she flew over it. Her stomach clenched, her thighs shook, and she tried to curl up into a ball to better weather the orgasmic storm, but could only lie on the bed and take the pleasure Kane was giving her.

Just when she thought he was going to let her come

down, he groaned and started fucking her. *Hard*. Her tits bounced up and down with every one of his thrusts—and just like that, Aspen was coming again.

"God, that feels so good! You have no idea," Kane ground out as he thrust forcefully in and out of her.

"I...think...I...do," Aspen said in time with his thrusts.

"I can't hold out—I'm coming," Kane growled between clenched teeth. Then he put a hand on Aspen's butt and pulled her against him, holding himself as far inside her as he could get, and came.

The groan that left his lips was porn worthy, giving Aspen shivers as she watched. The sight of him orgasming was *hot*. His eyes were closed, his head was thrown back, and she could feel him flexing deep inside her body. The condom prevented her from feeling his release, and she was almost glad. Their lovemaking was intense enough as it was; she wasn't sure she'd be able to handle more at that moment.

Without warning, Kane's eyes opened and he looked at her. He seemed almost pissed, but Aspen knew he wasn't. "Fuck," he muttered, then in one fluid movement, he rolled onto his side, keeping her hips flush against his own. He ended up on his back with Aspen draped over him. She curled her legs up and sat astride him.

Smiling, she rolled her hips, and he groaned. "Are you trying to kill me?" he asked.

Aspen knew she probably looked like a loon. A huge smile on her face, her hair likely in disarray, her chest blotchy from her orgasm, her boobs practically in his face...but she didn't care.

"What a way to go," she quipped.

Then Kane smiled, and Aspen's heart almost stopped.

She'd never seen him so...content. She loved that she'd been the one to put that look on his face. "You called me darling," she said inanely.

"I did," he agreed. "Told you, when we're in bed, you're my darling. Outside it, you're my *chérie*, *liebling*, *dorogoy*, or *gráinne*. Now, as much as I want you to stay exactly where you are, I need to deal with this condom."

Aspen wrinkled her nose. She didn't want to move.

Kane brought a hand up to her face and smoothed a piece of unruly hair back over her ear. "I know. I don't want to move either. I like where I am more than you know."

Sighing, Aspen lifted off his lap, and they both hissed when he slipped out of her body. His cock landed on his stomach with a soft plop. She couldn't help but giggle.

"You laughing at my manhood?" Kane mock growled.

"No, never," she hurried to reassure him.

Kane chuckled. "Don't move, I'll be right back."

Then he climbed out of the bed and walked toward the bathroom. Aspen didn't look away. She devoured him with her eyes. His ass was a work of art. She wasn't sure there was an ounce of fat on him. He was walking back toward her within fifteen seconds, and she didn't bother to hide the fact she was ogling his front side as he returned to the bed.

His cock was long; no wonder she'd felt him so deeply inside her. He wasn't overly thick, but it was almost hard to believe she'd taken him so easily, considering how long it had been since she'd slept with a man.

Instead of climbing back into the bed next to her, Kane leaned over, grabbed her hips, and physically dragged her ass to the side of the bed. He kneeled on the floor and spread her legs as far as he could get them.

"Kane!" Aspen protested.

"Yeah?" he asked distractedly. He ran a thumb down her slit, spreading the evidence of her orgasms between her folds.

"What are you doing?"

"Having a snack," he said with a grin, then his head dropped—and Aspen couldn't do anything but hang on for dear life as he ate her out as if he'd never get enough.

Brain had no idea what time it was, and he didn't care either. He held Aspen against him and smiled when she snored slightly. They hadn't left the bed since they'd arrived home from the carnival. Making love that first time had taken the edge off his desire, but he hadn't been nearly done with her.

With Aspen, he didn't feel like the outcast he'd been for most of his life. He'd never felt as deep a connection with anyone as he felt with her. Neither had Brain ever felt like he *needed* sex. He'd remained a virgin well past the age most boys experimented with sex. Because he'd never been around girls his own age until he was in his twenties, he hadn't felt the urge to fuck just for the sake of fucking.

But with Aspen, he found he couldn't get enough. Before today, he hadn't been confident in his abilities to make sex good for her, but once he had her in his arms, instinct took over. Feeling her orgasm when he was buried deep inside her hot, wet pussy had been an experience he knew he'd never forget. Watching her writhe under him, lost in the pleasure he'd given her, and then to feel her lose it again when he'd fucked her had made him feel more like a man than ever before.

Then he'd had to taste her, to examine her up close and personal. He'd eaten her to another orgasm, using his fingers to stimulate her, and once again, feeling her internal muscles flutter against his fingers was fascinating...a gift. He'd let her rest for a while, but when he couldn't hold himself back anymore, he'd feasted on her tits until she'd woken up, and then he'd taken her again.

The condoms were a pain in the ass, but he hoped there would come a time in the near future when they trusted each other enough to ditch them.

Aspen was also a wildcat; she gave as good as she got. When she'd wrapped her lips around his dick and looked up at him, he'd almost blown in her mouth in seconds.

In short, everything about Aspen was perfect. And he was head over heels in love with her. Even though that should've scared the shit out of him, it didn't.

She shifted in his arms, and Brain let her go. She rolled onto her side, and he cuddled up behind her. Her ass wiggled and pressed back against his groin, immediately making him hard. But Brain didn't plan on doing anything about that at the moment. He had a feeling he'd be hard around her all the time now. Wrapping an arm around her waist, he pulled her closer.

"Kane?"

"Yeah, darling?"

"Love you."

He froze.

When she didn't say anything else, he whispered, "Aspen?"

No answer. She was exhausted and probably had no idea she'd even spoken.

Closing his eyes, Brain knew he'd never forget this moment. Sure, she'd been mostly unconscious when she'd said the words, but he'd do whatever it took to get her to say them when she was awake.

For now, he simply kissed the top of her head and whispered, "Love you too."

Then he closed his eyes and slept.

* * *

Derek Spence paced his apartment, mumbling to himself.

He knew he should get over the fact Mesmer had dumped him...but he couldn't. She'd rejected him. Then she'd *humiliated* him by kissing that asshole in the bar. It was obvious she hadn't even known the guy until that night. If she thought she was fooling him, she was an even bigger idiot than he thought.

But of *course* the guy wasn't just anyone. He was a fucking Delta. They thought they were better than everyone else on base.

Derek knew he would've been able to find Akhund if he'd had just a little more time. But no, that fucking Delta and his team had to come in, and he'd been kicked off the search. To add insult to injury, they'd found and killed the terrorist within days of their arrival in Afghanistan.

Not only that—Derek had been given a reprimand. A fucking *reprimand!* It would be on his record forever. It was bullshit!

He'd done everything the Army had ever asked him to.

He'd put his life on the line time after time, and this was the thanks he got? A reprimand for trying to do his job?

Of *course* he hadn't been able to find Akhund. He had a huge handicap.

Mesmer.

He didn't know any other Ranger team who had to put up with a chick. She was slower, weaker, a definite handicap in every way. He'd been *this* close to finding Akhund when her incompetence had ruined everything. She should've been fine on her own; a *man* would've been. And Derek was convinced she'd encouraged the other men to complain to the major about what had happened, resulting in that fucking reprimand in his file.

It should've been Mesmer. Someone should've realized that having women on Ranger teams was a bad idea. That they couldn't handle intense combat situations. But no, she and her fucking Delta buddies were waltzing around post as if they were fucking royalty!

Yes. That fucking reprimand was all Mesmer's fault. If he didn't have to put up with her on *his* teams, they would've caught Akhund easily, and he'd have gotten a goddamn commendation.

She had to pay for fucking everything up. She *and* that asshole Delta had to pay.

He wasn't sure how, or when, but he'd make sure Mesmer regretted dumping him, regretted ruining his perfect record. And make sure that Delta regretted ever kissing her that night in the bar.

No one made Derek Spence look bad. He was a fucking Ranger—and he'd show the world he was no one to be messed with.

CHAPTER FIFTEEN

The next week was idyllic for Aspen. She'd spent every night with Kane and, if possible, she felt even closer to him now than she did a week ago. Yes, the sex between them was amazing, but when they were both too tired to do more than fall into bed, having him hold her was just as intimate as the nights when they made love.

They were both busy at work. Aspen had begun the process to leave the Army. It was both sad and exciting at the same time. She'd started looking at her options for working as a paramedic and had to decide if she wanted to stay in Killeen, or branch out and look in Temple or Georgetown. She didn't want to get too far from Fort Hood, as that's where Kane was at the moment.

The good thing about being a paramedic was that if Kane was moved from the Texas area, she could find another job no matter where they went. Of course, there was always the chance she and Kane wouldn't stay together, but at the moment, a breakup seemed unlikely.

The only thing disrupting her current contentment was—randomly enough—the weather.

Three days ago, the national weather service had said there was an eighty-five percent chance that Hurricane Florence would make a direct hit on the Galveston area. It had been upgraded to a category two, and wasn't expected to grow stronger, but because of other storms that had hit Houston, everyone was concerned about the wind stream shifting and forcing the storm to hover over the area for twenty-four hours or more.

Unfortunately, the forecasters were right, and the sustained rain bands brought massive amounts of rain to the coast and the surrounding area, including Houston. National Guard troops had already been sent in to assist in both the rescue operation for people trapped in their houses and cars, as well as to try to maintain order until the water receded.

Aspen was at Kane's once more, and they were still asleep when his phone rang. She rolled with him as he reached for it.

"Hello?"

Aspen looked at the clock and saw that it was four thirty-two in the morning.

"Right. We're on our way," Kane said to whoever was on the other end, then he clicked off the phone and tightened his arms around her.

"Who was that?" she asked.

"Trigger. We're heading out this morning to go down to Houston."

Aspen got up on an elbow and looked at him. The light they'd forgotten to turn off in the bathroom gave the room enough illumination for her to see. "We?"

"Yeah. You, me, the rest of the guys on the team. We."

"Are you sure it's okay if I go with you?"

"Of course. Why wouldn't it be?" he asked. "We've talked about this. You already got clearance from your major, and our commander is thrilled we'll have a combat medic with us."

"I just...I don't know. I've never really been asked to be a part of a team like this before."

Kane didn't laugh at her, he simply brought his hand up to her face and brushed his thumb over her cheek. "The day after you told the major you were getting out, he had your replacement assigned to the Rangers. You haven't seen Buckland, Hamilton, or any of the others since then. Besides, for this mission, there aren't really 'teams.' We're all going down there, and we'll split up as necessary to operate the inflatable boats and rescue people."

"Okay."

"I'd like you to stay with me while we're there, though. The team might be split up, but I want you and I to stay together. I'm trying not to be overly assholish about this, but desperate people do desperate things. And if something happened to you and I wasn't there to help...I'm not sure I'd be able to forgive myself."

Aspen felt kinda gooey inside that Kane was as worried about her as he was.

"And you haven't worked in a rescue situation like this before," he went on, as if he was still trying to convince her. "Yes, there was plenty of time for people to evacuate, but many don't have the money or anywhere else to go, so they stay. When the water rises, they panic, and they'll do whatever they can to survive. Not to mention the assholes who take advantage of those who've fled by breaking into homes and businesses. It can be dangerous, and I can't stand the thought of losing you when we're just now settling into our new normal."

Aspen smiled. "I'm thinking I need to stick around to protect *you*. Having a tried-and-true combat medic at your side can come in handy."

"Definitely," he agreed. "And you're right, I could get a blister or a paper cut and need you to kiss it and make it better."

Aspen rolled her eyes. Her man was a goof.

Her man. Damn, she liked that.

"We need to get up and head to the post to pack our stuff and get on the road," he said reluctantly.

"Do we have time for a shower?" Aspen asked. The question had been asked innocently enough, but the look in Kane's eyes when he answered was anything but.

"Yeah, but to save time, we should probably take it together."

And just like that, Aspen was turned way the hell on. "You think?" she asked with a raised eyebrow.

"Definitely," Kane said, then he rolled over, bringing her with him, and swung his legs over the side of the mattress. Aspen held on as he stood, loving the feel of his hardening cock against her backside. One thing about her man, he never had a problem getting it up.

He carried her into the bathroom, leaning over and turning on the water in the shower to allow it time to warm up. Then she let her legs drop.

"I'll brush my teeth while you use the bathroom, then we'll switch," he told her.

Aspen nodded.

In minutes, they were in the shower, and Kane went to

his knees in front of her and used his hands to spread her thighs. Licking his lips, he looked up and said, "Gotta make sure you're nice and clean here." Without waiting for a reply, he lowered his head...and Aspen forgot about everything else. Houston. The storm. Getting out of the Army. All she could think about was how good Kane made her feel.

As amazing as the morning had been, Brain was now one hundred percent focused on the job at hand. They'd arrived at the post and met up with his team. Then they'd been herded into a large two-and-a-half-ton truck and made the four-hour trip down to Houston, part of a convoy of other trucks and Humvees. Based on where the flooding was the worst, they'd spent the first couple hours putting up tents in an empty big box parking lot nearby to use as a staging area, and then had been in strategy meetings for the last hour.

The rain had continued to come down that afternoon, alternating between periods of relatively easy drizzle to absolute downpours. Everyone knew the situation was desperate for those who were trapped. The Army was working with the city, which was taking 9-1-1 calls and attempting to get assistance to those in need.

Throughout the afternoon, Aspen remained by his side. Well, not right at his side, but nearby. She worked with other medics to figure out the best way to split everyone up so they'd have the most coverage. Some of the locals had learned they were there, as well, and had come over to find out as much information as they could about what was going on and to ask them to check on loved ones. Aspen did her best to keep them occupied so the authorities could assign search parties to go on rescue runs when necessary.

Brain hadn't been happy to learn that Derek had volunteered to come to Houston. Although it wasn't as if he had any say in who volunteered and who didn't. The immature asshole kept shooting Aspen dirty looks, but she was ignoring him, too busy for his nonsense. Brain made a mental note to keep her as far away from Spence as possible. He hoped he wouldn't be a problem, as the middle of a humanitarian mission to help Houstonians wasn't the place for a showdown.

From the moment they'd arrived at the staging point, things had been hectic, and Brain was relieved when they got the go-ahead to start rescuing people. Some of the teams drove the big deuce-and-a-half trucks and others were taking boats the Army had acquired. Others still were teaming with locals who had shown up with their personal boats.

Brain and Aspen hopped into one of the large inflatable boats that the Coast Guard had brought with them and headed out for their first mission. With the Coastie steering, Brain and Aspen hopped in and out of the boat to enter flooded homes, checking for anyone who might be trapped.

During their first run, they brought a family of four back to the staging area, as well as their two dogs. On the second trip, they found an elderly couple who hadn't been able to flee and were trapped in their one-story house. And so it went.

Hours later, Brain had no idea how many trips they'd

made into the flooded streets of the city and back to the staging area, but it was a lot. He was exhausted, and he knew Aspen had to be tired too, but he'd never know it by looking at her. During their last few rescues, she was the one who'd made contact with the civilians who needed help, and he was the muscle, which was fine with him. Aspen was much friendlier than he was, able to calm the people they were rescuing.

He also had to give it to the men and women who were driving the boats. Brain and Aspen had used many different vessels for their rescues. After helping citizens to the tents, they climbed into whichever craft was ready upon returning to the launch area. So they'd had a different driver with each rescue, but thus far, they'd all done an amazing job of avoiding the dangers in the water.

And there was no doubt that being in the water was dangerous. There were submerged cars, road signs, and large chunks of debris that the people steering the boats had to avoid. Not to mention the downed power lines and even the occasional alligator.

"How're you holding up?" Brain asked Aspen when they were on their way back to the staging area for what seemed like the thousandth time.

"I'm good," she said.

There were three people sitting in the bottom of the boat, huddled together and crying with relief that they'd been plucked out of their car, which the driver had stupidly driven into a flooded street. The current had swept the car about a hundred feet downstream until it had gotten stuck against a bunch of trees. The trio had managed to climb onto the roof and hang onto the trees, but with the water moving as fast as it was, they couldn't swim to safety. They'd yelled and gotten the attention of someone nearby, who had relayed their position to the Army.

"You are, aren't you?" Brain asked Aspen.

She gave him a small, tired smile. It was dark outside by now, and he couldn't see her face very well. But every now and then they'd pass a streetlight that was still on, and he saw her eyes were on his. She looked...radiant. She was in her element, and it showed.

"I love this," she said. "Not people being hurt or scared, but being able to help them. Somehow finding the right words to make them relax and trust that I'm going to get them out of whatever situation they're in. I love having the ability to bandage up their hurts and reassure them that they're all right, that we're going to get them to safety."

"It's addicting," Brain said with a nod. This was the first time in hours they'd had a moment to talk. Really talk. "You're going to be an amazing addition to a rescue squad," he told her.

She tilted her head, looking slightly skeptical.

"You are," he insisted. "You know how to take instruction from someone else, but at the same time, you can think on your feet. Look at us, we've worked together flawlessly. I swear several times today you read my mind. I know whoever hires you is gonna think they hit the jackpot once you get on staff."

"Thanks," Aspen said. "You haven't been so bad yourself out here. I'm not sure what I would've done without you. That one couple that only spoke Spanish was so freaked out, I couldn't have gotten them out of their house if you hadn't been there to explain what was going on. And how lucky was it that we were sent to rescue that Japanese guy? He thought we were leaving him behind, and was desperate enough to leap into the water when we had to back up and come at him from a different angle. He would've been electrocuted if you hadn't told him what we were doing before he tried to swim out to us."

Brain shrugged. "As I said, we're a good team."

"We are, aren't we?" Aspen said.

Not able to stop himself, Brain lifted a gloved hand and tucked a piece of hair behind her ear. They were both soaking wet, as the rain still hadn't let up, and she had a streak of dirt across her cheek. But he'd never seen anyone as beautiful as Aspen in all his life.

Shouts sounded ahead of them, and Brain dropped his hand and took a deep breath. It was time to get back to work. He wasn't sure how many more trips they'd be allowed to take, but he knew Aspen wouldn't ask to take a break. She was stubborn, like he was, and the urgency to keep going, to rescue more people, was pressing on them all.

When they neared the edge of the water, both Brain and Aspen jumped off and held out their hands to help the trio off the boat. They walked them the few blocks to the staging area and showed them where to check in. Aspen reassured them once again that someone would help them get in touch with their families.

She turned to head back to the boats, but Brain caught her arm. "Time for a break, *chérie*."

"You're slipping," she said with a tired grin. "You've already used that one a few times before."

Brain shook his head. "Hey, I know a lot of languages,

but eventually I'm gonna run out. Besides, I thought all women loved French?"

Aspen shrugged. "I have to say that while I love hearing you call me darling in all the languages you know, I'm pretty partial to the English version...simply because of when you use it."

And just like that, Brain felt himself getting turned on. He mock frowned at her. "You can't say that sort of shit here, where I can't do anything about it."

"Oh...sorry," she trilled, not looking or sounding sorry in the least.

"Come on," he told her, grabbing her hand and pulling her toward a large tent that was filled with donated food and drinks from local businesses. "Time to refuel, then we can head back out."

He saw her frown.

Brain stopped and put his hands on her shoulders. "You have to take care of yourself first. You won't be any good to anyone else if you fall over from exhaustion or because you haven't kept yourself hydrated or fueled."

Aspen took a deep breath. "I know. I just...I keep hearing their cries for help in my head, and it makes me want to get right back out there."

"We won't take a long break. Just enough to get some calories and water into you. Okay?"

"Okay. Kane?"

"Yeah?"

"I'm glad I came."

He smiled at her. "Me too."

"You don't miss working with your team?" she asked.

He took her hand again and headed for the food tent once more. "Not like you're thinking. I mean, yeah, we work really well together, but this isn't exactly a war zone. During the rescues, we have to worry more about inanimate hazards, like being electrocuted or debris in the water, rather than the two-legged variety. Believe it or not, we can operate without being joined at the hip," he teased, happy to see Aspen return his smile.

"True. Besides, you have me," she sassed.

"I have you," Brain agreed solemnly.

Aspen glanced over at him, and he knew she heard the sincerity and admiration in his tone.

The food tent was surprisingly busy. There were military personnel as well as local civilians sitting and standing around, eating donated pizza, subs, and other snacks. Brain pulled Aspen into a line and they both filled plates with food. They stood off to the side of the tent, eating while standing up. Their clothes were soaked and, now that they weren't in the middle of a high-stakes rescue, Brain could feel the stress of the night pressing down on him. He wanted nothing more than to take a long, hot shower, change into dry clothes, and sleep for a day.

But rest would come after the job was done. The rain was supposed to continue through the night and then taper off...finally. The city needed the break, and the drains needed time to do their thing.

"You ready to go catch another boat?" Aspen asked after they'd both eaten most of the items on their plates.

"Ready as ever," Brain said. He caught Aspen's hand in his before she could head out of the tent. "Aspen?"

"Yeah?" she asked after turning toward him.

"If I forget to say it later, you're amazing."

She smiled. "Back at'cha, Kane."

Then, hand in hand, they headed into the rainy night to rescue some more stranded citizens.

* * *

Aspen was beyond tired. She felt like she did when she'd gone through the training to be attached to a Ranger unit. Every muscle in her body hurt and her wet clothes seemed to suck the energy right out of her. The darkness made everything look sinister and scary, and she wanted nothing more than to lie down on the ground and tell Kane to go on without her.

But she wasn't a quitter. And there were people out there who needed help. If she didn't go, who would? They'd have to wait that much longer for someone to get to them. There might be someone hurt, bleeding, or having a heart attack, who needed medical attention. She hated to think that someone could die just because she was a little tired. That was unacceptable.

So as exhausted as she was, she'd keep going for as long as her body would allow. And hearing Kane say he thought she was amazing did wonders for her energy levels. She could probably go on until she dropped over dead, as long as he was proud of her.

Working with him had been a pleasant surprise. She'd been nervous, because they'd never had to work side by side before. And it was *nothing* like working with some of the macho Rangers. He listened to her, didn't try to tell her how to do everything as if she were a child, and he deferred to her in almost all of the medical situations they'd encountered. He treated her as if she was a true member of their team, and it felt so good.

This was what she'd wanted when she'd signed up to be a combat medic. To work with others who didn't care about anything other than accomplishing their mission. Instead, she'd had to fight to be seen as competent by the very people she should've been able to trust implicitly.

"Fuck," Kane said under his breath as they approached the landing area for the boats.

Surprised at the venom in his tone, Aspen looked up. She'd been lost in her head and hadn't realized there was only one boat waiting at the moment. It was an aluminum fishing boat, probably donated to the rescue efforts by a local civilian.

And Derek was at the controls.

Kane's steps slowed, but Aspen clenched her teeth in determination. Yes, she hated Derek, but she could put aside their differences for the greater good. She just hoped he could too.

"Thank God!" Derek shouted, frantically waving at them to hurry. "During my last run, I heard about a pregnant woman who was in active labor. We need to get back there ASAP. Get in and let's go!"

Breaking into a jog, Aspen hurried for the boat. By the time she got to it, she was dragging Kane. "Come on," she urged, lifting her leg to step into the boat. But Kane held her back, not letting her get in.

"Why didn't you stop and get her when you first heard about her?" Kane asked Derek.

"Because the boat was already full. I had a woman with three kids, the youngest was two. They were freaked out, and there was no way we would've all fit in here if we'd gone back. Look, the longer you stand there, the worse her condition could be. She might have that baby and bleed out, or she could even lose it. You comin' or not?"

Aspen hadn't delivered a lot of babies, but she'd seen her share of bad outcomes when it came to giving birth. She remembered the baby she'd delivered while in Afghanistan, how good it had felt to hold the healthy infant in her hands. She couldn't let another woman suffer if she could do something to help her.

"Kane?" she questioned. She hoped he wasn't the kind of man to let his personal grievances get in the way of doing what was right.

She breathed out a sigh of relief when he gave her a brief nod and shifted his grip to her arm to help her step into the boat.

"How far away is she?" Kane asked.

"Not too far," Derek said, backing the boat up the second Kane's foot left dry land, not even giving him time to sit before he was revving the engine and flying away from the staging area.

Aspen frowned and held the edge of the boat for dear life. She understood the need for urgency, but none of the other drivers they'd had that night had driven as recklessly as it seemed Derek was.

"Slow down, man!" Kane yelled, obviously feeling the same unease as Aspen.

"Gotta get to her!" Derek shouted back.

The rain pelted Aspen's face, making it impossible for her to keep her eyes open. She ducked her head into her shoulder and squeezed her eyes shut. She held on to the side of the aluminum boat with all her might and prayed that they made it to the pregnant woman in one piece.

How long they drove, Aspen had no idea, but she'd

never been so happy to feel the boat slowing down. She lifted her head and looked around. She had no clue where they were; nothing looked familiar. There were no lights on anywhere. She could see the vague shape of townhouses all around them in the darkness, but the electricity had obviously gone out in this part of the city.

"We're almost there," Derek said. It was much easier to hear him, now that they weren't driving a million miles an hour. The rain still fell steadily, making it even harder to see.

"Keep an eye out, I don't know exactly which townhouse is hers. The other lady said she thought she was three or four units down from hers," Derek told them.

Which didn't exactly help, since Aspen didn't know where the original rescue had taken place. She was sitting toward the front of the boat, and Kane was more toward the middle. She glanced over her shoulder, noting Derek still sitting in the back next to the engine. Kane gave her a chin lift and a reassuring smile, which she appreciated.

Aspen turned back around and leaned forward, trying to see through the darkness, looking for debris in the fast-moving water, as well as any sign of the townhouse in question.

The boat rocked a bit, but Aspen ignored it, concentrating too hard on finding the pregnant woman in distress.

But she couldn't ignore the loud thud behind her—or the way the boat suddenly swayed back and forth alarmingly before a splash sounded.

Spinning around, she blinked in confusion.

Derek was standing in the back of the boat with an oar in his hand—and Kane was nowhere to be seen.

She heard something brush the boat and turned...only to see a body floating, facedown, quickly being washed away.

Aspen made a noise in the back of her throat and stared at Derek in disbelief.

"Hope his head is harder than it looks," he snarled. "He's not so tough *now*, is he?"

In a flash, Aspen realized that Derek had clobbered Kane upside the head with the oar—and she was probably next.

She could stay in the boat and fight Derek, or she could bail and save Kane.

It was an easy decision.

Taking a deep breath, Aspen threw herself to the left and over the side of the boat. The current immediately tugged at her, pulling her in the same direction she'd last seen Kane.

When her head popped up from the murky water, she heard Derek laughing. "Good luck getting back to base!" he called out, then he gunned the engine on the boat and zoomed away.

Knowing she should be outraged that Derek had left them in the middle of nowhere, Aspen couldn't waste energy on anything other than finding Kane. He was unconscious and likely only had seconds to live.

She swam as fast as she could with the current, hoping to catch up to Kane, and as luck would have it, crashed right into him as she frantically pinwheeled her arms. Grunting, she turned him over onto his back, which wasn't easy in the middle of the fast-moving water.

She couldn't touch the ground beneath her and

couldn't see anywhere to drag Kane's unconscious body to get traction, in case she needed to do CPR.

Frantically, she put one hand on his chest to try to feel for movement, and she almost panicked when she couldn't detect that he was breathing.

Knowing nothing about this was ideal, she turned his head, covered his lips with hers, and blew.

Then she did it again, and again.

She had to get him breathing!

She could feel his heart now, sluggishly beating under her hand, but if she had to do chest compressions, they were screwed.

After one more long rescue breath, Kane gagged. Water spewed out of his mouth, and as gross as it was, Aspen was almost delirious with joy.

"That's it...throw it all up. Get it out," she told him.

She hoped he'd open his eyes and tell her that he was all right, but he never did.

Using her legs to keep them afloat, Aspen looked around for a direction she could go to get them out of the water. She might've gotten Kane breathing again, but he wasn't out of trouble, far from it. She could barely make out a dark splotch high on his forehead, and she knew he was bleeding.

"Damn you, Derek," she hissed as she put her arm around Kane's chest and began to swim sideways. She didn't know where the current would take them, and the last thing she wanted was to end up in a river and headed out to the gulf.

She was relieved to see the townhouses were relatively nearby now. They were all dark, but maybe she could get to one and break inside.

Her body trembling with exertion and adrenaline, Aspen used one arm and her legs to propel them in the direction of the closest building. Hoping she didn't get turned around in the current.

She almost cried when she saw a townhouse dead ahead.

It took ten more minutes of fighting the current, but she finally managed to get to the steps leading up to the house at the end of the row. There was a wrought-iron rail along either side of the stairs, and she used it to help pull herself and Kane onto the steps. They were fully submerged, but the landing had only a couple inches of water. Using all her strength, Aspen hauled Kane's dead weight up to it. She straddled his head and reached up for the doorknob, praying that maybe, just maybe, it would be unlocked. But of course it wasn't.

Since she didn't fit on the small landing with Kane, she eased herself down on the first step, the water lapping at her hips.

Leaning over Kane, she tried to feel his head where she'd seen the blood.

She felt the warm sensation immediately, and knew the wound was still bleeding. Putting her hand over his head, she could literally feel the way his skin had split open when Derek had hit him.

Anger rose within her again. Hot and hard.

Derek had lied to them from the start. There was no pregnant woman. No one in trouble. She didn't know if he'd thought of the scheme right there on the spot, when he'd seen her and Kane coming toward him, or if he'd planned to hurt them from the second he knew they'd all be together in Houston.

It was shocking to realize he'd gone so far off the deep end. What other reason could there be? He'd tried to *murder* them! How had a decorated and respected Army Ranger fallen so low? And why? They hadn't even dated very long! Two measly dates. Why had he gotten so enraged just because she didn't want to see him anymore?

Nothing about the situation made sense...and now Kane was lying unconscious and bleeding in the middle of the night, miles away from anyone.

Aspen didn't have any of her medical supplies, they were both soaking wet, and the water contained who knew *what* kind of contaminants.

"Kane?" she semi-yelled, hoping he'd be able to hear her. "I need you to wake up now. We're in deep shit."

She waited, but there was no movement from the man she loved with all her heart. She pressed harder on his head wound, hoping like hell she'd be able to slow the bleeding. She put her free hand on the side of Kane's neck, where she could feel his pulse throbbing under the vulnerable skin there. Then she lay her head on his chest, listening to his heart.

There was absolutely nothing she could do right then but hope and pray they'd be missed, and someone would come looking for them. It was a long shot, as she had no idea how far Derek had driven them from the staging area, but surely one of Kane's team would eventually wonder where he was.

She had to cling to that hope—because the alternative was unthinkable.

Feeling overwhelmed, and more frightened than she'd been in her life, Aspen closed her eyes. The scent of oil and sewage was all around her, and she didn't even want to think about what was in the water she was sitting in. At least she'd gotten Kane out of it.

"Wake up, Kane," she whispered. "You have to wake up."

But he didn't even twitch.

CHAPTER SIXTEEN

"There's been an accident!" one of the Coasties shouted as he ran past Trigger and the rest of the Deltas on his way to where the boats had parked, a couple blocks from the staging area.

Without hesitation, all six men followed the man from the Coast Guard.

As they ran, Trigger shouted to Lefty, "Where's Brain?"

"Don't know. Haven't seen him in hours," Lefty returned.

Trigger shouted to the others, "Anyone seen Brain and Aspen lately?"

No one had.

Trigger mentally swore. It was possible they were still out on another boat, rescuing people, but throughout the night, they'd all managed to touch base here and there, even if it was in passing.

But if no one had seen or heard from either of them in hours, something was wrong. Trigger knew it without question. He'd never doubted his sixth senses before, and wasn't about to start now.

"What happened?" Doc asked one of the men rushing to get the boats ready to head out to wherever the accident had occurred.

"I don't know the details, but a boat hit a downed power line, and I guess because of the gas in the tank, there was an explosion."

Trigger winced.

"Who was onboard?" Grover barked out.

"No one knows. The boat was outside our search parameters, and we're still trying to account for all the vessels under our command," the Coastie said distractedly. "We could use your help if you're willing," he added.

Without hesitation, the six Deltas jumped into the two boats heading out to check on the situation.

Trigger, Lefty, and Oz were in one, with Doc, Grover, and Lucky in the other. After a very long, dark night, the sun was finally beginning to inch over the horizon. Everywhere Trigger looked was devastation. Trees down, debris in the streets, and cars abandoned and floating as far as he could see.

The water was receding, but not quickly enough. A small benefit to the rescue boats, as it meant they could get to the area where the explosion was reported.

Trigger couldn't shake the horrible feeling that Brain and Aspen were involved. There was no reason for them not to have been seen in hours, and the only conclusion he could come to was that they were somehow in the boat that had exploded.

He felt sick inside. The entire team knew the time might come when they lost a man on a dangerous mission overseas, but to die here in the States because of a freak accident was too awful to think about.

Not to mention...Brain hadn't had his team at his back. That ate at Trigger more than anything else. They'd always had each other's backs, and the thought of his friend hurt and dying alone was almost more than he could bear.

Then Trigger remembered that Brain wasn't alone. He had Aspen.

The farther they got from the staging area, the poorer the area became. This wasn't a good part of town on the best of days, but as the water receded, Trigger knew looting would break out and desperate citizens would do whatever it took to survive, including possibly attacking them on their boats for whatever they could get...water, food, first-aid supplies.

The boats slowed as they neared the area where reports of an explosion were heard. Trigger, Lefty, and Oz leaned forward, all their attention on searching for anything out of the ordinary.

Within a minute, Grover shouted from the other boat and pointed off to the right. Both boats immediately turned in that direction.

Trigger winced as they came upon an aluminum boat spinning in circles in a whirlpool. The back end had been blown off the boat, and there was no sign of the motor...or of anyone who might've been inside.

"Shit! Look up," the Coastie driving Trigger's boat said in a horrified tone.

In tandem, Trigger, Lefty, and Oz looked into the trees above their heads. Without the flooding, the tops of the trees would've normally stood at least thirty feet above ground, but because of the water level, they were almost right under the lowest leaves.

And stuck in the tree branches was a leg. There was a boot on the foot, but the rest of the body wasn't attached to the limb.

Trigger looked left, then right, and used his chin to point out what he was seeing. "There's the rest of him."

A torso was draped over another thick branch, with an arm on another.

"That's Spence," Oz said quietly.

Trigger took a second look. "*Fuck*," he swore.

The other boat pulled up alongside, and Lucky said, "Isn't that Sergeant Spence?"

"Yeah," Trigger said solemnly.

"What happened?" Doc asked.

"If I had to guess, I'd say he caught a downed line with his motor. Probably spun the boat around and hit another live wire. The sparks probably caught the gas tank on fire and blew," Lucky suggested.

Trigger's stomach rolled. He didn't like the man, but his death had certainly been gruesome.

"Hey, look!" Lefty shouted, pointing toward the still-spinning boat. Even though half of it was missing, it hadn't completely sunk, the swirling of the water keeping it afloat.

Trigger glanced over—and his adrenaline spiked.

At the front of the boat, wedged under a seat, was a black bag with a red cross.

Aspen's medical bag. He'd recognize it anywhere. She'd told the team once that she'd gone out and bought her own bag because the Army-issued ones were all too big for her frame, and she preferred a more comfortable and reliable bag to hold her supplies.

And if Aspen had been in the boat, so had Brain.

But where were they now?

"Spread out!" Trigger barked, immediately looking around to see if he could spot any sign of his teammate and his woman.

"That's Aspen's bag," Lucky said unnecessarily.

"I know. They were in that boat," Trigger said.

"If they were in there when the back blew off, they might've survived," Doc added.

"Maybe," Trigger said, but another thought came to him. He pulled out his walkie-talkie and asked to speak with the major in charge of organizing the rescue effort from the staging area.

As the Coastie drove the boat slowly around the area where they'd found Spence's body, searching for Brain and Aspen, Trigger had a quick conversation with the major. When he put down his radio, his lips pressed together grimly.

"What?" Oz asked.

"No one was authorized to come out this far, as we already knew. In fact, it was strictly prohibited."

"What were they doing out here then?" Lefty asked.

"The major also told me he's got a local on his hands who's not happy about his boat being stolen. He'd brought it in to assist in the rescues, said he left it to take a piss, and when he came back, it was gone."

"You thinkin' what I'm thinkin'?" Oz asked.

"If you're thinkin' Spence decided this was the perfect time and place to deal with his bullshit juvenile anger toward Aspen, and possibly Brain as well, then yeah."

"Fuck," Lefty swore. "So where are they?"

"Don't know. But we need to find them. *Now*," Trigger said.

He whistled at the other boat, and when it came close, he explained his suspicions to his teammates.

"We should report back to base," the Coastie driving the other boat said.

"Negative," Grover growled. "We'll radio back the coordinates of Spence's body, but we aren't leaving until we find our teammate."

The driver blinked in surprise but immediately nodded.

"They could be almost anywhere," Trigger said. "Lucky, you guys go down the next street over. We'll head down this one. We stay near each other; don't go driving off. This isn't the best part of town to be alone in. Got it?"

"Got it," everyone agreed.

"They're around here somewhere," Trigger mumbled as they began their search pattern.

"Brain's a tough son-of-a-bitch," Lefty agreed.

"And there's no way he'd let anything happen to Aspen," Oz added.

Trigger didn't want to think about what Spence might've done to his friend and Aspen. All sorts of worst-case scenarios ran through his head, but he refused to give them any more than a passing thought. Brain was counting on his team to keep a level head and find them. And that's what they were going to do.

* * *

Aspen shivered on the step she was still sitting on. The

water had receded enough that she was no longer waist deep in the foul-smelling stuff, but the roads were still flooded, and she and Kane weren't going anywhere. She'd thought about trying to break a window to get inside the dilapidated house, but wasn't willing to leave Kane to do so.

She'd heard an explosion hours earlier, when it was still dark, but no one had come to investigate as far as she could tell. Aspen thought she'd heard noises closer by a few times, but after yelling for help until she was hoarse, no one had appeared.

Now the sun had risen, giving the area an unearthly feel. Everywhere she looked was water. There were no signs of any people, only a few birds chirping merrily in the trees and the sound of water rushing by in the street.

Kane hadn't woken up yet either, which was scaring the shit out of Aspen. He'd stirred a few times but hadn't said anything. It was obvious he had a head injury, most certainly a concussion, but maybe something worse. Without him being awake to talk to her, she couldn't be sure.

She'd fallen asleep with her head on his chest once, but the nightmares had come immediately, waking her up and keeping her from even attempting to get any rest after that.

She was terrified Kane would die. She'd never forgive herself if that happened, because it was *her* fault he was lying so still under her. If she hadn't approached him in the bar, Derek wouldn't even have known he existed.

But then again, she wouldn't have fallen in love either.

Just when Aspen was coming to terms with the fact

that she was going to have to leave Kane and swim somewhere to find help, she thought she heard something.

Tilting her head to the side, she held her breath and listened...

A boat motor!

She'd know that sound anywhere after spending so much time on them the night before.

She wanted to stand up and scream for help, but she knew they'd never be able to hear her over the motor. She had to pray they'd turn down the street she was on so she could get their attention.

"Please, please, please," she whispered. "Kane, help's coming. Hang on just a little longer," she told him. She'd been talking to him for the last couple hours, believing that even though he was unconscious, a part of him could still hear her.

When the motor got louder, Aspen slowly stood. She wobbled a bit and grabbed onto the wrought-iron railing to keep herself from falling face first into the murky water a few steps down.

She fumbled with the buttons on her BDU top. She had to get it off to use it to flag down the boat. They'd never see her otherwise. Her fingers shook with adrenaline and cold. She'd been submersed in the chilly flood waters for hours.

She shrugged the camouflage jacket off just as she saw the boat turn down the street.

Holding onto the railing with one hand, she waved the jacket over her head with the other. "Here! Over here!" she cried out, her voice sounding weak to her own ears.

Taking a deep breath, she screamed as loud as she could. *"Helllllllp!"*

Miraculously, the boat picked up speed and came hurtling toward them. For just a second, Aspen thought they were going to plow right into the steps, but when it got close, it slowed, sending a wave crashing onto the step she was standing on.

The sight of Trigger, Lefty, and Oz at the front of the boat made her knees go weak.

She collapsed back onto the step and reached for Kane. "They found us," she told him. "Your team found us! Just keep hanging on. We'll get you some help and you'll be fine."

Then Trigger was there. Crouching next to her on the step. He put his oh-so-warm hand on her cheek and turned her to look at him. "Are you hurt?"

She shook her head frantically. "No, but Kane is! Derek said there was a pregnant woman out here who needed help, and we were at the front of the boat looking for any sign of her townhouse when he swung an oar at Kane and knocked him in the head. He fell overboard and was face-down for I don't know how long. He wasn't breathing, and I gave him rescue breaths. I managed to get him here, but he hasn't woken up. I'm so scared something's seriously wrong, Trigger!" Aspen knew her words were slurred, and she was talking way too fast, but she had to let someone know what happened, especially when Derek was still on the loose.

"Take a deep breath, Aspen," Trigger ordered.

She did.

"Another."

After the second, she felt a bit better.

"Are *you* hurt?" Trigger asked again.

"No. Cold, tired, and scared to death, but not hurt.

The second I realized what Derek had done, I bailed out of the boat. I wanted to get to Kane, but I also didn't want Derek to get his hands on me. He's gonna make up a story to spin this," she warned Trigger. "But I'm not lying! He ambushed Kane."

"I believe you, but Derek's—"

Aspen interrupted him as she thought of something else. "And Kane knew something was up," she continued, her voice filled with anguish. "He was hesitant to get in the boat with him, but I didn't give him a choice—"

"Derek's dead," Trigger said bluntly. Then he gently moved her out of the way as Lefty and Oz stepped out of the boat and came toward them. They lifted Kane as if he weighed no more than a child, carrying him to the boat.

Aspen watched worriedly...until Trigger's words sank in. "*What?* How?"

"I'm not exactly sure, but it looks like he ran over a live wire. It got tangled in the boat and it blew."

"Are you sure he's dead?" Aspen asked.

"I'm sure. His torso was dangling over one tree branch, his arm over another, and his leg was hanging from a third. He's dead, sweetheart."

Aspen wanted to feel bad. At one time, she'd actually liked Derek. But after what he'd said to her the other day, and especially after what he'd done a few hours ago...she couldn't feel anything but relief that they didn't have to worry about him retaliating against them ever again.

She nodded at Trigger and tried to step into the water to get to the boat, but once again, her body betrayed her. She staggered and would've gone down if Trigger hadn't picked her up. One arm went behind her back and the other under her knees.

"I've got you," he said as he carried her to the boat. Lefty and Oz reached for her and easily got her settled in the bottom of the inflatable boat next to Kane. She put her hand on his chest, where it had been most of the last few hours, and closed her eyes in relief when she felt his heart beating. She leaned over him, listening as Lefty talked to the rest of the team via walkie-talkie. Telling them they'd found Kane and her, and requesting they meet up at the next street over.

"We're safe," she told Kane. "Trigger found us. You can wake up now."

But he didn't.

Someone draped an emergency warming blanket across her shoulders, and another over Kane, but she didn't move her hand, keeping her eyes on his face. She prayed for a flicker of his eyelids or any movement of his lips to indicate that he'd heard her, but he stayed still and silent in the bottom of the boat.

"We need an ambulance to meet us at the boat launch," Trigger told someone over the radio. "We've got a man down."

Closing her eyes, Aspen rested her head on Kane's chest once more and let herself relax for the first time in hours. The men surrounding her might not be her team, but they were her friends. They'd take care of Kane. They'd make sure he didn't die.

Aspen didn't know what she'd do if he didn't make it.

He had to be all right. He just had to.

CHAPTER SEVENTEEN

Aspen sat in Kane's hospital room and stared blankly ahead of her. When they'd gotten back to the boat launch at the staging area, an ambulance had been waiting. She'd refused to leave Kane's side, and reluctantly, the paramedics had let her accompany them.

Trigger and the rest of the team had somehow beat them to the hospital and were waiting for her when Kane had been wheeled away. She'd tried to follow, but Grover and Oz held her back.

When she began to fight them, Lefty had stepped in, telling her to calm down.

"He's in good hands, Aspen. You have to let him go."

She'd shaken her head, frantic. "No. I can't!"

"It's time to take care of yourself," Lefty said sternly.

"I'm fine," she'd insisted.

"You aren't. You're soaked to the bone. You're shaking like a leaf, and I'm guessing weak as hell. You know as well as I do that Brain would be pissed if we didn't take care of you. At least let one of the nurses take your vitals. Check

299

you over. As soon as they know something about Brain, they'll tell us."

His words somehow penetrated the fog of panic that had taken over. Aspen grabbed his wrists and stared into his eyes. "Is he going to be all right?"

"Yes."

There was no hesitation in Lefty's answer.

"Brain's got a hard head. And he's stubborn. And he knows he's got you waiting for him. He'll be fine."

Taking a deep breath, Aspen had finally agreed to let someone check her out. She'd been led to a room and given a pair of scrubs to change into. She didn't have any underwear, but that didn't matter. The scrubs were warm, and it felt heavenly not to have something wet against her skin. She'd lain down on the bed in the room, and Grover had come in to keep her company while she'd waited for the nurse.

She must've fallen asleep, because when she woke up, it was Lucky sitting in the room with her. He'd immediately called for the nurse, refused to tell Aspen how much time had passed, and stepped out while the nurse did her thing.

After she was deemed to be suffering from exhaustion and exposure, and nothing more serious, Trigger had shown up and taken her to sit in Kane's room, where she was now.

The doctors weren't sure what the extent of the damage to his head was, as Kane hadn't woken up yet. But they'd done an X-ray of his lungs and they were clear. He had the beginnings of an infection, probably from whatever had been in the water that got into his bloodstream from the cut on his head, and a dozen stitches to close the gash where Derek had hit him, but otherwise his vitals looked good.

Even with the nap she'd gotten, Aspen was exhausted. She felt like she was a hundred and four years old. She knew she should eat, but nothing appealed.

"The authorities went back out and recovered Spence's body," Trigger told her.

Aspen merely nodded.

"It'll be up to you to tell your major and the other authorities what happened."

"Oh, I'm going to," she said with determination. "It's one thing for Derek to treat me like shit because I'm a woman; it's another thing altogether to attempt to *murder* someone. I'm going to do whatever it takes to make sure I get justice for Kane."

"He's gonna be all right," Trigger told her.

"I hope so..."

"He *is*," Trigger insisted. "He's got a damn hard head and we've been through situations worse than this."

Aspen nodded. "I just... He's so still. I hate that. The Kane I know is always moving. Sometimes it's subtle, but even when we're just sitting on the couch, his fingers are stroking the back of my hand or his foot is tapping the floor. I hate seeing him like this."

"I know. I never really took notice of it before, but you're right. Have faith in the doctors...and Brain himself. And—it has to be said—you're pretty damn amazing. We all thought so after seeing you in action in combat, but seeing how fiercely you protected Brain...well...thank you."

"You don't have to thank me for that," Aspen told him. "He means everything to me." Then she sighed and stared off into space and muttered, "I swear to God, all this better not be for nothing."

"What do you mean?" Trigger asked. "All what?"

"All the hell I've been through to help pave the way for women in combat medics," she said tiredly. "I worked my ass off to be the best medic I could be, Trigger, and what did I get in return? Hatred because of my gender. Harassment. I had to prove myself over and over, and even after I'd been in the job for years, I still got passed over for men who had way less experience than me. Someday, I hope women can do whatever job they want for our country and be respected for it."

"I hope so too," Trigger said. "And for what it's worth... you impressed the hell out of a lot of people today. Even though they didn't know what happened out there, they know you put your own life at risk to save Brain. They knew he wasn't breathing, and that you gave him rescue breaths until he was again. They know you dragged him through the floodwaters to a relatively safe place, and that you never left his side. I have no doubt that one day, women will stand shoulder to shoulder with their male counterparts on the battlefield and no one will even think twice about it."

"I hope so," she whispered. "I'm tired, Trigger. So fucking tired of it all."

"Come here," Trigger said, putting an arm around her shoulders and pulling her into him. It was an awkward embrace, since they were both sitting on separate chairs, but Aspen put her head on his shoulder and relaxed. She didn't close her eyes; she kept her gaze on Kane, willing him to wake up and tell everyone he was perfectly fine and start bitching about getting the hell out of the hospital.

Time went by. Trigger left and Oz took his place. Then Grover came in. But Aspen didn't move. She didn't leave to eat something, as the guys encouraged, and she didn't leave to take a shower. She was going to sit right where she was until Kane opened his eyes and she knew for certain he was going to be all right.

It was a couple hours later when Aspen first saw his eyelids twitching.

Lucky was sitting with her, and she scared him to death when she leaped up and rushed to Kane's side.

She hovered over him, putting a hand on Kane's cheek and brushing her thumb back and forth. "Kane? That's it, open your eyes. I'm here. You're safe. We're okay. You're in the hospital, and I know it smells funny, but you need to open your eyes for me."

She watched as his lids lifted but then slammed shut.

"Lucky, turn off the lights," Aspen ordered, not taking her hands from the man she loved. "Try again, that's it."

Slowly, ever so slowly, Kane's eyes opened...and she was staring into his beautiful eyes. "Hi," she whispered.

Kane's brows furrowed. "Aspen?"

"Yeah, it's me."

"My head hurts," he said in a low, scratchy voice.

"I know, and I'm sorry."

"Please move aside," the nurse said brusquely, putting a hand on Aspen's shoulder, gently pushing her away from Kane.

Aspen was reluctant to move, but when Lucky took her arm, she let him steer her to the edge of the room. A doctor rushed in next and asked everyone to leave while he looked over Kane.

Outside the room, Aspen paced impatiently with the rest of Kane's team.

"How can you all look so calm?" she asked with irritation.

"Because he's gonna be fine," Doc told her.

"You don't know that," she grumbled.

"He knew who you were," Lucky said with a smile. "He'll be fine."

That was true, and Aspen relaxed. She'd previously worried that he might've gotten his brain so scrambled, he'd experience amnesia. It happened all the time, but she was glad that didn't seem to be the case.

After ten minutes, the doctor stuck his head out the door. "Is one of you Trigger?"

"That's me," Trigger told him.

"Can you please come in?"

Aspen took a step forward. *She* wanted to see Kane.

"Just a little bit longer, Aspen. Trust me," Trigger told her.

She huffed out a breath, but nodded.

Ten more long minutes passed, and just when Aspen didn't think she'd be able to wait another second, the doctor, nurse, and Trigger reappeared. The staff headed down the hall, but Trigger remained in front of the door to Kane's room.

"Well? What'd they say?" Lefty asked.

Trigger sighed. "Brain's gonna be okay. He has a concussion, and the beginnings of pneumonia. The doc thinks it's because not all of the water got out of his lungs after he started breathing again. But the infection should clear up soon enough because they're pumping him full of antibiotics."

"Can we go in?" Aspen asked impatiently. She couldn't wait to hear Kane's voice again. To see for herself that he really was all right.

"He doesn't want to see anyone," Trigger said quietly.

Aspen stared at him in confusion. "He doesn't want to see you guys? Why not?"

"He doesn't want to see *any* of us," Trigger clarified. "Not even you, sweetheart."

Her adrenaline spiked even as her stomach bottomed out. "Why not? What's wrong?"

"He's got some memory loss, and he isn't feeling very steady about it."

Aspen froze. "What? What does that mean? He said my name. He remembers me!"

"He does," Trigger agreed. "And he knows the rest of us too. He knows that he's Delta, and can recall most of his childhood. But he hasn't been able to recall one word of the languages he's learned over the years."

Aspen blinked. "And?"

"And what?"

"And what else can't he remember?"

"That's it, so far. He knows everything that happened out there, but he's taking the fact that he's lost the ability to speak all those languages pretty hard."

Aspen didn't understand. "I don't care how many languages he speaks," she said. "I'm going in." She tried to push Trigger to the side and slip by him, but the other man stood firm.

"No. He needs time, Aspen," Trigger said.

"He needs *me*," she countered.

"Let her in," Grover said quietly from behind her.

"Grover—" Trigger started, but Lucky took his arm

and pulled him aside, letting Aspen push past him and into the room.

"This is a mistake," Trigger told his team. "He's *not* in a good frame of mind."

Aspen heard the guys crowd into the room behind her, but she only had eyes for Kane. He was sitting up in bed with a few pillows behind him, staring out the window.

"Hey," she said lightly. "You look a lot better than you did a few hours ago," she teased.

But when Kane turned to look at her...she saw none of the man she'd grown to love in his eyes. They were cold and hard, and it was all she could do not to take a step back.

"I told Trigger I didn't want to see you."

Aspen winced. That hurt. Trigger had claimed he didn't want to see *anyone*, not her specifically. "I needed to make sure you were all right."

"I'm fine," he said in a monotone. "You've seen, now you can go."

Aspen frowned. "Kane, what's wrong?"

He was silent for a beat. Then, "I think it's best if we gave each other some space."

The ache his words caused was so painful, Aspen brought a hand up to her chest to make sure she didn't have a knife sticking out of her heart. "What?" she whispered.

"Things have moved really fast between us. I think we need to slow down."

Her mind was spinning, and she couldn't figure out why he was saying these things. She knew sometimes people with head wounds had personality changes, but most of the time the change was temporary. "Okay, I'll head back to the tent city and visit tomorrow."

Kane slowly shook his head. "Don't. The last thing I need is another ex-boyfriend of yours getting the wrong idea and deciding if he can't have you, no one can. I need some *space*, Aspen."

His words were intentionally upsetting. While she was still reeling from the abrupt change of heart on his side, she was also a little pissed. "You know I don't have any other exes."

"Do I?" he asked.

Okay, *that* was ridiculous. "So...what? This is it?"

Kane shrugged.

Fighting tears, refusing to let him see how much he'd wounded her, Aspen nodded. "I'm glad you're all right," she said, her throat tight. "I guess I'll see you around."

She waited a breathless moment for him to say he'd been wrong, that he needed her, and for him to thank her for saving his life. But he just sat on the bed like a statue and stared at her with blank eyes. She might as well have been a stranger to him at that moment.

Aspen wanted to believe it was because he didn't remember the last week they'd spent together. How they'd made slow, sweet love...but that wasn't it.

He remembered. He just didn't care.

Derek trying to kill him had changed things. Maybe for good.

Feeling as if she'd lost something precious that she'd never find again, Aspen nodded once again and blindly turned for the door. The other guys stepped back, clearing the way for her, but no one tried to stop her.

She walked into the hallway and hesitated, not sure

which way to go. She had no idea which direction the waiting room was, or how to get out of the building. And she *had* to get out of there. Get back to the staging area and stay busy. Anything to not think about what had just happened.

* * *

Brain sat on his bed and stared straight ahead. He tried to think of the word for water in Kurdish, but it wouldn't come to him. He tried Italian. Then French.

Nothing. The foreign words that had lived inside his brain for so long had disappeared. They'd been his constant companion for almost his entire life. And now they were gone.

"What the fuck did you just do?" Trigger growled.

Not surprised by the venom in his friend's voice, Brain turned to look at him. "It was for the best," he said quietly.

"For who?" Trigger asked.

"Her," Brain said immediately.

"That's such bullshit, and you know it," Lefty added. "Aspen saved your *life*."

"And I'm thankful. But then again, she was the reason I was lying facedown in floodwater unconscious in the first place, wasn't she?" The words spilled out without thought, and Brain regretted them the moment they were out.

"What the *fuck*?" Oz exclaimed.

"Are you seriously that stupid?" Lucky asked.

"The doc was wrong. He's obviously got brain damage," Grover said with a shake of his head.

"The second she realized what happened, Aspen threw

herself overboard after you," Lefty seethed. "Into the fucking floodwaters that were full of sewage and live electrical wires. You weren't breathing, and she gave you rescue breaths until you started breathing on your own again! Then she hauled you who the hell knows how far to the closest available flat surface. *Then* she sat in those same floodwaters looking after your ass for hours until we found you.

"She was willing to fight the nurses for the right to stay by your side, but we convinced her to get looked over first. She fell asleep the second she lay down, her body just shutting down, but when she woke up, she barely tolerated anyone checking on her wellbeing before she was in here, waiting for you to wake up. She hasn't eaten. She hasn't slept again. She hasn't showered. Her first concern was *you*. Then you have the *nerve* to tell her you need some fucking space? What the hell's wrong with you?"

Brain's heart hurt at hearing everything that Aspen had been through. He'd known she was strong before, but hearing about all she'd done—for *him*—made him realize he hadn't really had a clue before. He remembered her saying that she loved him, and the pain in his heart increased tenfold. "I'm not the man she used to know."

"*God*, you're a dumbass!" Oz railed.

"I know, that's why I'm freeing her!" Brain shouted.

The room was silent after his outburst.

Then Grover bit out, "Explain."

He sighed, suddenly exhausted. "I'm the brain. The guy the team relies on to talk to locals when we're on a mission. I can't do that anymore."

"Seriously?" Doc asked when he stopped talking. "You're being ridiculous!"

Brain pressed his lips together. How could he explain how he was feeling? He loved these guys like they were his brothers, but they would never understand. He felt as if a part of his brain was missing. He felt like half the man he used to be, and he didn't want to bring Aspen down into the depths of despair he was currently feeling.

"First, that makes no fucking sense," Lucky bit out. "Yes, you're smart. And I'm not saying that you knowing all those languages didn't come in handy, but it's not as if we're helpless without you. Basically, you're telling us the only reason our missions succeeded was because you were able to chat with the locals."

Brain shrugged.

"Conceited asshole," Oz muttered.

"Everyone calm the fuck down," Trigger said, holding his hands up. "Shit, we're gonna get in so much trouble. The doctor said not to agitate him, and we've certainly fucking failed in that regard." He turned to Brain. "First of all, did you not hear the doctor when he said there's a chance the loss of those languages isn't permanent? Your brain took a hell of a hit. It's bruised and swollen. When you have time to rest, there's a chance the languages will come back."

Brain shrugged. "I'm a skeptic. What can I say?"

"You're an asshole," Lefty said under his breath.

"Second," Trigger went on, ignoring his teammate's snarky comment, "Aspen would never pity you or love you less if you could only speak English for the rest of your life. You're doing her a disservice by even thinking she'd be that much of a bitch."

Brain knew his friend was right, but he kept his mouth shut.

"And third, throwing Derek in her face wasn't cool," Trigger said quietly. "And you know it. You were desperate to get her to leave, and you said the one thing you knew would accomplish that by bringing up her ex. You weren't conscious, man; you didn't see her. Lefty was right. She was frantic, fighting anyone who dared get between her and the man she loved."

Brain closed his eyes. He thought about how Aspen looked when he'd first opened his eyes. She was exhausted. She had dark circles under her eyes and her hair was in tangles around her head. She was wearing a pair of scrubs that were too big, and he could still see the horror of their ordeal in every line of her face. As well as the worry for *him*.

And what had he done? Had he taken her in his arms and told her everything would be all right? No. He'd pushed her away.

He hadn't lain a hand on her, but he might as well have punched her in the face.

"He's finally getting it," Grover said.

Brain wanted to call out for Aspen. Tell her to come back, that he hadn't meant anything he'd said...but he knew it was too late. She was long gone. Probably already on her way back to the staging area.

He felt a hand on his shoulder, and Brain opened his eyes.

"She loves you. She'll forgive you," Trigger said.

"She's stubborn," Brain whispered.

"So are you," Lefty said from next to Trigger.

"I'm scared," Brain said softly. He wouldn't admit that to anyone but the six men standing around his hospital bed. "I don't know how to be anyone but the brain."

"How about you just be Kane for a while?" Oz said quietly.

"Aspen doesn't love you because you can speak two dozen languages," Grover said. "She loves you because you're you."

"Just like we do," Lucky added. "You're not on this team because you can speak Farsi. You're on this team because you've earned it. Because you're the best of the best. I don't care how many languages you can swear in when we're on patrol. I only care about how accurate your aim is and that you have my back."

"Thinking your only contribution to this team is your brain is shortsighted and ridiculous," Trigger added. "You're Kane Temple, and you're a fucking Delta Force soldier. Period. Got it?"

"Got it," Brain said, his voice wavering a bit.

"Now, while you're lying there and relaxing your noggin so you can get out of this hospital, you'd better be thinking of ways to apologize to Aspen," Lefty said.

Brain nodded. He still wasn't one hundred percent positive Aspen wasn't better off without him, but he had a knot in his stomach that told him he'd fucked up. Huge. He felt hollow inside, knowing she wasn't waiting nearby. Knowing he couldn't just pick up the phone and call her to hear her voice.

"Get better, man," Oz said, squeezing his calf before he turned and headed for the door.

"See you soon," Grover said as he followed Oz.

The other guys each said their goodbyes, and when Trigger turned to leave as well, Brain stopped him. "Trigger?"

"Yeah?"

"Will you keep an eye on her? You know how unruly those tent cities can get."

"Of course. We all will. Can I give you some more advice?"

Brain nodded.

"Don't wait too long to get your head together. Aspen doesn't give a flying fuck about how smart you are or aren't. She's going to be getting out of the Army soon, and she could get a job in any city in the country. She's gonna need a damn good reason to stick around the Killeen area."

The thought of Aspen leaving made the knot in his belly grow exponentially. Brain actually felt nauseous as a result. Or maybe it was because of the pounding in his head. He wasn't sure. "Maybe Gillian can check on her too?"

"That's a given. And you're going to have to put up with her and Kinley, and probably Devyn too, coming over and telling you what an idiot you are."

That made Brain smile. "They like Aspen that much?"

"You know they do. She's one of the crew now," Trigger said. "She and Gillian text each other all the time."

Brain loved that for Aspen.

"I'm going now. I'll come back tomorrow morning to check on you."

"Thanks. Trigger?"

"Yeah?"

"What happened to Derek?"

Trigger was silent for a moment. Then he said, "Karma. That's what happened. He ran over a live wire and blew himself up."

"Seriously?"

"Yup."

"Good riddance."

"Exactly. Get some sleep, your head will feel better when you wake up later."

"How'd you know my head was hurting?" Brain asked.

"Because I know you," Trigger said simply, then he turned and left the room, shutting off the light closest to the door on his way out.

The sudden darkness felt heavenly, and Brain lowered the bed until he was lying down once again. He felt like shit, his head hurt like hell, and the damn emptiness in his brain was driving him crazy.

But underneath it all was the knowledge that he'd hurt the one person in the world who he knew without a doubt would do anything for him.

"I'm sorry," he whispered before falling into a deep healing sleep.

CHAPTER EIGHTEEN

One week.

Seven long days. That's how long it had been since Brain had seen or talked to Aspen. He'd been held in the hospital for four days because of an infection and concern over the swelling of his brain. When he'd gotten back to his house, he'd had a constant stream of guests to look after him...but not the one person he most wanted to see.

He'd thought about calling her, but didn't want to risk her hanging up on him before he could say what he needed to. He couldn't just drive himself to her apartment because he hadn't been cleared to get behind the wheel of a car until today.

But what he did have was a lot of time to think.

Think about what happened down in Houston with Spence. How he'd clearly snapped.

Brain hadn't wanted to get into the boat, but he'd done it anyway. It had been stupid to put his back to the man, but he literally had no clue Spence would've tried to fucking *kill* him.

He'd felt some kind of sixth sense and turned at the last second, only to find the oar coming right at him. Brain hadn't had time to duck, and he didn't remember actually getting hit. He'd been immediately knocked unconscious and didn't recall anything until he'd woken up in the hospital.

But his friends had been happy to give him all the gory details. He knew he'd been floating facedown in the flood-waters when Aspen had jumped in after him. Brain ached to see her. To apologize. To beg her for forgiveness. But he'd been biding his time, hoping to be one hundred percent better before he went to her. The last thing he wanted was to blurt out more bullshit and ruin his chances of winning her back.

Brain had no idea if she would even take him back, but he was going to do everything in his power to convince her that he'd been an idiot, and that he loved her.

And today was the day.

The memorial for Spence was being held this morning. Under any other circumstance, Brain wouldn't have gone anywhere near the chapel. The man had tried to kill him, after all. But Grover had told him Aspen was going to attend. He had no idea why she'd want to go, but he did want to support her however he could.

He'd finally been given approval by the post doctor to drive, so after Brain put on his dress green uniform and the sunglasses he wore because of the constant headache he still had, he climbed into his Challenger and headed for the base chapel.

The parking lot was full, but not overly so, and Brain easily found a space to park. Taking a deep breath, and knowing the next half hour wasn't going to be easy, he walked into the chapel.

It looked like the service had just started, and Brain immediately spotted Aspen. She was also wearing her dress green uniform and was sitting in one of the back pews, behind the rest of the mourners. She sat alone, her spine ramrod straight as she stared at the chaplain.

Brain slipped into the pew and sat next to her, holding his breath. But other than a quick sideways glance, she didn't acknowledge him in any way. Not that he thought she'd make a scene; that wasn't her way. But Brain hadn't been sure of his reception.

The next twenty minutes were tough. Listening to the post chaplain praise Spence, talk about what a good man he was and how his death was a great loss to both the Army and his family, was a joke. It was a hard pill to swallow that the man who'd done his best to kill him was being lauded as if he were a hero.

But finally the service was over. And Brain turned to Aspen. "Hey."

"Hi," she said evenly, no emotion showing on her face.

"This is the last place I expected you to be this morning," he said.

She shrugged.

Brain took her in. She looked rough. Her face was pale, and she still had circles under her eyes. If he wasn't mistaken, her heart rate was too fast. He could see it pulsing in her neck.

"Can we talk?" he blurted, wanting more than ever to take her in his arms and comfort her.

Aspen nodded, and Brain sighed in relief.

"But not here," she said.

"Of course," he said immediately, standing and holding out a hand for her.

To his surprise, she took it.

He'd never felt relief as great as he did right at that moment. She hadn't slapped his hand away. Didn't tell him to get lost.

He began to hope that maybe, just maybe, he hadn't lost her forever.

The second she was standing, Aspen dropped his hand, and Brain tried not to be too disappointed. He gestured for her to precede him out of the pew, and she slipped by him into the aisle. She didn't indicate in any way that she wanted to wait and talk to Spence's relatives, which was a relief.

Once outside, Brain slipped his sunglasses back on his face, wincing at the bright sunlight and how it made his head throb. "Do you want to grab a coffee with me?" he asked, feeling out of his depth and awkward, which he hated.

But Aspen shook her head. "No. How about meeting back at my place...say in about twenty minutes? That will give me time to get there and change first."

Brain nodded immediately. "Sounds good. I'll run home and change myself, if that's all right."

"Of course. See you soon." Then Aspen turned away from him and walked to her Elantra.

Brain had to force himself not to go after her when she staggered a bit, then straightened and unlocked her door. He had no idea what was going on with that small stumble...but he didn't like it.

He drove home as fast as he could and threw on a pair of jeans and an olive-green button-down shirt. It was a shirt Aspen had said she liked...before he'd been an idiot and pushed her away. She'd said it brought out the green in his hazel eyes. He was willing to do whatever it took to remind her how good they were together. That at one time, she'd liked him.

He was five minutes early when he pulled into the parking lot at her apartment, and Brain forced himself to sit there until their arranged meeting time came around. Then he practically jogged into the building and to her apartment. He knocked, then heard her shout that the door was open.

Frowning at the fact she'd not only left her door unlocked, but that she hadn't even checked to make sure it was him before telling him to enter, Brain pushed open the door. He shut and locked it behind him, taking a deep breath for courage before walking inside.

Aspen was sitting on her couch wearing a sweatshirt and cuddled under a fuzzy blanket. He took in the box of tissues, a glass of orange juice, and a stack of books on the table next to the couch, and asked, "Are you sick?"

Aspen's lips twitched. "Can't get anything by you, can I? Sit, Kane. We need to talk."

Those four words had struck terror in the hearts of many men over the ages, but Brain had expected them. That was why he was there in the first place. He steeled himself, and instead of sitting in the chair across from the couch, which seemed as if it was too far away, he took a seat on the couch next to her. Not touching, but being this close to her after everything he'd said seemed like a miracle.

Taking a deep breath, Brain blurted what he'd been thinking for seven long days.

"I love you."

* * *

Aspen felt like crap. After leaving the hospital in Houston, she'd been shell-shocked. Hurt, confused, and even a bit angry. The rain had finally stopped and the water had begun to recede. She'd gone back to the tent city, changed into a spare pair of BDUs that she'd brought, helped break down the tents and pack the trucks to go back to Fort Hood.

She'd kept to herself and spent the ride back to Killeen going over and over everything that had happened. Every muscle she possessed hurt, and she knew she'd have bruises springing up all over her body.

After helping unload the trucks, Aspen had gone back to her apartment and slept for twenty hours. When she woke, she'd felt even worse than when she'd fallen into bed the day before. She'd called her major and told him she was sick and had slept for another twelve hours.

After five days, she was finally feeling better, but her body wasn't quite back up to fighting form. She'd forced herself to get up and go to Derek's memorial service, but had planned to come straight home and back to bed.

Seeing Kane had been a surprise. Even more that he'd sat next to her and asked to talk.

She was all for that.

She'd changed into the most comfortable fat pants and sweatshirt she owned and waited with bated breath for him to arrive. It was past time to talk about everything that had happened. Clear the air.

Kane sat next to her on the couch, and just when she

opened her mouth to speak, he blurted out, "I love you. And I'm sorry."

Aspen blinked in surprise. "What?"

"I love you," he said again, firmer that time.

Aspen's heart was beating out of her chest, but she did her best to keep her emotions under control. "Last time I saw you, you broke up with me. I'm getting whiplash from your signals, Kane."

He sighed and ran a hand through his hair. "I know. And the only thing I have to say for myself is that I wasn't me in that hospital a week ago."

Aspen raised an eyebrow.

"I know that sounds like an excuse, but it's not. I'd just woken up, and was confused and depressed and hurting. I was so fucking happy to see you, but then the doctor kicked you out and began to inspect me."

"Inspect you?" Aspen asked with a small chuckle.

Kane's lips twitched, but he nodded. "You know what I mean. It felt like an inspection. I was relieved when I seemed to remember everything, but when he told the nurse something in Spanish, and she responded...I realized that I couldn't understand them. It completely freaked me out. Then I realized I didn't remember *any* of the languages I'd learned over the years. Not one. The words were just gone. It felt as if I had a hole in my head.

"Trigger came in, and I told him what was going on. He started asking questions about when and if I'd ever remember, and the doctor said he just didn't know. That the possibility of me getting that part of my memory back was sixty-forty. I...didn't handle it well."

Aspen snorted. "You think?"

Kane didn't smile, he just continued to stare at her.

"And now? Have you remembered?"

"Some," Kane admitted. "Words pop into my head here and there. It's a little disconcerting, actually, to be talking to someone and the word for 'red' or 'shirt' or even 'asshole' just comes to me."

"So that's why you're here? Because you're getting your memory back and you can be the 'brain' once more?" Aspen asked, a little harsher than she'd intended.

"No," Kane said immediately. "I knew from almost the second you left the hospital that I'd made a mistake. When you left, it was as if you took all the air from the room. Trigger and the rest of the guys also made no bones about the fact that I'd fucked up. I've missed you, *chérie*."

Aspen reached toward the end table, picked up her phone and studied it for a second, then looked back at him. "Funny, I haven't gotten any messages from you. You forget my number?"

"No. I was afraid you'd block me. Or just not answer. I did have Doc drive me by your apartment the other day. Your car was here, but when I knocked, you didn't answer. I figured you were avoiding me."

"When?" Aspen asked.

"Three days ago."

"I wasn't here," she told him. "Apparently, I picked up some nasty infection from sitting in the floodwaters for hours. I cut my hand on something, and all the creepy-crawlies got in that way...that's what the doctors think, at least. I was really sick a day or so after I got back, and I called Devyn. She came over and drove me to the post doctor. They made me stay the night at the hospital on post before letting me go home. I wasn't here when you came by, Kane. I would have answered the door if I'd've been here."

Kane looked alarmed. "Are you all right now? Should you have been out and about today? I should go and let you get some sleep."

Aspen reached out and touched Kane's arm, feeling the same electricity shoot through her hand as she had the first time she'd touched him. "I'm okay," she said.

"Fuck," he swore, grabbing hold of her hand and holding it tightly in both of his. "I had so many antibiotics being pumped into me in the Houston hospital, I guess that helped stave off any major infection I might've gotten through the gash on my head."

Aspen nodded. "Yeah, I thought about that too. Your head still hurts though?"

"Now and then, yes. I've been wearing the sunglasses to help with that. Every day it's better, and the doctors say they think now that I've started to remember some of the languages I lost, they'll all come back when the swelling in my brain goes down completely."

"I'm glad."

"I was surprised you went to Derek's service," Kane asked.

Aspen let him change the topic. "I sat down with my major and told him everything that happened that night. From your hesitation to get into the boat in the first place, how I'd turned when I felt the boat rocking and saw Derek standing there with the oar in his hand, my decision to bail out of the boat after you instead of waiting around to see what Derek would do to me, the way he gunned it out of there, leaving us to our fates. It wasn't easy, and I was scared he wouldn't believe me, but he did.

"He told me that Derek had received a reprimand for his actions in Afghanistan. I hadn't known about that; no one did, apparently. But it was enough to push Derek over the edge, I guess. He lived and breathed the Army. And somehow, he ended up blaming me for all his own actions. The major said he'd make sure everything that happened was noted. I don't know where, or who will ever see it, but I felt better knowing the major believed me.

"Anyway...the bottom line is that Derek paid for his sins. He was a jerk, and discriminatory toward women in general, but for trying to kill you, he paid. Big time. Karma took care of him. I could've insisted the major do an investigation, get the Army's criminal investigation unit involved, but honestly, he can't be punished any more than he already has been. And there's little honor in dragging a dead man's name through the mud.

"If he was alive? You can bet your ass that I'd be screaming from the rooftops about what he did to you. But now? I'm just tired of it all. Karma did her thing, and I'm taking that as a hint to get on with my life."

"So why'd you attend today? It pissed me *way* the hell off to hear the chaplain going on about what a great person and soldier he was," Kane said.

Aspen nodded. "Yeah, that was hard to take. But I wanted to be a better person than Derek was. And I genuinely feel bad for his family. I also hoped it would give me closure on everything that happened."

"And did it?" Kane asked.

"Surprisingly...yeah. I can put it behind me and look forward to my new path in life."

"I'm not sure I can put it behind me so quickly," Kane admitted. "That asshole tried to *kill* me. And as long as assholes like Derek are allowed to hold leadership positions in the Army, things for women will never change. They can't be allowed free passes simply because the brass doesn't want to deal with the waves it'll make if they're called out on their behavior."

Aspen pressed her lips together. Kane's words meant the world to her. "I know you're right, but I just want to move on."

Kane stared at her for a long moment, then sighed. "I don't like it, and I hate that Spence is getting away with what he did...but for your sake, I'm willing to let this go."

Aspen started to thank him, but Kane spoke before she could say anything. "But I *am* going to have a long talk with the major. I know you already talked to him, but I'm sure you downplayed a lot of the shit Spence gave you. Probably reasoned that he wasn't treating you any differently than he was the others on his team. Which is bullshit. Someone needs to speak up on your behalf, and the behalf of all the women who will come after you, and that someone will be me."

"Thank you," she said quietly. "Because you're here and safe, I'm over it, but I can't help but think about little Annie and how enthusiastic she is about wanting to join the Army, possibly even walk in my footsteps. If having a talk with the major can do even a bit of good for women in the future, I'm okay with it."

Kane nodded. Then he looked down at his hands as if he was reluctant to say what he was thinking.

"What is it?" Aspen asked.

"I really am sorry for being a dick," he told her.

"I know. And I'd already forgiven you a week ago," she told him honestly.

"You did?" he asked in surprise.

"Yeah. Did you really think I was going to just walk away? Kane, I love you. I've loved you almost since that first kiss we shared in that bar. There was no way I was going to turn my back on everything we have just because you were throwing a hissy fit. I'd planned on giving you some space, then confronting you when you were well enough to go home. But then I got sick, and my plans were kind of sidelined."

"You love me," he said. It wasn't a question.

"Of course I do," Aspen said.

"I hurt you."

"You did. I've never felt such pain in my life as when you told me you needed space. But then I got mad. I'm afraid I thought a lot of bad words about you for a while. And when I finally calmed down enough to think about what happened, I realized that I'd pushed too hard. I was desperate to see you, and I should've listened when Trigger told me that you needed some peace and quiet."

Kane shook his head. "No, you didn't do anything wrong. It was all me. You just wanted to see me. The guys told me how you refused to leave my side while I was unconscious. You didn't eat, shower, sleep. Then the second I woke, I broke up with you."

"*Tried* to break up with me," Aspen corrected. "I wasn't going to let you go without a fight. I didn't give up during training, and I didn't give up when everyone tried to tell me I couldn't be a combat medic to a Ranger team. I certainly wasn't going to give up on you after one little misunderstanding."

"I don't deserve you," Kane whispered.

"Wrong. We deserve each other," Aspen told him. Then she turned her head and coughed into her sleeve.

"You're still sick," Kane said, sitting up straight. "You need to rest."

Aspen clutched his hand tighter. "I don't want you to go."

He looked surprised. "Oh, I'm not going anywhere," he assured. "You didn't leave me when I needed you most, and I'm not leaving this apartment until you're back to your old self."

Aspen smiled. "So we're okay?"

"We're more than okay," he told her. "I love you, you love me. You forgave me for being a dick, and I promise it won't happen again."

"I'm glad you're okay," she told him softly. "You scared the shit out of me."

Kane leaned forward slowly and kissed her on the forehead. Then he encouraged her to lie down on the couch, and he tucked in the blanket, making sure she was comfortable. He leaned over her and said, "I had the best combat medic looking after me, there was no doubt that I'd be all right in the end. Sleep, *querida*."

Happier than she'd been in days, Aspen slept.

* * *

"Oh, *fuck*," Brain gasped as Aspen bounced up and down on his cock.

It had been a month and a half since he'd almost lost her, and their relationship was more solid than ever. All the languages he'd lost had slowly come back, and he'd never been more content.

He had great friends, a job he enjoyed, and a woman who proved time and time again that she not only loved him, but she'd fight for him if necessary.

Aspen had gotten her discharge papers that afternoon, and they'd celebrated both her release from the Army and the job offer she'd received from Acadian Ambulance Service in Temple. He'd made them a nice dinner with extra-sweet frozen margaritas for Aspen, and topped it off with her favorite—a pound cake for dessert. After they were done eating, she'd dragged him up to his bedroom and pounced on him.

He was currently lying on his back, holding onto her hips as she rode him hard and fast. Her tits bounced with every thrust, and she moaned as she brought a hand down to flick her clit as she rode him. She was sexy as hell, and it was all Brain could to do hold back his own orgasm.

The second he felt her go over the edge, he grabbed her around the waist and rolled until she was on her back. Then he fucked her even harder. Almost overwhelmed by the feel of her inner muscles still fluttering all along his bare cock. They'd done away with condoms, and he'd never felt *anything* as good as being inside her bareback.

Way too soon, he was on the edge. He pushed inside her as far as he could and let himself go.

A minute or so later, he collapsed, making sure not to crush Aspen under him. He rolled them to their sides, felt her hot breaths against his neck, and closed his eyes in contentment.

He'd almost lost this.

He'd apologized so much that Aspen had ordered him not to say "I'm sorry" ever again in regard to what had happened in Houston. He'd agreed...but he still mentally apologized often.

"Congratulations," he said softly.

Aspen chuckled. "Thanks."

"For what it's worth, I'm proud of you. The city of Temple might not know it yet, but they're in the very best hands with you. When someone calls 9-1-1, they'll be lucky if it's you who shows up to help."

"I've got some classes I need to take to feel comfortable, especially when it comes to pediatrics, but I'm excited to get started and meet the other paramedics I'll be working with."

"They're going to love you," Brain told her, hoping that was true.

But Aspen merely shrugged. "Even if they don't, I'm okay. I have you and your team. And Gillian, Kinley, and Devyn. I don't need to be best friends with my coworkers, because I've got all of you."

"Damn straight," Brain told her. "When are you moving in for good?" he asked.

Aspen picked up her head and stared at him. "I wasn't sure you were ready for that."

"Not ready?" Brain scoffed. "Woman, I've been begging you to stay every night for the last month."

"If you're sure..." she said, letting her voice trail off.

"I'm sure," Brain confirmed. "More than sure. You're just wasting money renting that apartment since you're at my house all the time anyway. I want you *here*. In my bed. In my shower. In my kitchen. I know this house is small, but eventually we'll get a bigger one."

"It's perfect," Aspen said with a smile.

Brain snorted, and the movement made his cock slip

out from between her legs, causing them both to groan.

"I hate losing you," she said.

"You'll never lose me, darling," Brain told her. Then leaned down and kissed her. Long and slow, just how they both liked it.

Winnie Morrison looked over at her neighbor's house and smiled at seeing Kane's sleek black car parked in his driveway. He loved that car. And the fact that it wasn't sitting safe and secure in his garage could only mean Aspen's car was currently occupying the space. It was obvious he loved her more than he loved his car, which reminded Winnie of her late husband.

Steve had been the love of her life. He'd passed away five years ago, and not a day went by when she didn't miss him. Didn't miss the way he'd held her hand, or changed the light bulbs without complaint, or chopped the vegetables for salads because he knew she hated doing so.

But she'd had over fifty-five years with him, and she was content with how her life had gone. She was ninety-one, and didn't have a lot of time left. But she wasn't dead yet.

So when her granddaughter, Jayme, asked if she could come stay with Winnie for a while, she had enthusiastically agreed. Watching Kane mow her yard in nothing but his shorts was entertaining, sure, but she was bored most days. It would be nice having Jayme around.

Not to mention, at thirty-two, it was past time for her granddaughter to be married. But Jayme was stubborn. And picky.

Winnie wasn't going to let that stop her though. She'd found someone who would be perfect for her Jayme. She'd met the young man—everyone seemed young to Winnie— at the grocery store, and they'd become fast friends. He'd called her several times to chat, and he'd even stopped by the other day just to check on her and see if she needed anything. He was respectful, courteous, good-looking— and most importantly, single.

Smiling to herself, Winnie hadn't felt this much antici- pation and excitement in a very long time. She might be old, but she still remembered the butterflies she got when she'd first met Steve. She wanted that for Jayme.

Turning away from the window, Winnie began to plot. She couldn't wait for Jayme to arrive.

Sierra sat quietly in a chair in the middle of a dilapidated house, desperately trying to get her hands untied. It was no use; all she managed to do was tighten the knots in the ropes holding her to the chair even more than they already were. Tears threatened, but she fought against them. She felt as if all she'd been doing was crying.

It was hard to understand how she'd even gotten here in the first place.

She'd just finished a shift at the chow hall and was headed back to her tent when she'd been grabbed from behind, a sack shoved over her head, and then forced into the back of a vehicle. A man put a knife against her throat and told her that if she made a sound, he'd gut her like a fish.

So she'd lain there, silent and trembling, as they drove

right past the guards at the entrance to the post.

She'd been moved from house to house ever since, and paraded with glee in front of the insurgents.

In the midst of her reminiscences, a man she recognized entered the room where she was being held captive and dropped a familiar-looking duffle bag at her feet.

She stared at the bag in dismay. It was hers. She'd been so excited when she'd found it at an Army surplus store back in the States, before she'd left for Afghanistan.

"In case you're wondering if anyone is looking for you, they aren't," said the man. She'd seen him around base. He was an interpreter. Muhammad Qahhar. Someone trusted enough to mingle amongst the American servicemen and women. "They think you left. That you couldn't handle the job. No one cares about you, devil woman. You're ours."

"What are you going to do to me?" she asked.

"You're a training tool for my men," he said.

Sierra didn't want to know what that meant, but she couldn't stop herself from asking, "What do you mean?"

"They need to learn how to get information from our captives. How to inflict just enough pain to make someone want to tell us everything, but not enough to kill them. You'll be our test subject. We'll use you to hone our skills, so when it's time, and America sends their best soldiers to take us down, we'll be skilled enough to send all you Westerners running back home with your tails between your legs."

Sierra was horrified. They were going to torture her for *practice*?

"Please, let me go! I won't say anything to anyone."

"No," the man said succinctly before turning to two other men who had come into the room with him. Sierra hadn't even noticed them before; she'd been concentrating too hard on the man she'd known as an interpreter...and her bag. "Are the caves ready?" he asked.

"Yes, Shahzada," the other man said.

Sierra blinked in recognition. Shahzada was the name of the leader of the insurgents in the area. *Muhammad* was Shahzada? Oh, shit. He moved freely on the base. He was trusted by everyone. Clearly, no one even suspected he was the very terrorist they were searching for.

Right there, under the noses of the men and women Sierra had gotten to know while working on the base.

"Good. Take her there and do as you've been instructed. We'll see how many other contractors we can grab to keep her company. Eventually the Americans will catch on, and they will send their so-called *elite* forces to try to stop us. By then, we'll be ready for them."

Shahzada smiled gleefully as he turned to Sierra. "You and the others will be instrumental in getting your people to leave our lands. You should be proud."

Proud? No, she wasn't proud—she was terrified.

Sierra couldn't stop herself from flinching away from the men who came forward. She had no idea what was in store for her, but she knew it wasn't going to be good.

Someone, somewhere, had to figure out that she hadn't just up and left the base, right?

She had to be strong, stay alive, so she could tell someone that Muhammad was Shahzada. She might not be a soldier, but she loved her country—and Sierra wouldn't go down without a fight.

Her last thought before a fist came toward her face, making it impossible to think about anything, was the larger-than-life soldier, Grover. She'd sent him a letter, explaining that she preferred more personal handwritten letters to email, and that she was looking forward to getting to know him. When he got it, and realized she wasn't sending any others, surely he'd think something was wrong. Right?

* * *

Oz was lying on his couch with his hand behind his head, watching football and trying to ignore the argument he could easily hear from the apartment next to his. He'd been listening to the asshole tear into his girlfriend for at least an hour. This wasn't the first argument he'd overheard either. As far as he could tell, the guy had never smacked her around, but he knew better than most how badly words could hurt.

He and his sister had grown up with a father exactly like the jerk he could hear yelling next door. They hadn't ever been able to do anything right and had spent their childhoods trying to be quiet, staying out of the way of their dad. Their mom had walked out when Oz was still a baby, and he'd never known her. His sister, Becky, was six years older than him, and yet it had been Oz who'd done what he could to try to protect her.

His sister had never been able to shake free of the abuse they'd suffered. She'd dated a man who was just like their father, except he didn't hesitate to use his fists to get his point across. Oz had tried to help Becky more than once after she'd left home and while he was still in high school. He'd sent money so she could get away from her abusive boyfriend, but she'd always ended up going back to the guy.

Their father had died right before Oz graduated, and when Becky showed up to his funeral obviously on some sort of drug, Oz was done. He'd helped her as best he could, but until she wanted to help herself, he couldn't do anything more.

Oz hadn't talked to Becky in over a decade. Right after he'd graduated from high school and joined the Army, he'd had to concentrate on his own future.

He regretted that now. Wished he'd been strong enough to help Becky more than he had.

Listening to his neighbor get verbally abused through the walls brought all the memories to the surface that he'd done his best to bury.

"You're trash, Riley! Always have been, always will be!" the man screamed.

"Kick him out," Oz muttered under his breath.

"Screw you!" the woman yelled back. "Get out."

"That'a girl," Oz said with a nod of his head. "Stay firm. Don't let him talk his way back in."

"You'll be begging for me to come back," the man warned.

She laughed. "No, I won't. All you do is sit around and play video games all day. We're *done*."

"Fine. You're an ice-cold bitch anyway. Frigid as fuck."

"Out!" the woman yelled.

Getting up from his couch, Oz wandered over to his door and opened it. He wanted the asshole she was kicking out to know that she wasn't entirely without protection. Oz was a big man. At six foot five, he was an imposing figure, and he didn't think the guy from next door would do anything as long as he was watching.

Oz had seen his neighbor around, though he hadn't

said more than a polite "hello" and "good morning" in passing. But he'd be damned if he let the verbal abuse turn into something physical.

He leaned against his doorway and crossed his arms over his chest, looking as intimidating as he could. Three seconds later, his neighbor's door opened and the guy stalked out. He turned back and opened his mouth to hurl one last insult...when he saw Oz.

"You aren't worth it," the man sneered to his neighbor, then stalked down the hall, past Oz's door, and disappeared into the stairwell.

Turning to his right, Oz saw the woman standing in her doorway. She blushed when she saw him looking at her. She was a petite thing, at least a foot shorter than he was. She had long brown hair that curled at the ends and big hazel eyes. She looked stressed, but he could also see the relief in her eyes.

"You all right?" he asked.

She nodded. "Thanks."

"You're better off without him," Oz couldn't help but add.

"I know," his neighbor said.

He was glad to see she wasn't breaking down in hysterics. He supposed she'd probably be upset later, and he couldn't blame her, but for now she was holding herself together.

"I'm Oz," he said with a small lift of his chin.

"Riley," she reciprocated.

Oz opened his mouth to say something else, but he heard the elevator down the hall ding and turned to see who was getting off. If it was Riley's ex returning, he was going to make sure the man understood once and for all he wasn't welcome back.

But instead, a man wearing a suit and tie, along with a kid who was around nine or ten, walked down the hall toward them.

Oz frowned—and was even more confused when the man stopped in front of him.

"Porter Reed?" he asked.

"That's me," Oz told him.

"I work with the Texas Department of Family and Protection Services, the Child Protective Services section. Do you have a sister named Rebecca Reed?"

"Yes."

"I regret to inform you that your sister has passed away under unfortunate circumstances. You're listed as next of kin, and this is your nephew, Logan Reed."

Oz blinked in surprise, his neighbor forgotten, the argument he'd overheard gone from his head as if it hadn't happened. All he could do was stare down at the little boy who was trying to be brave, but was obviously scared to death.

He opened his mouth to protest, to say that the kid couldn't be his nephew, that he hadn't even known his sister *had* a kid. But then the little boy looked up...and Oz got a look at his eyes.

The kid had lived through hell. He could see it in his gaze, along with terror as he looked up at the strange man he'd never met. A man who could hurt him, as he'd obviously been hurt in the past.

But it was the gray color of his eyes, just like Oz's own, that convinced him the boy had his blood running through his veins.

And as if a switch was flicked inside him, Oz instantly knew he'd do whatever it took to protect the boy. If Becky was truly dead, and CPS was at his doorstep, Logan had no one else to look after him. To keep him safe.

Moving slowly, so as not to alarm the boy more than he already was, Oz crouched down so he could look Logan in the eyes. He held out his hand and said softly, "Hi, Logan. I'm Oz. Your uncle. And no one is *ever* going to hurt you again."

*

To find out who Winnie sets up her granddaughter, Jayme, with...check out *Shielding Jayme*! This novella will be offered in an anthology in December 2020, but if you want it as an individual book, you can certainly get it that way too!

And, Wow, does Oz have his work cut out for him with his nephew...and what's going to happen with his neighbor? Check out *Shielding Riley to find out!*

Want to talk to other Susan Stoker fans? Join my reader group, Susan Stoker's Stalkers, on Facebook!

JOIN my Newsletter and find out about sales, free books, contests and new releases before anyone else!!
Click HERE

Want to know when my books go on sale? Follow me on Bookbub HERE!

Also by Susan Stoker

Delta Team Two Series

Shielding Gillian
Shielding Kinley
Shielding Aspen (Oct 2020)
Shielding Jayme (novella) (Jan 2021)
Shielding Riley (Jan 2021)
Shielding Devyn (May 2021)
Shielding Ember (Sep 2021)
Shielding Sierra (TBA)

SEAL of Protection Series

Protecting Caroline
Protecting Alabama
Protecting Fiona
Marrying Caroline (novella)
Protecting Summer
Protecting Cheyenne
Protecting Jessyka
Protecting Julie (novella)
Protecting Melody
Protecting the Future
Protecting Kiera (novella)
Protecting Alabama's Kids (novella)
Protecting Dakota

SEAL of Protection: Legacy Series

Securing Caite
Securing Brenae (novella)
Securing Sidney

Securing Piper
Securing Zoey
Securing Avery
Securing Kalee
Securing Jane (Feb 2021)

SEAL Team Hawaii Series

Finding Elodie (Apr 2021)
Finding Lexie (Aug 2021)
Finding Kenna (Oct 2021)
Finding Monica (TBA)
Finding Carly (TBA)
Finding Ashlyn (TBA)
Finding Jodelle (TBA)

Delta Force Heroes Series

Rescuing Rayne
Rescuing Aimee (novella)
Rescuing Emily
Rescuing Harley
Marrying Emily (novella)
Rescuing Kassie
Rescuing Bryn
Rescuing Casey
Rescuing Sadie (novella)
Rescuing Wendy
Rescuing Mary
Rescuing Macie (novella)

Badge of Honor: Texas Heroes Series

Justice for Mackenzie
Justice for Mickie

Justice for Corrie
Justice for Laine (novella)
Shelter for Elizabeth
Justice for Boone
Shelter for Adeline
Shelter for Sophie
Justice for Erin
Justice for Milena
Shelter for Blythe
Justice for Hope
Shelter for Quinn
Shelter for Koren
Shelter for Penelope

Ace Security Series

Claiming Grace
Claiming Alexis
Claiming Bailey
Claiming Felicity
Claiming Sarah

Mountain Mercenaries Series

Defending Allye
Defending Chloe
Defending Morgan
Defending Harlow
Defending Everly
Defending Zara
Defending Raven

Silverstone Series

Trusting Skylar (Dec 2020)

Trusting Taylor (Mar 2021)
Trusting Molly (July 2021)
Trusting Cassidy (Dec 2021)

Stand Alone

The Guardian Mist
Nature's Rift
A Princess for Cale
A Moment in Time- A Collection of Short Stories
Lambert's Lady

Special Operations Fan Fiction

http://www.AcesPress.com

Beyond Reality Series

Outback Hearts
Flaming Hearts
Frozen Hearts

Writing as Annie George:

Stepbrother Virgin (erotic novella)

ABOUT THE AUTHOR

New York Times, USA Today and *Wall Street Journal* Best-selling Author Susan Stoker has a heart as big as the state of Tennessee where she lives, but this all American girl has also spent the last fourteen years living in Missouri, California, Colorado, Indiana, and Texas. She's married to a retired Army man who now gets to follow *her* around the country.

She debuted her first series in 2014 and quickly followed that up with the SEAL of Protection Series, which solidified her love of writing and creating stories readers can get lost in.

If you enjoyed this book, or any book, please consider leaving a review. It's appreciated by authors more than you'll know.

www.stokeraces.com
www.AcesPress.com
susan@stokeraces.com

Made in the USA
Middletown, DE
19 October 2020